The True True Story of Raja the Gullible

(and His Mother)

Also by Rabih Alameddine

RABIH ALAMEDDINE

The True True Story of Raja the Gullible

(and His Mother)

Grove Press
New York

Audre Lorde, excerpt from "Inheritance — His" from *The Collected Poems of Audre Lorde*. Reprinted with the permission of W.W. Norton & Company, Inc.

FIRST EDITION

Printed in the United States of America

First Grove Atlantic hardcover edition: September 2025

The book is set in 12-pt. Cochin LT by Alpha Design & Composition of Pittsfield, NH.

Library of Congress Cataloging-in-Publication data is available for this title.

ISBN 978-0-8021-6647-0
eISBN 978-0-8021-6648-7

Grove Press
an imprint of Grove Atlantic
154 West 14th Street
New York, NY 10011

Distributed by Publishers Group West

groveatlantic.com

25 26 27 28   10 9 8 7 6 5 4 3 2 1

To Marsha
who must now read this

Our deepest bonds remain
the mirror and the gun.

—Audre Lorde

I
(2023)

This morning, my mother sat in front of me, covered neck to toe in a red-checkered, black-streaked wax tablecloth we'd been using as a hairdresser cape for a few years—fastened with a binder clip, of course. I'd been her designated hair colorist since she'd stopped trusting professionals while still in her early forties. She cursed the entire trade when one poor sod mistakenly dyed her hair a deep russet—and he was a poor sod because he was still a young apprentice at the time. He was all she could afford. My father had my mother, all of us, on a strict budget. Every now and then, I would ask if she could sit down on the floor between my legs so I didn't have to stand while dyeing her hair. She refused, of course. I had to suffer for her elegance, she'd say.

My mother had intimate relationships with mirrors. With a tilt of her dark eyes, she stared at her reflection, at her pale neck furrowed with tiny blue veins, at the white roots in her hair, the part in the middle looking like a road marker separating two lanes. She told me she hated this mirror, the whole vanity, she was going to buy a new one. She felt certain she could find a reasonably priced one that was more beautiful than that dissembling thing before her. Mirrors are fleeting, I said, they retain nothing. There was going to be a new her in a few minutes. I began to brush dark into light. A mirror kept no record of metamorphosis.

She snorted. "You're breaking house rules again," she said.

"That wasn't philosophizing."

"Sure sounded like it. Forgetful mirrors and all that."

"You look beautiful."

"I'm old."

Told her I was as well. I pointed to my hair, which was already whiter than hers. The original red turned a weird blondish in my forties, and white in my fifties, which I liked the most since it didn't stand out as much.

"You're in extreme middle age," she said. "You're not allowed to be old. That would make me ancient."

"But you are ancient."

"Fuck your mother."

Her favorite expression, which always sounded off coming from her, even after years of hearing it. Anyone else saying it barely registered, but of course, my mother saying it to me was always strange.

Her head lurched right slightly and abruptly. She noticed. I noticed. Both pretended we didn't. The dye brush remained steady in my hand. She was still in great health for her age. She swore she still could, if needed, climb the three flights of stairs to our apartment when the building's diesel generator was asleep. Yet her body had been failing her at a faster rate, tentative tics growing more assured. At times her hands shook so much that she developed this habit of sitting with one nestled atop the other in her lap like napping kittens.

"Why don't you let me dye your hair?"

"Now, why would I do that?"

"Because you'd look younger. We can probably find a dye that would make it look more natural than your original, which God knows was a color not found in nature."

4

"How could it be not found in nature when it was my natural hair color?"

"You should let me dye your hair because I'd like it. It would remind me how I used to comb your hair as a boy."

"You never combed my hair. Not once."

"Of course I did. You can't remember anything. We agree on that at least. Your memory is worse than mine."

"And we never agreed on that. You have the worst memory in the history of mankind. If there was an oblivion Olympics, you'd win a gold medal in every category."

"I wonder what the categories would be. I'd ask you but I'm sure you forgot."

"Ha! Don't make me laugh, Zalfa, or I might end up dyeing your ear black."

"Let me dye your hair. Maybe you'd find a boyfriend."

"How? It hasn't helped you any."

"Fuck your mother."

The boy on the second-floor balcony across the street admired the lush, bent oak below my building. I was swaddled in nightclothes, whereas he was shirtless. He stepped back from the concrete railing, showing me he was wearing a pair of skimpy white briefs with a red pack of cigarettes held tightly by the waistband against his hip bone. He delicately picked out a cigarette, lit it, took a long puff, and scratched his beard before exhaling. Lusty. Were he wearing something more than underwear, I would have expected him to rearrange his privates before throwing a smiling glance up my way. It was a flirting game he liked to play. He wouldn't look up until his performance was done. It was never overt—plausible deniability forever an option. He was meticulously polite when he encountered me on the street, whether by himself or accompanied, always nice to the neighborhood homosexual. He didn't return to the railing, didn't want to block my view. How old was the little scoundrel? Twenty, twenty-one? Probably horny. I hadn't seen his girlfriend in a while.

He enjoyed the show. I enjoyed the show, but I wished I could explain that it wasn't a desire for him I felt. I longed for the desire I used to feel for a boy like him when I was younger, a nostalgia of sorts, the deliciousness of hunger, the flush of blood. I longed for longing; I desired desire. I used to get indomitable erections when I saw a stunning guy like him, and as I aged, I've slid a spiral from lust to an acute echo of yearning. The helpless longing of a ghost. My mind now titillated by the memory, not the vision.

I wished to send him a thank-you card for reminding me.

On cue, the boy tipped slightly backward as though about to lose his balance and topple. He slid his palm across his chest, through the vortex of hair around his navel, and rearranged his dick in the white briefs. He looked up slyly, knowing I was mesmerized. My heart went out to him.

"Is the neighbor boy on the balcony?" my mother yelled from the kitchen. "I can invite him for lunch if you want. If you let me dye your hair, he'd probably accept."

"I can't even remember what to do with a boy like him."

"Speaking of the oblivion Olympics," she said. "I'm making coffee. Want some?"

My mother made little studied noises in the small room, a thud of a dropped book, a squeak of a table lamp being

moved (probably), a not-so-soft sigh followed by a cavernous cough. She wanted me in the room, needed to talk.

Wedged into the corner, the bed my mother sat on had no
headboard or footboard, just a box spring and mattress with
sheets and a bedcover, an Indian kantha of the most glorious
lemon yellow and pink. My mother leaned her head to one side
as though she was trying to decipher one of Picasso's Cubist
paintings. She petted a purring Monet somewhat distractedly
with her right hand, while his twin, Manet, lay curled on the
farthest pillow. Her left hand rested on the bed, feet on the
scuffed linoleum floor, a mirror image of Wyeth's Christina.
With the room so tiny, her legs almost reached the far wall. I
was only able to see the back of her head, her black-black hair
reaching below her shoulder. I wondered if she was or had been
crying. Not for Nahed's departure, I thought. Her tears were
triggered primarily by kitsch these days: bad movies, sappy
Christmas cards, and poorly dubbed Turkish soap operas. She
turned to face me. Her pinched lips had no specific meaning.
When she'd reached eighty, her thin lips began to form an
inverse crescent. She countered by pursing them regularly.

"This room wouldn't feel so suffocating if we put in a
window, even if it's a small one," she said, allowing herself
another sigh. "I'm going to miss her terribly."

"I know," I said. "So will I."

A dog barked in the distance—not any dog, it was Eddie,
the golden retriever who lived on the fourth-floor balcony of
the building next door. Neither Monet nor Manet flinched.
The whole neighborhood loved the dog yet hated his habit of
barking at birds. In March of the previous year, two mourning
doves tried to nest along the eaves of the balcony below. Eddie
barked for a whole week before the doves decided to relocate

to a more upscale, less boisterous neighborhood. Eddie was by no means the loudest disturber. My cousin Nahed had to endure the sounds of human debauchery cascading from the room above at strange hours. Our neighbor was fucking his Sri Lankan maid whenever his wife left the house. Nahed allowed it a few times, after which, with my mother's blessing and mine, she stomped up the stairs, rang the doorbell, and threatened the husband with exposure if he didn't immediately halt this most unsensual of rackets. He did stop, he had to, but not before accusing her of being unneighborly.

"Will you?" my mother asked. "Do you miss her mother? Or will you just miss Nahed?"

"I will miss both."

"See, I told you. You never listen to me."

"Say thank you."

"Must I?"

"Yes," I said. "You must."

"Thank you, you little shit."

"You're welcome."

Nahed had left us early that morning, back to her apartment, which had taken two and a half years to resuscitate. My mother had wanted us to bid her farewell and accompany her to the apartment, to wave to her as she entered the building's lobby. Since Nahed was our houseguest, my mother insisted we do so even though neither of us had a car. The only way my mother was able to let it go was when my cousin pretended to be insulted that she was called a houseguest. She'd been living with us, with me, for those two and a half years — remarkably, two and a half years to the day.

"I need to clean the room," my mother said, "but I don't feel like it. What should we do tonight, the two of us?

8

I don't want to be alone, so no reading for you. Want to get stupid and play canasta? You have enough edibles, right?"

"Yes, but we don't have enough food in the house."

"Fuck your mother, mister." She stood up, casually smoothed her dress before twirling once. "I can still eat as much as I want."

At some point after Nahed and her mother moved into our inconvenient abode, my mother discovered dope. When she was high, she got the munchies, but it wasn't for something as childish as snacks. She would eat everything in the fridge and then start cooking two different kinds of stews and scarf it all. Never gained weight.

"Bring out the drugs," my mother said. "Let's get stupid."

She intended for us to build a new mood in our home.

She braced her bare feet against the railing as if testing its solidity, her ankles looking shapeless and slightly puffy. The purple veins seemed pronounced as the tawny evening glow turned mauve. Her mouth hung open, her lips loose, her hair vigorously brushed. Across the street, the building sides glistened, the air grew luminous. The bougainvillea below wouldn't let up on its vinous rustle, its stray flowers falling upon a giant heap of plastic garbage bags that looked like a slumbering prehistoric beast. The city shimmered, shadowless now, mysterious in these last lights. My mother stared at the seated man on the second-floor balcony, probably the flirty young man's father. She wouldn't move her eyes, a rigid gaze directed to the left of her legs, through the railings, down on to the man's pipe as it glowed, waned, glowed again.

The building's generator kicked in, announcing the time to be five thirty. I was able to rise off my rocking chair on the second attempt. I turned off our small generator at the end of the veranda. Before my mother arrived, I'd had it closer to the door. Moving it to its current location was one of her many demands. She needed it as far away from the clothesline as possible, not wanting the drying laundry to pick up any generator dust particles, which she insisted were flecks of grease. When the big building generator was on, hanging laundry had to be taken back off the line, brought out again when it went off. Our schedules were determined by the generators.

"I don't feel anything," she said, "or not much. Do you think I've grown inured to the drugs?"

"Of course not," I said. "You're so stupid right now, totally wasted."

I felt as if heaven had dropped behind my eyelids, as if I were being hugged by an angel.

"You're stupid," she said, "not me. Fuck your mother. Does this mean that I shouldn't have another?"

"Absolutely not. I should send you to your room."

"Such a sourpuss." Her hands tried first to compose her hair, then tried to rub the wildness and the chemistry from her eyes. "I will sleep well tonight. I don't think I'll remember my dreams, though. I never do if I have edibles. Am I talking too much again? You'll never believe who visited in my dream last night. Mr. Cat. He showed up as if he'd been around all this time. You know I adore Monet and Manet, but they're no Mr. Cat. No cat is or will ever be. All these years and I still think of him almost every day."

When I was young and gullible, I used drugs hoping to travel to far-flung imaginings, to undertake glorious exploits of the mind, a trip to the moon on gossamer wings. Now that I'm old and gullible, I hope for the greatest of all adventures: a night of unbroken sleep.

Laundry rejuvenated my mother. Cleanliness made her happy. Washed away old sins, old mistakes flushed in the rinse. The sun was shining, the day absently warm, so my mother ran the washing machine. She came out onto the balcony, beaming at me, at the world, looking years younger, carrying a basket brimming with wet bundles. I was on my second cup of tea, getting ready to walk to school. My tie on but not yet my jacket.

"Do you have time to help," she asked, laying the basket at her feet.

"Not much," I said. "Maybe a little."

Our first day of not-gray. Rains had been persistent for a few days. She stood in the healing light, her eyes shut for a moment. The sun was supposed to add wrinkles, but she looked younger, as though her life was to be extended for a dozen years. She pinned a wet nightgown to the line.

"Hand me the stuff and I'll pin," she said. "Pull your tie back before you get your hands wet."

Piece by piece, I handed, and she pinned, her dresses, my shirts, hers, her bras, her underwear, not mine. We moved together, coordinated, in silence, which was unusual for her. Something was on her mind.

"We're happy," she said. "Aren't we?"

"Yes, we are," I said.

"I thought so," she said. "You can go to work now. I'll make you something good for dinner."

II
(2001 – 2021)
The Banking Collapse
The Covid Pandemic

I begin this story with the lie, and like a great whale leading other sea creatures in her wake, it was followed by a whole pod. I wish I can say I had doubts. I didn't. I jonahed that whale, swam right through and settled in. Gullibility and I have always been chummy. In my defense, the offer seemed real, and in a sense, it was, and when it arrived, I was desperate. Hook, line, and harpoon. I was in.

An organization called the American Excellence Foundation sent me an email on Friday evening, July 23, 2021. The foundation was based in the state of Virginia all the way over in America, and in spite of the name, its mission was supposed to be global, as in, it claimed to be a nonprofit fighting disease, poverty, hunger, and inequity around the world. Impressive, and I was impressed, particularly with the content of the email: yada, yada, yada, they were great, blah, blah, blah, I was great, yada, yada, yada, and my literary sensibility was both courageous and excellent, if not exactly American, blah, blah, so they'd like to offer me a residency at their subtly restored, bucolic farm in central Virginia for three months, where they'd board me, feed me, pay me one hundred dollars a day, and provide me the space and unfettered time to work on whatever I was working on.

The only hesitation I felt when I received that email was that I wasn't working on anything, hadn't worked on anything for more than twenty-five years, and had no intention of working on anything in the future either. I had written a book, you see, twenty-five years earlier. But I'm not a writer, not really. I wrote a book, that was it. It was an accident.

No, the lie wasn't that I had received an offer as a writer and I wasn't. I never claimed to be. I taught French philosophy at a high school. I was sixty-one years old when the damn offer arrived, and I'd been teaching the same class at the same school in Beirut for thirty-six years.

My high school alma mater offered me the job in the summer of 1985 during the middle of the civil war. I was to start teaching that fall, and I was worried that since I'd be spending most of my time in French, my Japanese might atrophy. I began a writing project in Japanese, an essay dealing with taking long walks in Beirut while that civil war was going on. I thought I'd work on whatever it was that I was writing during the summer and finish it before I started teaching, for the practice, mind you, just to improve my written Japanese. I ended up working on the project for nine years. Turned out to be a book of ninety-six pages. Taking so much time to finish such a small book should have been a signal to anyone and everyone that I was not a writer. I wasn't supposed to publish it either, had no intention of doing so. The writing started out as an exercise, which turned into a private endeavor meant to clear my mind, to disentangle my feelings of what happened during the war, to the people, to the city itself. I didn't write about myself at all, just stories of the war and the city. I described battle remnants, memories and traumas etched into concrete. Up there was where a sniper camped, shooting no less than seventeen people, including Mrs. Bharat and Samira, her Ethiopian maid, down this street. The big hole over there was made with an RPG that missed its target by about twenty meters. I wrote it as a Lebanese stroller dissociating from his surroundings, pretending to be Japanese. The only person who had read any of it was Mrs. Murata, a neighbor who was responsible for my fascination with Japan and had moved back to Tokyo at the beginning of the Lebanese civil war. I received an email sometime in the nineties from her niece Himari informing me that Mrs. Murata had passed away, and that she, Himari, had found my manuscript in her aunt's papers. She wondered if I'd allow her to show it to an editor friend of hers. I found out later she'd already done so long before she received my permission.

A small press published my bizarrerie of a book, stupidly titled *A Walk with the Japanese Ghosts of Beirut*. Through no fault of my own, it did rather well—okay, it did very well. It became somewhat of a phenomenon in Japan, primarily because of its exoticness. I mean, here was one of those Arabs, barely a level above a brute, who could write a book in our hallowed language. Not that my use of language was beautiful, not baroque or flowery, but simple, like the walks I took—straightforward, but allegedly able to plummet its reader into immeasurable depths. Apparently, I'd spent nine years perfecting the tone that would make the book devastating and excruciatingly poignant, not that I'd spent nine years because I found the language so difficult, nine years trying to light a small fire with the ill-formed, wet branches of my Japanese sentences.

When I say the book did well, I don't mean in biblical proportions. It was not Harry Potter, Gibran, or the Bible. It sold well for what it was. It was translated into twenty-three languages but never made a bestseller list in any country. It did well in that I was invited to read or talk about my book by a few universities and literary festivals. I was able to travel the world on other people's money. Okay, it did well enough that I made a tidy sum of cash from publisher advances, and I put all of it away, never spent any of it, because I was terrified I would have no money to live on when I grew old, as I was right now, and I knew I could be fired at any point from my job.

I wasn't completely candid when I wrote that teaching French philosophy was the only job I ever had. Not that it was a lie—I used to moonlight as a performance artist, a controversial one, even, but I didn't earn any money that way. My art was not my job. Teaching my teenage brats was.

Here, I would like to address my feelings about my book. Whenever I spoke of it in a deprecating manner, I was accused of exhibiting a perverse reverse humility, a conceit fishing for praise. Worse, a German reviewer called me a naïf master. I was neither. He compared my book to W. G. Sebald's works, particularly *The Rings of Saturn* and, dear lord, *Austerlitz*. I know I had no say in how a reviewer saw my work, but I was filled with shame. Mortified, even. To this day, I dreamed of visiting Winfried's grave in the churchyard of St. Andrews, kneeling, and begging his forgiveness. It might not have been my fault, but I was ever so sorry.

Yes, my book's narrator was a walker, like Sebald's, but the tradition of walker-narrators was as old as writing itself. It was true I wrote about the vilification of the other, but that was only concerning Beirut at a specific time. Sebald tackled the whole history of persecution. He was a master, and I a peon. The problem with the comparison was that one of the master's strokes of genius was his use of nineteenth-century prose, updated of course, to write about the great melancholy of the twentieth century. He used hypotaxis unlike anything I had seen before. Me? I could barely subordinate a clause, and I certainly couldn't do it in Japanese.

I was no master. Writing in that pristine language would forever be a struggle.

Yet I was no naïf. I might have been younger when I wrote it, but I had been reading extensively, the poets, the philosophers, the great novelists. I read them all in four languages. I knew what a great book was supposed to read like. It was never my intention to write one, nor could I, since I spent all my writing time trying to figure out how a Japanese sentence worked.

When I said I didn't consider my book that great, I wasn't being humble or arrogant. I was speaking the truth.

Now, did I earn a lot of money from it? I did. Let's just say that after the book was published in all the different languages, I had low to mid-six figures in my savings account, in dollars no less. I refused to touch the money. Okay, so that wasn't true either. In 2001, my mother became depressed that she was aging so quickly and earnestly. All of us, her family—my father, my brother, and I—disapproved of plastic surgery, but my mother apparently did not; well, obviously did not. My father refused to pay for any of it. I doubt he could have anyway. My brother, the soulless dentist, aka the stupid one, whined that he had his wife and kids to worry about; he couldn't help. My mother turned to her homosexual, nonbreeding son, who happened to be very gullible. I have always been susceptible to my mother's minor needs and exigencies. I began many a battle feeling indomitable and ended up prostrate and vanquished, my mother's flag fluttering, its pole staked right through my heart. I knew of no one else who could use sighs as a lethal weapon. Twenty thousand dollars was what she wanted, and that's what I gave her. In fairness, as I look back now, I can state that it was the best money I ever spent. You should have seen her face, literally and figuratively. She looked so good and was happy again—so, so happy. The knife pruned and joy bloomed.

Other than that, I didn't spend any of it. I lived off my meagre salary. The bank was giving such high interest on savings that I was making plenty. I thought that when I retired, I would be able to do so comfortably. I'd be able to travel, spend time on the beaches of Tunisia, have shopping sprees in Milan. I had a good plan. And I lost everything, everything. The politicians and bankers stole all our money. Everyone's savings—poof. The whole country. There was nothing I could do about it. My dreams did not fade; they imploded. And even though having a job meant I was luckier than most everyone else in this bloodthirsty bitch of a country, I would never be able to retire. I was a serf.

Do you see now why I so easily believed that lie of an invitation?

And my mother said, "Go to America, Raja, go, go, go, so we can have more space in your apartment for a few months."

Yes, my name is Raja.

Call me Raja the Imbecile.

Welcome to my stupid life.

Let's talk about my mother for a bit, shall we?

You would think that after siphoning off twenty thousand from my bank account, Zalfa wouldn't ask for another big favor. Okay, so the thought might have crossed your mind, but it didn't mine. As I said earlier, call me Raja the Gullible.

In June 2005 my brother Farouk had his fourth child — maybe third, but who keeps track of such things? My mother was happy for two days, at which point my dad died. She mourned for a month or two, wore black for a year, returning to color and unabashed happiness in June of 2006. Sixty-eight at the time, she developed new routines, filled her leisure with civilized vices. Her mornings were devoted to taking adult courses at the university, primarily cultural studies and painting. Her watercolors were awful, but she was proud of them — no one could possibly inform her otherwise. She loved her cultural studies and would try to convince disinterested family members to pick up a Conrad or a Dickens. She was over the moon when one day her class was assigned *A Walk with the Japanese Ghosts of Beirut*. She wouldn't stop talking about it for months. "No, of course he isn't as great as Conrad," I once heard her say, "but his next book will be. Just you wait. He's writing a masterpiece."

She used her afternoons to visit family, play cards with friends, and — what brought her the most joy — babysit her grandchildren. She couldn't abide being alone, so she stuffed her life with people. If she wasn't with people, she was on the phone. She believed mobile phones were invented with her in mind. She was happy. She was independent for the first time in her life, and after spending so many years as a subaltern to an incompatible husband, she flourished. He left her nothing other than the apartment we grew up in, his gas-guzzling, exhaust-pipe-missing junker of a car, and a few thousand dollars in their bank account. He would have spent that money had he known he was going to die from a heart attack that sunny day in June.

But her inheritance didn't last because, you should know, my brother was a dick, and always had been.

Sometime in 2012, I received a call from my brother, seemingly in a panic. Could he talk to me in confidence? Could he rely on me not to share what he was about to tell me with anyone, not my mother, not his wife, not anyone? Sure, I said, not thinking much about it. His secrets, like him, were boring.

He needed money, obviously. I couldn't imagine him asking me for any other kind of help. I'd been expecting the call for quite a few years. He wouldn't specify how much he needed at first. I assumed that was because he didn't know how much I had in my bank account. My secrets were more interesting than his.

He was in trouble, he bleated, deep trouble. He was whisking his family out of the country, couldn't risk lingering in Beirut. He gave his notice at the clinic, but he already had a job lined up in Dubai, because, you know, dentists were in demand. He'd already sold his apartment and both their cars.

That was fast, I said. What good fortune to have found buyers so quickly!

Why did he have to disappear? Loan sharks, yes, loan sharks. My first thought was that at least the lie was original. He must have thought hard to come up with it, or maybe his wife did. He told me he had borrowed money from a usurer, feeling certain he would be able to pay it back not just promptly, but ahead of schedule even. Things fell apart, though. He hadn't realized how these people operated. I wouldn't believe it if he told me. Now, they were threatening him and his family. It would have been acceptable if he was the one being imperiled, but they were going to come after his kids. That would not do. Could I loan him some money?

My brother was as transparent as a piece of glass, only not as smart.

No, I said. I heard his shock behind the momentary silence. I did not mention that if the situation was reversed, he wouldn't give a single penny or pence or piastre, that he had lied to me, and about me, more times than an accountant could count. I didn't bring up that when one of his sons was five, he called me an ass, and when I asked him why he did that, he said everyone in his family called me an ass at home. I did not tell my witless brother that we haven't had a meaningful conversation ever. I didn't say any of that. I said no.

I disliked my brother. He loathed me.

When I was four, seven-year-old Farouk told me that when I, a newborn, was brought home for the first time and placed in the crib that once belonged to him, he had tried to strangle me in my sleep. Every night, he told me, when he and baby me were left in our room with the lights out, he would get out of bed, walk over to my crib, extend his hands through the bars, and strangle me. You wouldn't die, he told me.

He was always a failure. He was always a liar. He was always a pig.

When we were younger, he wore the look of a prize pig; when he grew up, a defeated one, having lost the prize along the way.

I could imagine the discombobulation of his porcine brain trying to digest my rejection over the phone. But, but,

but, you gave mother twenty thousand to get her face done. This was more important. This was an emergency. He was flabbergasted when I did not budge.

I should have told my mother right then and there. It might not have changed anything, but my telling her could have been a warning, preparation for what was to come. He told her the loan shark fabrication, but with her, he held a better hand. He was leaving the country and wouldn't be able to return, and he was taking her grandchildren. He was her eldest. She was blind to his mediocrity and his failings. She loved him absolutely and his children even more. She couldn't bear the idea of losing them. Yes, she told him, she would give him whatever she had. She would sell her apartment, her only home since she got married, sell the junker, close out her bank account. He could have all that.

But then she shocked him by demanding that she emigrate with them. She would have no home, nowhere to live, no family without him and his kids. They must take her. He hadn't thought through his plan because, you know, he's not terribly bright (I know I've mentioned this more than once, but trust me, it bears repeating). Maybe he expected her to move in with her sister and be taken care of by her. Maybe he thought she'd move in with me. But there was only one deal she was willing to make. She'd give him everything, never thinking about me. He could take all she had, but he had to take her as well, since she would have nothing left. My mother loved him so. She sold everything, even the furniture. My duplicitous brother had her ship the Persian carpets—because they would look good in the apartment in Dubai—but not my mother's adored sixteen-seat dining room table that had been in her family for generations. She should sell it, he told her, there was no time for sentimentality.

I knew something was wrong as soon as she called, announcing she wished to visit me. My mother never did that. One of my pet peeves was that she showed up at my apartment whenever she pleased, any day, any time. My apartment was one street over from hers, a five-minute walk, and she used that as a reason to drop in, to check in on me, as she liked to say. When I'd complain, she'd insist she need not change her behavior, since I rarely had any visitors.

That day, she didn't use her key, but rang the doorbell. I practically had to pick myself off the floor to answer. Who was this woman before me? I asked her what was going on, but she wanted to have coffee first before we talked. She didn't even berate me for not having had the kettle brewing before her arrival. Head bowed, her eyes looking at her next step, she slow-walked into the kitchen like a wounded animal, dragging not a limb but her whole body. She wore black, a dress I hadn't seen since my father's mourning period. I thought she was going to tell me she had cancer or something equally horrific.

We faced each other across the speckled-top kitchen table, perfectly black coffee in tiny white cups, which both of us were unable to pick up with shaky hands. I had to be gentle; she seemed more fragile than the porcelain.

She told me in a muffled voice that she sold everything and was leaving.

"What the hell?" I yelled. "Are you insane? You fell for his lies again. I can't believe this."

"You don't understand." She wouldn't look at me, kept staring at the coffee, which was slowly dissipating heat and losing vitality. A crack of light seeping from the kitchen window's tie-up curtain fell on her hand like an annunciation.

"Of course I understand," I railed. "And so do you. He wants what he cannot have. Ever since I can remember, he's lived as if the world owed him. He uses people, and you let him."

She still wouldn't look at me. I had to stand up and turn my back to her. I didn't want her to see my face in such agitation. I stomped to the sink, dumping the coffee without having had a single sip. I couldn't figure out which made me rage more, that my brother was destroying her life or that he, like my irksome father, could turn her, my oak, into a simpering willow.

"I can't let you go," I said. "No, you will not go. I won't allow it."

I didn't have to turn around to face her. I heard the chair slide on the linoleum. She had to regain her full height for what was to come.

"I don't need your fucking permission, you little shit."

"That's because you're stupid."

We both swiveled to confront each other with only enough space between us for accusing fingers. I could smell her amber and orange flower body lotion, the scent of sumac under her fingernails. She glared at me. Luckily, she had to do so while looking up because she was shorter than me. Not by much, but in war, every inch mattered. And into the spiral we dove.

"You're the one who's stupid," she yelled. "Not me."

"You're so stupid. Even this coffee cup is smarter than you."

"I can't believe I raised such a stupid son."

"You did raise a stupid son and you're following his stupid braying all the way to the stupid city of Dubai. I can't believe you bought the loan shark story."

"Not all of us can afford to be as cynical as stupid you. Fuck your mother. Now, this stupid coffee is cold. Make me another stupid cup. I can't believe you talk to your mother this way. May your house crumble. Do you have anything to eat in your stupid refrigerator? You made me hungry."

She turned to the fridge, and I turned toward the burner with a new kettle.

"I can't even smell the cardamom in your coffee," she bellowed into the coolness of the freezer section, "which means you're buying cheap beans again." Her bony behind showed from behind the refrigerator door. "Just because you prefer drinking tea doesn't mean I have to suffer."

"Don't change the stupid subject."

"Oh, heaven. Is this okra stew? Do you have rice, or must I eat it straight out of the pot? How come you're never prepared for your mother's visits?"

"Well, we no longer have to worry about that, now do we?"

The riceless microwaved okra stew was dutifully massacred. She dabbed her lips with her handkerchief. Before her I placed another cup of Turkish coffee, hot enough to send bandeaus of translucent smoke reeling upward. She explained her closing of bank accounts. Her home was sold to a nice couple with three children, which the apartment needed. She felt it was a family home, not that of a single woman. And the couple was nice enough to buy most of the furniture in the apartment. She'd wanted to sell everything inside for one price, but Farouk refused, itemizing and pricing everything, including the silverware.

"How could you sell everything?" I asked. "Did you not consider I might want something?"

"Of course not," she said. "You wouldn't want anything of mine. You're so peculiar. Look at this place. It's so spare, nothing is out of place. If you add anything here, you might have a heart attack and the whole building might collapse from shock."

"You so love to exaggerate, don't you?"

My dull-witted brother was organizing the move, the sales, the financing. By the time they were to leave in seven days, my mother's home would no longer belong to her, and no trace of her would remain in her homeland. My brother had at first wanted to travel with the truck carrying their belongings, but his wife convinced him it was a bad idea. I wondered whether he mentioned this to my mother hoping for her to suggest that she ride with the truck.

"How are they fitting everything in one truck?" I asked. "Is the idiot too cheap to hire two? Your table alone might take up the entire space."

"We're not taking the table," she said, in a surprisingly nonchalant tone. She sipped her coffee, looking up at the ceiling as if having a chat with God, a divine klatch. "It's old and falling apart. The owners didn't want it at first, but Farouk gave them a deal, just three hundred dollars for the table and chairs. I have a feeling they might keep some of the chairs and use the table for firewood, which is a shame if you ask me. I know it's not worth much, but it's oddly charming."

"You sold the table?" I must have sounded severe because she recoiled, her starched face momentarily static, her hair melding into the chairback, her eyes screaming in alarm. "How could you?"

Her hand jerked, almost spilling coffee on her black sweater. It took her a second to gather her composure and put the cup back onto its saucer. "We couldn't take it with us. Farouk didn't want it, neither did my sister. Selling it was the only option."

"No, it wasn't the only option. I'll take it."

"You can't," she said. Her voice trembled like a trapped insect. "Where will you put it?" She sipped the remaining coffee with wobbly deliberation.

"Here," I said. "I'll use it instead of this one."

"Stop it," she said. "It wouldn't fit. The apartment is small as it is. Kitchen and living room in an open space. Put that table here, and you'd hardly be able to move around."

"That's my problem, not yours. I want our table. It's part of my family. Did you forget I danced naked on it once? Do you remember? Farouk couldn't wait until Father came home so he would spank me."

"Of course I remember," she said.

"I want the table."

"No," she said. She seemed to be wilting once again before my eyes, folding hedgehoglike into herself. "You can't. I won't let you do this to yourself. It would ruin this apartment and all the work you did on it. You must stop living in the past. Time to move on."

She'd regressed to the whispering, the inability to look anywhere but downward, the slumped shoulders.

Sometimes, it took me a while to figure out what was happening before my unseeing eyes.

"Why are you so stupid?" I yelled, standing up. "I want the stupid table."

"You're the stupid one," she yelled, standing up. "You can't have the stupid table."

I walked to the cabinet where I stored the can of Danish cookies, opened it, and removed three crisp hundred-dollar bills. I slapped them on the table. "Here's the money for the stupid table, three hundred dollars. I want my table."

"I will not take your money, you little shit," she said.

"It's not for you," I said. "It's for my stupid brother. I don't want him to ever think I owe him anything. And I'm not going to pay more for it. You two were willing to let it go for three hundred so that's the price. I'll pay to transport it over here and that's it. It's my stupid table now."

"I won't allow you to talk about your stupid brother this way," she said, as she grabbed the bills and stuffed them in her pocket. "You're such an ungrateful son. The table is going to ruin this place, and you're going to break your neck trying to maneuver your pudgy ass around it every time you walk from the sofa to the kitchen. You're so stupid. You want the table, you can have it. I can't wait to visit from my comfortable home in Dubai and watch your bounteous behind stuck in one of these corners. 'Help me, help me, I can't move. My mother was right. I shouldn't have brought this humongous table into my tiny apartment, but I was stupid and obstinate.' You'll have to butter the walls so your ass can slide across. Stupid you. I'm emigrating to Dubai, and you're going to miss me so much you're going to be crying like a stupid baby for months. You should go back to wearing mascara so you can email me photos of you looking like a sad clown with dark streaks on your cheeks. Fuck your mother. I'm leaving now."

And off to Dubai she went.

Now, you might rightly ask why I would want the table. Let me tell you. It was true what my mother said at the time, that it was too big. What need would I have for a sixteen-seat table when I scarcely had any visitors? The largest number of people I'd ever had at one time in my apartment was five, and that happened once, maybe twice. The table was so immense that if I needed to walk from my living room to the kitchen, I had to squeeze my butt between it and the wall, sliding crablike. I've had to have two sets of cleaning utensils—two mops, two pails, two squeegees—one for the kitchen, and one for the rest of the house. To open one of the windows, I would have to either crawl on the table or get to it by going out to the veranda. The monstrosity swallowed any sense my apartment might have had. Feng shui turned to folly. But what can I say, I loved it. Our history was carved into it. My mother was right in that I enjoyed living in the days of yesteryear, though unlike her, I realized a while ago I need not suffocate under the swaddle of my past. I could and did leave some of it behind. I had so much of it after all.

That stupid table meant the world to me.

And it did to my mother as well. When her grandfather Melhem, the village carpenter, wanted to marry my great-grandmother Nazek, he realized his modest lifestyle might not impress his future in-laws. He was wrong—no one in the village owned anything of any significance, not land or houses, maybe a cow or a mule, a goat or some sheep. They were all mountain peasants. My mother's generation was the first to go to school, the first literate one. In any case, her grandfather wanted to show his intended wife and her family where he wished to be, not where he was. He carved this table by hand, beginning it in early summer, but unable to finish it before the rains arrived. That thing didn't fit into any of the two rooms of his house. Like Monet—the painter, not my troublemaking cat—he worked on his masterpiece en plein air. He did try to varnish it as he worked but wasn't able to halt the water damage. Continent-like stains, as well as island archipelagos, bloomed on various locations. He tried painting the table white before presenting it to his wife, but, thankfully, he wasn't a good painter. Snow-colored chips began to flake off within less than a year and he had to strip off the paint, restoring it to its original disaster, the greatest dining table ever created.

It spent at least two and a half years outdoors because my great-grandfather Melhem was married quite a long time before he was able to add an extension to the two-room house that could accommodate such a colossus. My kitchen cum dining table lived with nothing between it and the stars, lived happily in the mountains for a while, but, obviously, it wasn't an *ever after*—a full *happily ever after* is unthinkable in Lebanon. After the three contiguous catastrophes, the last days of Ottoman rule, the First World War, and the famine, my mother's family felt it had no choice but to follow the village river all the way down to its death and dissolution in Beirut.

Now, when a caterpillar is ready for the pupa state, it builds a silky cocoon or shiny chrysalis around itself and begins to dissolve into soup—the brain, the body, the whole thing turns to soup. After a while, this soup reconstitutes itself into a splendid butterfly or maybe a pesky moth that would live out its short life trying to fuck a light. What I had always found incredible was that if you trained a caterpillar to do a certain thing, then the butterfly would remember how to do that thing, even though the caterpillar's brain and nervous system had dissolved and gone through a soup process. So, when my mother's family tumbled into Beirut leaving their ancestral village behind, they may have lived city lives, may have worked at city jobs, but even after that miraculous transformation, they remained peasants. And I, an heir to all their genes, to all the soup, that is.

My mother once told me she'd inherited the table—and not her sister or brother, who were both older—because she'd always loved it, but also because her family understood before she did that she'd married a miser. My mother swore that all through her marriage, and for a few years after she was widowed, she wouldn't allow herself even a mildly negative thought of my father. It was only after she moved in with me that she began to entertain the possibility that he might not have been the perfect husband for her, and a bit later realized he might not have been the perfect husband for anybody. Her horrid experience in Dubai might have had something to do with the awakening.

She had left for Dubai, and her first return visit back to Beirut, for her brother's funeral, would not be before a full fourteen months had passed. That was the longest time we'd been apart. She called regularly from Dubai, every few days or so, and sounded all right on the phone — not exactly happy, but all right. She knew just the right amount of cheer to use on me, and I, Gullible Raja, believed her. Maybe I did because I desperately wanted to, maybe because I lacked the necessary imagination to understand what my brother and his wife were willing to put her through, or how my mother could let them do those things. She was always inexplicably timid when dealing with my father or brother. It did not occur to me that my heartless brother would have her on an even stricter budget than my father ever did. She was allowed no money for anything, since my brother and his wife were offering room and board. Every time I would ask on the phone whether she was coming to visit, she'd come up with one excuse after another: The grandchildren needed her tutoring, her daughter-in-law needed an appendectomy, trivial things like that. It was when I saw her walk out through the automatic doors at the airport that I understood she wasn't doing all right. I tried various ways to get her to tell me what was going on, but she deflected all. She stayed with me for only four days, to attend the funeral and obsequies, but had to return quickly because she was needed. My brother and his family couldn't come to the funeral because they were so busy, avoiding loan sharks, one presumed, and they certainly couldn't make do without her.

Like most people, I have many regrets, but not recognizing what was going on, not inveigling her to tell me, might be the top of the list — well, maybe top five, or maybe top ten. I've screwed up quite a bit.

Her sister passed away five months later, and that time she couldn't make the funeral, which boggled my mind. She gave some idiotic excuse. She was needed to drive the kids to school or something like that, and she'd already called her nieces and nephews offering condolences. I tried to buy her ticket, but she wouldn't budge — she just wouldn't.

Almost two years into her stay, she was able to convince my brother to let her take classes again. There was some organization run by and for Lebanese expats called *Université pour tous* that offered continuing education classes in French. She called the admissions office to register. The director herself talked to her, telling my mother she had been one of my brats some twenty years earlier. I was her favorite teacher, she said, but unfortunately, she couldn't let my mother take any of the classes because her French wasn't good enough. My mother broke down, that being the final affront. I happened to call her the next day, and for the first time since she moved, she didn't hold back, letting loose with a barrage. She wailed over the phone, told me my brother and his wife were treating her like a maid, they didn't allow her use of the cars unless they needed her to drive their kids somewhere, that they forced her to wash all the pots and pans even though they had a dishwasher because they thought the machine would ruin them. She spent most days by herself. She sometimes went for a week or so without leaving the apartment. Her room had hardwood floors, pine paneling on the walls, and wooden beams on the ceiling. It looked and felt like a sauna. She was suffocating. In between sobs she would ask why a modern apartment in the desert had beams as if it was some chalet in the Alps. She hated everything. Nothing in her life was working. And the worst part was my brother and his wife no longer allowed her to dye her hair because it cost too much and they told her she was too old to worry about her vanity.

"Bastards," I yelled into the phone.

"And now I'm told my French isn't good enough. I can't take it anymore."

"Don't do anything crazy," I said.

"Oh, I can't kill them," she said, "as much as I want to. I must think of the children."

I told her to pack her bags. I called the airline and bought her a first-class ticket to Beirut whose price included a limousine to pick her up. I couldn't rely on the stupids to drive her. I then called the director, my old student, yelling at her for thirty minutes. She didn't dare hang up on me. She kept trying to convince me that my mother's French was not good enough because their classes were sometimes taught by French expats. I told her she should change the organization's name to *Université pour la haute bourgeoisie* and hung up. I hoped I was no longer her favorite teacher.

When I saw my mother at the airport, rolling her baggage cart, showing wide strips of white hair on each side of her part, I realized that the next time I saw my stupid brother, I would kill him. With my bare hands.

And you need not worry. I wouldn't see him again. I refused to talk to him, let alone get together with him.

I believe the first time she considered that her husband might not have been an ideal one happened after about a week. She and I had spent that week in shock, trying to come to terms with the fact that she, I, and the dining table were going to be stuck together in my compact apartment for the rest of our lives, neither one of us having ever imagined we would be there. I'd left home as soon as I graduated college at twenty-one, wanting to break any reliance on my parents. And now here we were. She and I had exhausted ourselves, moving things around the apartment to accommodate her and her meagre possessions, never stopping for fear of having to talk about how we ended up in that situation. Standing at the kitchen counter building sandwiches for our dinner, her back to me, she looked up at the disappearing sun in the window, and mused, "I guess he didn't make my life comfortable."

I wasn't sure what she was talking about and told her so.

"Your father," she said, not looking back. "I'm talking about your father. I always thought he, unlike most other husbands I knew, worked hard to make my life comfortable. I no longer do. He was a bit selfish."

"A bit?" I asked. "You think he was only a bit selfish?"

"Why do you have to exaggerate all the time? Always drama. What was your first drag name again?"

She knew the answer, so I wasn't going to give her the pleasure of my reply.

"Hyperbolea, yes, that's it. The Geisha Hyperbolea, always and forever."

That was not exactly true. My first drag name was the Geisha Steatopygia, but that didn't last more than a week or two since no one knew the word and I would have had to explain. I soon transformed into the Geisha Hyperbolea, who had a longer incarnation than her predecessor, the poor Steatopygia.

I should have been more upset with her insults. I should have yelled at her. Though I made sure not to show it, I was pleased she was recuperating, rebirthing herself back to the mother I knew. But it would take another month or so for Zalfa the Indomitable to return to me. I was coming home from work, having had another exhausting class with my brats. I tried to come into the apartment as quietly as possible to lie down on my bed for a few minutes before having to face anyone—well, having to face my mother. I was about to walk into my room when I heard soft sniffles in the kitchen. I looked in on her, realized it was no mere sniffling. She was weeping, slumped on the giant table, her head resting on her forearm. I asked if she was all right, surprising her upright.

"Yes, I'm doing fine," she said, "but your father was a dick."

"You don't have to tell me."

"And your brother is a dick too."

"You should try telling him," I said. "You'd feel better, believe me. Do what I did. Call him and tell him he's a charmless, heartless, witless, withered soul of a person who suffers from social halitosis and then hang up on him. It's like filling your heart with helium that will lift it up to the skies. Try it."

"Oh, shut up. You don't understand anything." She shook a forefinger at me, and then both hands. "Now, come squeeze your big butt through here and sit next to me. We should talk, and I don't want to do it from so far away." And she was back, my mother, who could metamorphose from tearful to imperious in less time than it took for anyone to say *What the hell*. "See, if you had a skinny ass like mine, you'd be able to maneuver around the table easier, but you have a fat ass. Don't look at me that way. I'm not saying you're fat, just that your ass is."

She proceeded to set the conditions of our living together. She would try to respect the fact that it was my apartment, but she couldn't guarantee it, since, you know, she was my mother. She was going to do all the cooking because everyone knew I wasn't the best cook. She would oversee food shopping because I didn't care for quality as much as she. Cleaning, we could both do, ditto for laundry, but she was not going to wash my underwear. She was over washing men's underwear. Maybe I could hire a part-time housecleaner. The Japanese mahogany lintel I'd placed on the table must go. She didn't care where I put it. It was pretty and all that, but who would place a part of a door as a centerpiece? No, only flowers in a nice vase go on the table. And the coup de grâce: She didn't think it was right for her to keep asking me for money, and no, she couldn't possibly be given an allowance. What was I thinking? She was no child, no teenager. I had to give her access to my bank account—the checking account, not my savings account, at least not yet.

To this day, I'm not sure how or why I agreed to her conditions, and so easily. I didn't argue. I didn't mention that I was the one being inconvenienced. I didn't bring up the fact that I was saving her from the horrible choices she'd made, from how terribly she was treated, from the humiliating life she was living. I agreed. I moved the lintel to my bedroom. She had been so oppressed with gloom in that fake shiny city. I couldn't bear it.

Now, where was I?

So, my mother moved in with me in 2014 or maybe the beginning of 2015. I remember it was winter, a heavy rainstorm sopping and mopping the streets of Beirut. Surprisingly, we adjusted to living together well and rather quickly. Our temperaments were supposed to be incompatible. I loved quiet, and she hated it. She hated being alone, and I loved it. We adjusted. I had to adapt more. She was used to living with others, whereas I hadn't in years. She was supposed to be habituated to compromise. In the end, we were able to live together because we both understood that if we did what she wanted, we would both be happier. That was not to say I kowtowed to her every whim. I had some boundaries, which she crossed every now and then, claiming that at her age, she couldn't be expected to remember where the lines were drawn. Some rules were not to be broken: She couldn't have too many friends over at the same time, and my father's family were not allowed anywhere near my home, particularly Aunt Yasmine. My mother could visit her as often as she wished, but my father's evil sister wasn't allowed to pass under our lintel. I still carried the childhood scars of all our battles, the ones I was forced to engage in and those I avoided.

We lived at peace for a few years, only one fight every week or so, or maybe it seemed harmonious compared to what was to happen after. Self-delusion was our sustenance. Not just the two of us, but the whole country. Living under avaricious and murderous governments that had replaced other avaricious and murderous governments, bordered by more avaricious and murderous governments, denial of reality became a mode of survival. I'd return home after a rough day with my brats to find my mother playing cards with three or four of her friends, only able to sit at a right angle at the giant table since one side was pushed against the wall. She would have a snack waiting for me at the kitchen's end of the table. The ladies would giggle as I maneuvered across to get the sandwich. Among her usual guests at least two or three wouldn't be able to squeeze through to the kitchen. And of course, my mother would lie, telling them how hard we worked to get the table moved, how much we both loved it, and that soon we would have it sanded and varnished to regain the freshness it never had. We spent our evenings reading or watching bad television shows on pirated stations. She couldn't tear herself away from series that always ended with justice triumphant. At dinners, she'd force me to tell her about my day. I couldn't get out of that no matter how hard I tried. She made me break one of my steadfast rules, telling her about my brats. My mother missed her calling. She would have had a remarkable career as a manager of a black site. She used enhanced interrogation techniques that were more sophisticated than anything developed by the CIA. Never had I ever spoken to anyone about my students outside of school, never mentioned any names or repeated what happened in my classes. My mother finagled her way into getting to know what happened with every brat. Professional boundaries be damned, she couldn't fathom why I would wish to have any. Worse, she sometimes knew who the brats' parents were or their grandparents and was more than willing to tell me all the family gossip she'd heard. By the second year, she wanted us to save time by my handing over the roster. She, on more than one occasion, wanted me to invite the classes for dinner so she could meet them. I was strong enough to not allow that.

We thought we were happy, or at least content, before the first disaster struck — a Lebanese disaster, mind you, not some European or American one, like when the Dow Jones loses a hundred points, Facebook goes down for a day, or a ninetysomething-year-old monarch passes away and football games are canceled.

Lebanon is a nation of thieves; what the eye sees the hand filches. In the fall of 2019, news began to leak that the Lebanese banks had run out of money. Why? Because members of all branches of the government had been stealing everything. Lebanon had been run by mafias for generations, devouring all, budding twigs and dry, the whole tree even. Hume once said avarice spurs industry. I can't speak for the rest of the world, but in my country, avarice spurs nothing but a more wanton avarice. A collusion between the government, the central bank, and the big banks had been a giant Ponzi scheme with our savings. Once the mafiosos ran out of money to siphon off, they went for the reserves, emptying the deposits of the national bank. The savings of every Lebanese—every Lebanese who wasn't a criminal hiding money abroad—disappeared. The government would tell us the money wasn't gone, no sirree, the banks were holding it for us. We couldn't withdraw any of it because, you know, there was no cash anywhere. And there I go again, exaggerating. Everyone who had money in the bank could withdraw the equivalent of $100 a week . . . no, $100 a month . . . no, the equivalent of $50 a month. My mother refused my giving her an allowance since she wasn't a child. Well, our government considered us all children.

It took a little bit of time for us to figure out what happened, or for me at least. Our pilfering government trickle-truthed us. The process of realizing that my savings were gone lasted a month or so, yet it felt sudden. In one instant,

I lost everything, wiped out. Before I could do anything, before I could take a breath, I was done. I had lost a future. Whatever dream I had for my retirement, every image I had of myself past that moment, of myself to come, was disappeared. What was mine no longer belonged to me. Now, I was one of the fortunate ones, blessed, in fact. I had a job, and unlike those of most of my compatriots, my job would end up paying me in dollars.

As I watched my country implode, as the currency devalued at a vertigo-inducing rate, I kept trying to convince myself I was lucky. I tried to convince my mother. She would have none of it.

While I grieved for a lost future, my mother sought retribution and redress.

For the weeks that the banks wouldn't open, she roamed the apartment, imprecating vengeance upon every politician in Lebanon, upon the head of every banker, every militia leader, every mafioso. She wouldn't calm down. School had started again, and I would leave for work with her yelling at the ceiling and return to her yelling at the light fixtures. How dare they steal an eighty-one-year-old woman's savings? She was a widow and a grandmother. She almost slapped me when I tried to joke it was my savings that were gobbled up, not hers. I tried sitting her down and explaining that we would be all right, that I might not be making a lot of money, but I made enough for both of us to keep going. We just had to cut out a few things. We couldn't go out to eat, which we never did anyway. We couldn't go on a holiday, which we seldom did in any case. Basically, we would get by. She called me stupid, of course. What would happen were I to lose my job, if the school couldn't pay me any longer? It wasn't as if she could start working at her age. She insisted we were screwed. I worried that this anger and anxiety might generate cardiac issues.

She and I camped at the bank's doors on the day they were to open, joined by hundreds of others, maybe thousands. After a two-hour wait, we were told the bank wasn't going to open. I went back to work. My mother simmered on high dudgeon. She talked to Aunt Yasmine, whose family was in worse financial shape than we were. Aunt Yasmine had a friend who was best friends with our bank manager's secretary, a Miss Zainab, and got us an appointment with her at ten in the morning. I arrived from school, had to wade through a pack of howling customers, shoving my way toward the inner sanctum, only to arrive at a glassed-in office where my mother seemed to be creating a louder commotion than the entire horde. Three men waiting outside the office cheered her on, jumping up and down. They were missing pom-poms. You tell her, one screamed. Make them give us back our money. I could see my mother through the glass under flickering fluorescents, her legs intertwined with those of a tumbled chair, her arms gesticulating wildly, her purse swinging an arc, trying to make herself look bigger, what a naturalist would call a deimatic display, an insane one. The taller and larger Miss Zainab pushed her seat as far into the corner as she could, hoping the desk was a good-enough barrier. I was assailed by my mother's energy, by the sound of her fury as soon as I opened the door. The secretary gave me a most pitiful, imploring look. Between the two of us we were able to calm my mother a bit. I returned the chair to upright. Miss Zainab tried to tell us she was in the same boat, her money was in the bank as well and she was unable to access it. My mother called her a liar, of course. That she should be ashamed of herself for lying to a woman her mother's age. Miss Zainab kept insisting she was the secretary only, she couldn't do anything. My mother accused her of dissembling once again. The secretary, her face contorting in worry, pointed to the engraved sign on her desk that stated her name and position. My mother, moving forward in her seat, demanded to scream at the manager, who hadn't come in, of course, and probably wasn't going to for a long time. None of the big shots were going to be around. If she didn't desperately need the job, Miss Zainab would quit right that minute. Did we think she enjoyed being yelled at by my mother? It was when Miss Zainab whispered that she was afraid of what everyone was going to do to her that my mother softened. She switched moods. The bank manager hadn't provided the employees with any security that day, Miss Zainab said, and my mother began to commiserate with her, cursing bank managers and all politicians. Within a few moments, my mother was on the other side of the desk comforting a sobbing Miss Zainab. My mother wouldn't allow any harm to befall her, she would make sure all the men outside behaved themselves, nothing untoward would happen to the secretary, but was there any cash in the bank that my mother could withdraw because we needed the money, maybe like one hundred thousand dollars lying around somewhere not doing anything? No, of course there was nothing of that kind, and if there were, we couldn't withdraw any of it, and Miss Zainab couldn't do much, but she was going to make a call to her friend in withdrawals to see how much money was lying around and whether he could do anything. She made the call while my mother was still hugging her, my mother's size making her look almost like a stole around the secretary's shoulders. It turned out we could get some money out, but we had to be discreet, not tell anyone, walk to the third office in the back, and not take out our checkbook until we were inside. Her friend would give us something, but please don't tell anyone she did this because she would lose her job and the men outside would demand the same and she couldn't bear it. My mother asked for her boss's mobile number, which Miss Zainab refused to give out at first. My mother needed the number to make sure Miss Zainab, her new best friend, would have an easier time for the rest of the day. Upon leaving the glass office, my mother berated the waiting men for being rowdy. She told them the secretary was just the secretary, was one of us so they shouldn't disturb her, that they should call her boss instead. Would they like his number?

We left the bank with $4,350 in cash. It would be the last time we withdrew a substantial sum from our savings. Miss Zainab would answer my mother's calls all the time and would help as much as she could. The bank manager had to change his number.

I was able to blanch my feelings for a couple of weeks after the bank visit. As soon as I felt a simmer of anger, I would drown it in icy water. I couldn't have my mother worrying so much. One evening, I returned from school, heard the television news blaring from inside our apartment—my mother would take off her hearing aid when I was out of sight—and as soon as I opened the door, she turned the television off. Under normal circumstances, my mother had difficulties remaining still. When she felt guilty or was trying to hide something, she made small, hurried movements with neck and head, with her hands. A dimple appeared and disappeared on her chin when she was agitated, or when she lied. Even her knees vibrated, just as mine used to do so long ago when I was about to sit for a school exam. Neither one of us could ever win a hand in a poker game. I knew right away she didn't wish me to see something on the television.

"You didn't have to turn it off," I said.

"There's no need to watch," she said, standing up. She planted her hearing aid into both ears. "It's the same old same old, just the news." She smoothed her dress with a quick, deft movement of one hand while the other removed her glasses. "Do you want something to eat? I cooked a couple of eggplants." She walked toward the kitchen, squeezing herself by the table. "We shouldn't be watching too much television anyway. We should save on using the generator. Who knows how much diesel is going to cost now?"

"The television runs on the UPS battery," I said. "You know that."

I clicked the remote control, and my mother said, "Don't. You'll make yourself miserable. Turn it off."

"I can handle it," I said. "I'm curious."

Michel Q. flickered on the screen. Everything about him had changed since the last time I saw him in person except for his irksome laugh. He wore a wool mask all those years ago—a mask that couldn't mask his stupid laugh. Through the years, I studied the transformation, in newspaper photos, on television, from murdering hoodlum to militiaman to patriot to politician, a well-trodden path taken by everyone at the top. He was on the news that evening because he happened to be an assistant of some kind to the minister of finance. And he cracked joke after imbecilic joke while the people went broke.

"I want to kill him so badly," my mother, ensconced on the sofa right next to me, said. "I have been planning his murder for decades. I want to twist his neck like a chicken. I want to run a cheese grater down his repulsive face. Don't argue with me. I know I can't do anything to him, but I can still imagine how I will kill him. It gives me comfort."

My mother was the only one I'd told about my underground stay, and the truth was that no one else wanted to know. Only my mother asked. I returned home, and everyone assumed they knew what happened. My father didn't want to know; my aunts, my cousins, my brother, no one did. The lies became more intriguing than anything I had to say. I was a spy who worked both sides, I was brainwashed with drugs, I played Russian roulette every night with militiamen betting on my survival, and of course, what became Aunt Yasmine's go-to explanation: I was the whore of Babylon. Only my mother defended me. I was fifteen, I was her baby. She wouldn't allow anyone to say any of those things about me. They said them behind her back. At the time, I didn't want to tell her, I didn't want to tell anyone, I didn't even want to speak, but she always knew how to get me to talk, despite myself. She allowed me some time alone, sitting in the same room with me but not saying anything. I left the room only when we had to hide in the corridor from sniper fire and hoodlum bullets, Mr. Cat in my arms, always. But one evening, six weeks after my return, she explained that school was open the next day and I was to go, and she wasn't going to leave the room until I told her what had happened to me, in detail of course, in embarrassing detail, and after that we would never talk about it again and I would get over it. I did get over it. I am my mother's son, nothing if not resilient. But we had to talk again and again about what happened because Michel Q. the misery bringer kept popping up in photos all over the place.

"He's so ugly," my mother said. "He looks more botoxed every time I see him. He can't appear on television without being injected. He should try formaldehyde."

Surrounded by interviewers and reporters gaping at him like passersby at a car wreck, he gloated and gleamed. His eyes held a rapturous, demented sheen. He wore a bespoke Brioni that most likely cost more than all the articles of clothing that both my mother and I owned. Unfortunately for him, he had left the jacket unbuttoned. He was a rotund man whose pants followed the sagging curve of his ample belly, and whose pants would not have deserved a mention were it not for his being a homicidal psychopath. He blustered, made terrible puns, tried to sound clever. He hawked a couple of times, hoping to clear a phlegmy throat. I thought he was about to spit but he ended up swallowing. He brought up the hackneyed "Beirut is a phoenix forever rising from its ashes" quote, and weren't the Lebanese amazing because we always recovered. Civil war, no problem. Israeli invasion, no problem. Syrian invasion, no problem. Financial collapse, please. Our people were the most irrepressible, so we shouldn't blame the government for repressing. In brief, the government wasn't willing to provide any economic relief to those whose money was stolen by the members of that government.

"Have you considered going to therapy?" my mother asked.

"What?" I wasn't sure I heard her correctly.

"You know," she said, "you can see a therapist and you'll feel better."

"What are you talking about? I feel fine."

"I know, but you can feel even better. If you talk to someone about what happened, you wouldn't have to be so upset every time that stupid shit appeared on television."

"But I'm not upset."

I could feel it percolating. I was dipping my toes into the frenzied pool before plunging.

"You're yelling," she said.

"I'm upset with you, not because that stupid shit is on television."

"If you're not angry, how come you made me turn off the television when he came on."

I had to jump up. "Are you insane?" I yelled. "I didn't make you do anything. I turned the television on. You turned it off."

"See. You're so angry. A therapist can help you."

"I swear I'm going to lock you in a mental institution and throw away the key."

"I'm so scared," she said. "So scared. You wouldn't survive a day without me. Why, if I go away for one hour, Monet and Manet will scratch out your eyes. Each one of them takes one eye. You'll become blind like Oedipus, except you didn't kill your father and you certainly can't marry me. You make a stupid Oedipus, if you ask me."

"Please stop. Don't say another word. I might just jump off the balcony. I swear. I can't take it."

"Don't be so dramatic. Sit down." The remote was already in hand, her knuckles around it redder than the paler skin encircling them. "Let's talk about this like rational adults. Sit down. I'm just saying you get upset when you think of him. Remember Michel Q.'s son, huh, remember? You were scared you might have had to meet his father, that stupid shit. You can't deny that."

"First, that was twenty years ago, if not more," I said, rationally. "And second, any rational person would be. He's wanted to kill me for as long as I can remember."

The story went like this. On the first day of class so long ago, I read out the brat roster, and when I came across the name of the stupid shit's father, I knew I was in trouble. The son named after the grandfather, patriarchal evil in a continuous loop. Except that boy, Ghassan Q., proved to be a sweet, smart, beautiful eighteen-year-old boy, and kind, so kind. He fell in love with philosophy. The son of the man who had never opened a book in his life grew up to become the most voracious reader of any of the brats who had ever studied with me. I liked the boy quite a bit, still do. What terrified me was that I would have had to meet his parents the first week of January when we returned from break. It was a school tradition. I couldn't afford to have the stupid shit see me, let alone talk to him. I decided I would see as many parents as I could before I had to meet the stupid shit and then pretend to be severely sick and leave early. It turned out I need not have worried. Neither of Ghassan's parents showed up. They sent his Moroccan nanny, who had raised him since he was six. By the end of our scheduled twenty minutes, she was in tears. I had spent so much time praising her for raising such an amazing boy I hadn't noticed how overwhelmed she had become. I didn't lie or exaggerate. I told her how impressed I was with Ghassan, and she broke down.

I'd not told that story to anyone, never mentioned that the stupid shit's son was ever in my class, but of course, when my mother moved in, she forced me to tell her everything.

"I'm quite all right," I said. "No therapist could make me feel any better."

"I'm suggesting it for your own good," she said. "You can remain miserable if it makes you happy. I care about you, which is why I'm suggesting this. I don't like to watch you suffer."

"I suffer only because you drive me crazy."

"You know," she said, "I read in *Marie Claire* that if a son suffers from post-traumatic stress disorder, the mother suffers her own kind of post-traumatic stress disorder, but you never think of me."

"I can't stand you right now," I said. "Go to your room."

"You go to your room, you little shit. I can't believe you talk to me this way. I'm your mother. I'm not going to talk to you ever again."

I stood up, trying to go to my room, but she pulled my arm and I fell back to the sofa.

"Where are you going?" she said.

"To my room. You're not speaking to me."

"You can't go to your room," she said. "How can I not speak to you if you're not here for me to not speak to?"

"You make no sense," I said.

We remained next to each other, uncomfortable and irritated, watching and hating Monsieur Micho on the news. My mother and I bonded in our sulk.

＊　＊　＊

I should have known something was off, or maybe I should have known she was up to something, plotting some nefarious plan. She seemed happy, or maybe less upset. The country was in upheaval, demonstrations everywhere, unlike anything Lebanon had seen before. In every city, in every town and village, in Beirut, in Tripoli, in Nabatieh, people took to the streets to protest the government purloining everything they owned, and were joined by more and more, to protest other grievances and older pains, the injustice of living Lebanese. The army and police were shooting at the protesters. The people wanted all the politicians out, and the politicians wanted to break every bone in the country.

I would return home from school to find my mother whistling the latest pop songs by singers who were the same age as her grandchildren. In less than a week she'd gone from wanting to cheese-grate politician faces to communing with our bonsai maple, telling it how much she admired its fall colors. She walked around the apartment with the finger loops of her scissors poking out of her pocket. I couldn't figure what was going on. I asked her, of course, but she'd always been the queen of deflection. I was nowhere near as skillful as she was at extracting information, not knowing how to be as intrusive or irritating. Should I have told her to stop being happy and tell me what was going on?

I walked into class one morning knowing I would have to repeat what we'd already gone through the day before. They were probably still stuck on Mill and Kant, utilitarian versus normative ethical theories. Most of my brats couldn't grasp the difference between two vastly different positions. I knew I was pushing them, but I also knew that with one or two exceptions, they were up for it. We had a few minutes before the bell. Some of the students were still trickling in, all of them designer fashionable. When I was their age, we had to wear uniforms. Twenty years ago, the school decided that the older students no longer needed to appear homogenous, no uniforms after sixième, which I considered a mistake. They were smiling, looking somewhat devious, as if they had somehow found the questions for a pop quiz I was about to give. They were being too familiar for my liking.

A boy, Yusef, lounged on his desk chair, mushroom-cut hairstyle, white D&G shirt, indolence incarnate. He was probably my favorite brat of the current crop, the smartest. I told him to sit up straight. I had never had to do that before. They'd been respectful up to that point. Yusef was utterly comfortable with his queerness. He wore his femininity like a favorite pair of runners, and his classmates seemed to adore him. I liked and envied him.

The class would not bring up what was going on if I did not ask, so I did. And of course, it was Yusef who gleefully said, "We love your mother."

And once again I thought to myself that the egregious error of my life was never having shot my mother.

Monique: "She's amazing."

Mohammad: "She's so cool."

Georges: "Such a lady, so much class. I want to be as incredible as her when I'm eighty-one."

Manal: "Yes, so elegant, but when she needs to, she can curse like a taxi driver. She stood her ground and refused to budge."

She'd been going to the antigovernment demonstrations. I was stunned. I had told her a million times, if not two million, that she shouldn't. A few demonstrators had been killed—shot or beaten to death. Many were taken away and tortured by the police. Thugs associated with the ministry were attacking protesters randomly. The front was not a place for an old lady.

Rawi: "She was probably the oldest person there. Every time a policeman came close, she'd ask him if his mother knew what he was doing."

Marie: "She'd use the choicest of words, of course."

Nico: "She's inspiring."

How did they know she was my mother? She told them, of course. So many of my brats were there, not just this year's class. Apparently whenever she came across a younger person she would ask if they knew who I was, and younger meant anyone under fifty-five. She met dozens.

Yusef: "When the army threw tear gas, we all knew that she couldn't run fast enough. I tried to help her, but then my cousin came and carried her."

I remembered his cousin, a student of mine from ten years earlier, an attorney now, and an antigovernment demonstrator. And a carrier of my mother.

Yusef: "And your lesbian cousin is remarkable as well."

I didn't have a lesbian cousin.

Yusef: "Yes, you do. My gaydar is infallible. I can tell a lesbian if she is in another canton, and your cousin Nahed and I held up signs shoulder to shoulder."

I felt a migraine coming on. I called a halt to the conversation. No more talk of my mother in class. I made them get back to Kant, to Kant and his stupid imperatives.

I ought to kill my mother.

By now, you should be able to figure out what happened when I confronted her that evening. We had a big fight, calling each other stupid names, and she continued doing whatever she felt like, including going to demonstrations. Once she no longer needed to hide, she turned our big table into an arts-and-crafts one, making grander and more outrageous signs every day. A photo of her made the middle pages of a newspaper; she was holding up a sign that said, "This Grandmother Wants the Regime to Fall," which was followed by one that said, "This Grandmother Wants All the Brothers of Whores in Jail." Her favorite sign though, which few people understood, simply said, "Don't Make Me Bring My Son to the Next Demonstration."

Our argument was like every other one we'd had as adults. I screamed that she was risking her life and she screamed that it was her life to do with as she pleased, quickly deflecting to how could I be so stupid as not to know that my cousin was a lesbian, the cousin whom I had not spoken to since I'd left home to go to graduate school. I'd had no contact with her or her family. How would I know? Why would I care? No, just because Nahed and I were family black sheep did not mean we should care about one another. No, I hadn't heard of the scandal of her divorce, her husband leaving because he walked in on her doing the nasty with none other than his sister, doing it standing in the kitchen and not in bed. Everybody could have been gossiping about it for years, but I was obviously not listening. I did not care.

"Of course, you do," my mother said, now calm, almost serene, having won the fight as usual. Score was probably ten thousand her and zero Raja the Gullible, maybe one — I may have won one fight some time ago but can't be sure.

"You've grown conservative in your dotage," she said. "People change, but not in your imagination. You still see everyone like they were when you were ten. You must be starching your shirts too much because it has seeped into your brain, which has become stiff. Starch is causing rigor mortis of the mind. Your ostracizing Nahed hurts her feelings."

"Are you kidding me, Zalfa? She used to beat me up on a regular basis while all of you cheered her on. I'm the one hurting her feelings?"

"That's not fair," my mother said. "It wasn't just you. She beat up everybody."

"Her mother used to set her on me. She was like a pit bull."

"Remember how you used to tell me she looked like a Bulgarian weightlifter. You two must have been seven or eight. Well, she's been lifting weights for about thirty years. She looks astounding, still so active, unlike you."

"I am active. Dealing with you is the most tiring exercise."

"They say when her husband walked in on her, he went for a gun to shoot her, but thought better of it."

"Smart man," I said. "She would have pummeled him."

"See," my mother said. "I don't even have to tell you the punchline. No bullet would stop her, not Nahed, the mighty Bulgarian."

My mother and I bonded in our giggle.

"One of your students from this year's class," my mother said, "can't remember the name, tall girl, glasses, braids her hair into pigtails."

"Mirna," I said.

"Yes, Mirna. She told me her grandmother makes the best pickles in Lebanon and that she once pickled a jar of green tomatoes for each of Mirna's teachers. Everyone was delighted except for you, Mirna said. You refused the gift. The whole family felt hurt and shame that you would do such a thing. Who but you refuses gifts?"

"Of course I refuse gifts from students or their families. Do you not understand anything about ethics, about boundaries? What am I talking about? Of course you don't."

"Do you not understand anything about kindness? You can't turn down a gift. That's so insulting. Do you never think about anybody else? I would have loved some pickled green tomatoes. Did you ever consider that? In any case, Mirna said she would ask her grandmother to give me a jar. I can't wait."

"You can't accept a gift from one of my students," I yelled. "I will not allow it."

"Be quiet," she said. "I already accepted. And it's not a gift, since I promised Mirna a jar of my homemade lamb fat to give to her grandmother. It's a barter. I like Mirna."

* * *

A few weeks later, Randa, an older student, called the house phone. She apologized for disturbing me, but she was worried about my mother, who wasn't answering her cell phone. My mother was napping. Randa repeated the apology, saying she would call my mother directly in the evening. I had to ask how she knew my mother even though I was sure they'd met at a demonstration. She told me.

They met after the police tear-gassed them. Apparently, my mother was by then more prepared than Randa, having bottles of water and dishrags in a knapsack — a knapsack that belonged to me, as she told Randa right after inquiring if I had taught her. Randa, overwhelmed by tear gas and humiliation, bawled. My mother took over. She washed Randa's face, wiping tears, dust, and dregs of gas. When Randa complained that she was probably a mess, my mother smoothed her hair with water and searched through it for hairpins, which she pried open with her teeth, and used to tame stubborn strands.

Randa became my mother's devotee.

"You never tell me anything," my mother said when she came out of the room. "You keep so many juicy stories from me. And for what? To protect your students? They're the ones who have no problems telling these stories."

I tried, for the umpteenth time, to explain that I must respect their privacy and couldn't talk about them, whereas they could tell their tales to whomever they wished, even to a tattletale like her.

"But they talk about you all the time," she said. "Non-stop storytelling of Professeur Raja. You did this once and this one time you did that. Nonstop, I tell you."

"The only reason they talk about me," I said, "is because you keep asking them."

"Not true. I only ask them sometimes, not all the time. They talk about you because they adore you. As soon as Randa found out you're my son, she started telling me about you in class."

"And how did she find out I'm your son?"

"I asked if she was your student but I didn't ask her to tell me secrets. She volunteered them."

"I bet."

"She told me the priest story. That was funny."

"What priest story? I don't remember a priest story."

"She told me you were young, starting out. Early in the school year, you had talked about Nietzsche saying God is dead and you made her think a lot, so when she went home, she told her mother what you said, and her mother went berserk and called her priest, who ran over in full regalia with his thurible and holy water sprinkler to exorcize the demon of atheism from the apartment. Do you remember?"

"Vaguely," I said. "I'm sure it's true. The two subjects that usually cause parents the most concern are atheism and feminism. But all I remember from Randa was she was smart. She might be the best human rights attorney in town. I don't recall a priest story, though."

"Randa said that when she showed up to class the next day, she looked so red-eyed that you had to ask if things were okay. She snapped that it was your fault she couldn't get any sleep. The priest had burned so much frankincense in the apartment and particularly her room that she could barely breathe all night. Her mother forced her to wash her face and hair in the vapors of the burning incense as if the frankincense was soap. I thought it was the funniest thing. You should have told me that story even if you didn't remember it."

I couldn't stop my mother from demonstrating against the government, but our country's second disaster did — stopped her from doing anything. The Covid pandemic may not have been an exclusively Lebanese catastrophe, yet its local effect was unique. Yes, many perished alone and untouched. Hospitals were overwhelmed. Yes, we had to isolate, sequestering in our rooms and homes. Whatever was left of the economy ground to a halt. But in this country, the pandemic doused all rebellious flames, crushed any hope of changing the status quo. The populace fell, not the regime.

The quarantine affected my mother and me differently. She needed people, whereas I preferred to avoid them. She began to feel blue within a week of being isolated. She had kept herself busy since moving in with me, and suddenly, she had quite a bit more time to spare. She was unsure how to deal with the situation, and that not knowing made her anxious. I saw her confronting her image in the vanity mirror on more than one occasion. One time, I realized I hadn't seen or heard from her in a while. I found her in the bathroom with an old toothbrush, on her knees, scrubbing dirt that had accumulated in the indentations between the tiles. She'd been at it for hours. She spent most of her spare time on the cell phone or on the couch watching television. She didn't fight.

I reacted differently. Were it not for the fact that people were dying, I would have been having a great time. Quarantining in my own apartment because of a virulent virus wasn't a problem. The streets of Beirut were empty. How could I not be happy with that? No cars, no pollution — the city was usually crowned with a veil of dust and dirt, but the mourning shroud had been lifted. Beirut was delivered from itself. Its sparrows, starlings, and pigeons flew the skies unencumbered, seemingly the only thing moving in the city. I heard their electric chirps above all. I would walk out onto the balcony and could see forever, breathe sweet gardenia-scented air. I hadn't seen the mountains that clearly in years and years. I could almost see every fleck of snow on the peaks, a sight that nourished the eyes. No people — I could hear myself think. I enjoyed having no one intrude into my life. I had long ago mastered the language of solitude.

We spent the first month in each other's and the cats' company. We didn't leave the apartment much at first, if at all. I could say that Monet and Manet were overjoyed, but that would be overstating. The boys were over-content. Never had they had that much attention, switching laps every twenty minutes or so.

We had our groceries delivered and had to make sure they arrived when the building's generator was turned on. Otherwise, I would have to descend and ascend the stairs with them. If the groceries were left outside our door, my mother would spray the bags with diluted bleach before bringing them in, and then wash everything separately. If I had brought them up, she would spray me as well. Shoes had to be off and vigorously scrubbed. She changed to spraying me with bleachless antibacterial solutions because bleach thinned out the colors of my clothing. My red running shoes turned pink after two cleansings. She didn't change the solution when I told her it hurt me, informing me that one must suffer a little for good health. She did change it when it ruined clothing. If she or I had to pay the delivery boys, she had us microwave any new bills that came into the house and wash our hands while the nuking was going on. Much later, I would read that most currency was printed with ferrofluid, an ink that has magnetic iron in it, which should make microwaving it dangerous. Obviously, the Lebanese government was too cheap to use anything as sophisticated.

My mother was bored and I knew it, or I should say, she was bored and made sure to tell me she was at all times. I was teaching remotely. Before every class, before I sat in my chair, before I pried open the clamshell of a laptop, I would lock my bedroom door, which I never had to do before, because I knew she would find any excuse to interrupt my Zoom, to say hello to my brats. Even with the lock, she would knock every now and then to ask if I wanted tea or coffee.

A month into the quarantine, my mother and I started taking walks together. I walked regularly, since I had never owned a car, never felt comfortable behind a wheel with the insane traffic of the city. I shouldn't have said that. I probably wouldn't have driven even if I'd grown up in a place whose denizens followed traffic laws, say, Switzerland. I didn't care for cars as a child and didn't understand the other boys' fascination with them. I'd always been a congenital walker.

My mother, on the other hand, had driven all her life. Moving in with me was the first time in her life she lived in a household without access to an automobile. We could have bought one before the politicians stole all our money, but we decided against it. Ours was a garageless building, which was the reason I moved into it in the first place—cheaper rent. She moved around the city using taxis, Uber, the local jitney service, or what seemed to her most natural: making friends drive her.

I was not religious, but I walked religiously, in both senses of the adverb. I took long walks three or four times a week and I took them alone. Through the years, they offered me solace, stimulation, and rejuvenation. When the pandemic began, the government decreed that we should not be out in public and anyone doing so would receive a fine. Like almost every other law in the country, it was ignored. I walked with a mask, kept my distance, and felt safe. I needed that time alone. I assumed my mother understood without my having to explain it. Before the quarantine, she never asked to join, but then it seemed one day her sequestering impatience reached its peak. I was ready to leave on one of my walks when I found her, in a pink tracksuit and neon-orange espadrilles, holding the handle of her black handbag in front of her stomach with both hands, standing at the door. I could tell she was smiling behind her mask, but I wasn't able to tell whether she was doing so sheepishly or triumphantly.

"No," I said. I tried to nip her whims in the bud, eternally hoping that one day she might listen to me, and of course she wouldn't. And of course, she had her conditions for our walk. Obviously, we couldn't go beyond the neighborhood. Being eighty-two at the time, she couldn't walk too far, and more important, we had to return before the building's generator would be turned off; the generator could be shut off at any time, since we had a diesel shortage. She was bored enough that she would risk my carrying her up the stairs.

My walks were meditative? I could meditate in my room like normal people — well, like weird normal people who meditate.

She tried to indulge my preference for quietude, but that lasted about ten minutes of the first walk. The streets were not teeming with the usual hustle and bustle of Beirut, but there were enough people for her to greet everyone she came across, the neighbors she knew and those she didn't. She observed social distancing and wore her mask. Her first few conversations came across as yelling, since she feared not being heard, what with a mask covering her mouth and her listeners standing so far away. I had to mention it a few times before she corrected. When she met a new person, she would briefly remove her mask, then request the same of the newbie, so that they might see each other's faces like normal human beings, if only for a moment, a fleeting one. I had to loiter in her presence while she chatted. I would remind myself that we had limited time and my suffering would end at some point.

My boor of a father used to accuse my mother of having conversations just to fill the air with words. He was wrong about that, as he was about everything else. It was true that my mother talked quite a bit. She may not have suffered from logorrhea, but her chattiness certainly made me suffer. However, only a stupid man like my father, or maybe a deaf person, could fail to see that my mother used conversations in a myriad of ways, and for many reasons.

During the walks, she talked to everyone to ease anxieties, hers and her listeners'. Obviously, I'm not suggesting she did that with me. And she used different tones with women and men. With the former, my mother spoke gently, almost conspiratorially. The women weren't exactly talking as much as massaging each other with words. Platitudes and commiseration as shiatsu and aromatherapy. All she could do with men was to provide an ear. Without exception, every man we encountered wanted to complain and did not wish to be interrupted while he whined. Every man, no matter how old, would stop whatever he was doing when my mother said hello. He'd place his hands in his windbreaker — it might have been spring, but the weather could change at any moment, in his mind at least. He'd puff out his chest like a gibbon and let loose with a litany. The currency is freefalling so quickly no one has time to sneeze. Prices skyrocketing every minute. Who can afford anything? This Covid is a government conspiracy, an Iranian conspiracy, a Saudi or Israeli one. Could the situation possibly get any worse? How could a man support his family under such conditions? Always ending with how such injustices were heaped upon him. My mother's first hello was no mere word, but the tinkle of a Pavlovian bell. *Ding*, a conflagration of whining.

Every one of these men reminded me of my stupid father. I asked her once how she could listen to the same gripes over and over. She accused me of lacking compassion.

She thought the walks would make her feel better. They certainly distracted her, and she was able to meet and be entertained by a grand cast of new characters. She remained blue, however, maybe less mopey, but not yet hale. She couldn't visit her friends or her family, since none lived within walking distance. She mentioned Aunt Yasmine on a regular basis, how terrible her health was, how lonely she was with only her daughter, Nahed, for company. I refused to care.

The walks did not lift her sagging spirits, but it was on one of them that she met the woman who would, the one who would become my mother's friend, Madame Taweel. Only my mother would find a mentor at eighty-two, let alone the most inappropriate one. I couldn't imagine a worse woman that my mother could befriend, not at the time.

It was by no means an auspicious encounter, or it was, depending on whom you asked.

But allow me to start a bit earlier.

By the time my mother and Madame Taweel met, I'd been living in my apartment for almost forty years. The two of us, my apartment and I, had survived many things: the civil war, the Israeli siege and their bombing of the neighborhood, all the various militia occupations, and the worst disaster of all, the election, or the installation if you will, of one of the neighborhood's hoods as a member of parliament, when suddenly checkpoints sprouted around us like a winter fungus. Anytime I had to enter or leave my home, I had to show an ID to striplings in army fatigues and explain where I was going. Luckily, that shitshow lasted only one winter because our parliamentarian keeled over and died within a few months of being elected. The fungus was removed. In any case, we survived that and more. I was infrequently bothered by anyone. All I asked was that I be left alone, and the neighborhood obliged for the most part.

I'll get to Madame Taweel. Just allow me a moment to set it up.

I earned my undergraduate degree in 1981 and struck out on my own, or I should say, struck out with Mr. Cat. It was the right time. So many apartments were empty, so many abandoned. I was an anomaly in any number of ways. I was the only one in my class who didn't either emigrate (couldn't afford to and had nowhere to go) or stay in my parents' home. I had been saving money from my private teaching and found temporary work as a translator with a couple of embassies—not much work to speak of since we were in the midst of the war and the skeleton crews of those embassies were running on fumes. I could barely afford food, so I certainly didn't have enough to buy a diesel generator. As much as I loathed the idea, I needed a roommate. I had no idea how to look for one, since my circle of acquaintances was smaller than a hula hoop and I wasn't going to ask my family for help. For the first time in a long time, fate decided I needed a break. A girl from college, a third-year, made me a delectable offer. She did not wish to be my roommate, but she needed a room for afternoon assignations with a gorgeous boy she had no intention of marrying. I seemed to be a relatively clean person, and better yet, I didn't seem to have any friends that I talked to, so I was probably discreet. We could make a deal. We did.

N (I have kept my promise to be discreet) paid two years' rent on my guest room, such a boon, but used it for only four months because, you know, the Israelis invaded. She would leave for Montreal and become a regular, if minor, actor in a soap opera. We didn't interact much. She and her paramour used the apartment almost every afternoon for an hour or so and left as soon as they finished showering when we had water and earlier when we didn't. As much as I liked her, and I did quite a bit, as much as I admired her gumption, her no-nonsense approach, and her judicious use of makeup (she left behind a steamer of cosmetics with various shades of base, eyeliner, eye shadow, mascara, rouge, blush, lipstick, and lip gloss that I used for years after she was gone; we had the same coloring, after all) and as much as I often wished I could be N, she wasn't the important thread in this yarn. It was her boyfriend. And no, we didn't have sex or anything like that.

When the Israelis invaded, we all knew that they would come for Beirut no matter what lies they were telling. The city began to empty. A civil war was one thing, but another occupying foreign power was going to cause quite a bit more carnage. My family was fleeing to Damascus—all of them, my parents and Farouk, Aunt Yasmine and her brood. Even her husband, some minor muckety-muck in the army, wanted nothing to do with the Israelis. My mother begged me to come along, she walked over three times in one day to ask me to join them. They were all going to be staying with Syrian friends who had one extra bedroom. How were they going to fit? I told her I would rather be buried with Mr. Cat in my apartment, that I would rather subject him to a life with the Israelis than have him spend a minute with my father or Farouk after the years of mistreatment they put him through. Of course, I didn't miss the irony that I happened to tell her that as Mr. Cat purred ecstatically in her lap.

My family left, N left, everyone left, and Mr. Cat and I hunkered down in our apartment as the Israelis laid siege to Beirut. I had set myself up with enough bottled water, enough rice and lentils, enough gas cannisters, enough cat food to last us months if we were parsimonious. I didn't have electricity during the siege, so I spent most of my time reading by candlelight and experimenting with makeup. What can I say? I was bored and N left so much of it behind.

During one productive morning, after I'd made myself breakfast and transformed into drag geisha, I was feeling quite happy with myself despite my and my country's dire circumstances. Even wigless, I looked stupendous. This was before the Israelis began their crazy bombings, while they were still braying atop the surrounding hills, the Merkava tanks and F-16s ready but not yet firing. And someone knocked on my door. I was so scared I almost peed in my jerry-rigged kimono. I had no intention of opening the door, of course, but I tiptoed toward it. (I had no getas at the time, not that I was ever that fond of them.) Before I could stretch and look through the eyehole, I heard a whisper, "I know you're in there, Raja. Please open the door. It's me, Mansour." And since that was probably the most he'd ever said to me, he felt the need to add, "Mansour, N's friend."

We were both shocked when we saw each other. I looked fabulous and he bedraggled. I quickly dragged him inside (pun intended). The first thing he said when he sat down was "You look strange." I told him the word he was looking for was *beautiful*, maybe *charming*, or *delightful*.

I knew little about Mansour. In the four months since I first met him, he visited my apartment probably ninety times if not more, every afternoon. He sometimes arrived with N, sometimes after she did. He would acknowledge me with a nod of his head and traipse to the guest bedroom. He'd also nod as he left. I gathered he was a boy of few words. I knew he was in his early twenties, probably twenty-one or so, my age. I knew he was handsome, a rougher Cary Grant. Glittering, lustful eyes, dark, lush hair everywhere. Every time he passed me, I caught the terrifying smell of sweat and grease. I figured he worked with his hands. I had assumed he was Palestinian. Oh, and he wore fatigue pants, so he likely belonged to one of the militias.

He sat uncomfortably on the sofa, measuring me and not saying anything. I asked him why he chose to visit at such an inopportune time. We both knew N had left the country. He still didn't say anything.

"I can change," I said. "I wasn't expecting anyone. Was trying different looks. I can take off the makeup."

He was taken aback. No, it wasn't my looks that had him flummoxed. He hadn't slept in thirty-six hours. He felt a migraine coming on. It wasn't me. He needed my help. Would I let him use my extra room?

I hadn't expected that.

I felt torn. Now, N had paid for the room, so I should let him use it, but I didn't want a roommate while we were under siege. I told him that and added that I knew nothing about him. I didn't want a stranger living with me.

He began to explain. He wasn't exactly looking for a place to live, but for a hiding place when the time came. He was a mechanic, not a fighter. He could fight if he needed to, but his skills as a mechanic were in demand. He was the one who kept the fleet of jeeps crisscrossing the city, the vehicles that carried fighters and those that carried rocket launchers. He was working constantly for the heroic resistance, but at some point, probably sooner rather than later, the Israelis would overwhelm the resistance and take over the city. He couldn't risk being captured. The enemy didn't believe in nuance, couldn't tell the difference between a mechanic and a fighter. The Israelis would kill him for sure, probably torture him as well. He was too young to die, and truly, he didn't handle pain well. He had no one else. His entire family was in Jordan somewhere. He'd come to Beirut a few years ago because he thought he could make more money here. Worst decision he'd ever made. Would I please let him stay in my guest room when the time came?

I hesitated. I was sure it wasn't a smart idea to have a militia guy in my apartment when the Israelis strolled into Beirut, let alone a PLO guy, even if he was only a mechanic. And then, could I be confined in an apartment with another guy and keep my sanity? Could I afford to get involved? I should say no, but I couldn't. He looked terrified, vulnerable on the couch, slumped and fragile. His T-shirt screamed, "I need a good wash." His dark eyes beseeched me.

I knew he'd lied. I understood that he could never fight, whether he needed to or not. I guessed, correctly as it would turn out, that he had never fired a gun in his life. He wore his macho drag because he saw no other way of being. I said yes.

We were both wrong about many things. We thought the resistance would crumble, and the Israelis would march into Beirut with ease. We thought their bombing campaign would be brief. We assumed he would keep working until the last minute, at which point he'd hide in my guest room. He'd return to Jordan as soon as he was able. We turned out to be right about that at least.

The indiscriminate bombing was relentless; the resistance did not crack, at least not as quickly as we thought it would. And the Israelis didn't enter Beirut, not at first. They sent their genocidal cronies. But that part of our history, as cruel and insane as it was, doesn't much concern this story.

Less than forty-eight hours after I'd agreed to hide him, Mansour knocked on my door again. He was ready to go underground. Hades had gone aboveground. He was deserting, even if that was not the precise term since he didn't belong to an army. He could no longer stomach it — *it* being the bombings, the killings, the deaths, the lack of sleep, the exhaustion, the fear, the lack of a functioning toilet, or all of the above. He was a coward, he said. He wanted out.

He stayed with me for a couple of months before sneaking out of the country to Syria and then Jordan. It would be an exaggeration, and a romantic one at that, to suggest I wouldn't have survived the siege and the massacres that followed without his company. He was, however, a great help. He was terrified constantly, and my mothering him, my allaying his fears, distracted me from mine. I was able to keep my wits even when a handful of bullets decided to batter my bedroom windows and embed themselves in my walls.

In order for you to be apprised of all the facts, I'm going to admit here that I too lied. We did have sex. I tried to be discreet earlier because I'd promised him then that I wouldn't tell anyone. However, one must sacrifice discretion if it undermines a story. Would you believe two young men spent so many nights in a corridor, threatened by obliteration at any moment, while the hounds of Hades barked outside, and didn't have sex? Mansour was handsome, hirsute, and hung—very well-hung. I rode that beast as often as I could. I assume that after forty years Mansour, if he is still breathing, wouldn't much mind my telling about our having sex.

Why tell about what happened more than forty years ago? What has that to do with my story? Well, before he left, to thank me for "saving his life" as he called it, Mansour offered the greatest of gifts. He was a magnificent mechanic. He refurbished a small diesel generator, installed it on my balcony, and left clear instructions on how to care for it. I still use his generator to this day, the only one I've ever owned. Never had to have it fixed. The one thing I've done to it in the last forty years is move it to the end of the veranda when my mother suggested that the diesel fumes were greasing our laundry.

Now, what did that have to do with Madame Taweel? I'm getting to it, I swear.

Basically, Mansour's true gift was that in the last forty years, I was able to avoid dealing with the diesel-generator mafias. I thought I was blessed, couldn't believe my luck. And then, of course, my mother greeted Madame Taweel, the godfather of generator mafias.

My mother hadn't heard of Madame Taweel, surprising as it may seem, because she was in Dubai when Madame Taweel came to power, when she colonized our neighborhood. Before her, the neighborhood's capo was a man whose name I no longer recall. I never had any dealings with him, but my mother did, since the family's generator was a rental and the building they lived in subscribed to the man's giant generator. My father, like almost everyone in the neighborhood, had to pay a monthly fee to the man, whom my mother described as a listless seal. I had interactions with the seal's bodyguards, though, particularly when I was younger. Each time I passed by the stronghold—the top two floors of a building around the corner—one of his goons would let out a nasty catcall of some kind. It made them happy, didn't bother me. I had to give his goons some credit. There was always a confusion of supplicants in the lobby of the building, asking for extensions on their next rental payment, begging to have the generator fixed, all kinds of favors. Astonishingly, the seal's goons kept all these people in one line. Outside of little kids at schools, I'm not sure I can recall any Lebanese standing in line.

My mother told me about her one encounter with the listless seal. On a scorching day in August, a few years after my father died, 2008 or maybe 2009, my mother's small generator broke down, and worse, the seal's giant generator wasn't working either. What to do? Usually, when something like that happened, my mother relied on either my father or Farouk to deal with the problem. She no longer could. She put on her finest summer dress, sensible heels, sunglasses, grabbed her fake Chanel handbag, and marched toward the generator godfather's stronghold. She began to sweat as soon as she left the building, so she turned around, descended the stairs to the garage, and got in her car. It might be a ten-minute walk, if that, but she was going to drive, even if the junker's air conditioner barely functioned. There was a crowd on the building's ground floor, but the goons led her straight to the elevator. A Chanel handbag allowed you to get ahead in life, but only if no one could tell it was fake. She exited the elevator on the sixth floor to a surprise: On the edges of the well-varnished pine door of the apartment, beads of condensation formed like mother of pearl. The Sri Lankan maid led her into Siberia. This is how my mother described the scene. Dark, all the curtains and blinds drawn, the only light in the room emanating from two table lamps with thick shades. Almost every person in the neighborhood was in the room, either sitting on three large sofas and a dozen chairs or standing along the wall. The room smelled of camphor, candle wax, and lavender air freshener, and was as full of coughs and chairs as a hospital waiting room. The capo sat on a red velvet–upholstered, oversized fauteuil. His feet would not reach the marble floor. He positioned himself close to a door. Best of all, a slightly younger replica of him, the listless seal's pup, stood behind massaging his daddy's shoulders. And the room was so cold, air conditioners at full blast.

She walked up to the listless seal, but before she could say a word, he held up his palm and said, "I know. You want electricity, but why don't you have a cup of coffee before we talk?" On cue, another Sri Lankan maid appeared from the door that led to the kitchen, carrying at least a dozen cups of Turkish coffee and a sugar bowl with the smallest silver spoon my mother had ever seen. She helped herself to a cup, at which point the pup nodded his head toward the side wall, smiled at her, then nodded his head to his father, which my mother interpreted to mean "Please move your ass toward the wall because my dad is feeling stressed." The listless seal sighed forlornly and settled into his frown and furrowed chin.

It wasn't long before a seated woman spoke to no one in particular, but loud enough for everyone in the room to hear,

"I was planning on making ice cream this afternoon." The seal perked up. My mother was disappointed that he didn't flap his short arms. "Pistachio, of course," the woman said. "That's my specialty. Learned to make it from my mother, except I use both salep and clotted cream. I don't make it often, so I don't scrimp. And today's heat inspired me to try for the best ice cream ever. But I can't make it without power."

"But you can, madame, you can. The generator is being fixed as we speak." The godfather looked at his son. "The mechanics will have it running in a minute or so."

"That is welcome news," the woman said. "I have a hankering for ice cream. Would you allow me to send some for you and yours later this afternoon, you know, to sweeten your tongues a little?"

The whole room seemed to relax with the clinking of coffee cups and saucers, a few too many exhalations. A woman next to my mother spoke softly to another, "I'm glad she volunteered. I was about to offer my German chocolate cake, but I don't feel like baking today."

That the listless seal lasted as long as he did as the neighborhood's major generator was remarkable, a testament to some hidden skill. However, in spring of 2014, I was out on my balcony, morning tea in hand, watching night shadows recede to uncover my neighborhood, its early people, and its first indistinct rays of grayish light. I was getting ready for work. No power this early in the morning. The sparrows were up to their usual early mischief in the effulgent branches of the oak. The grocer, on his wicker stool in front of his shuttered store, smoked a cigarette and cogitated about eternity. The butcher, Abou Sami, and his assistant worked inside their shop by a single bulb running on a UPS battery, cow carcass hanging on hooks waiting to be quartered. With so little light, the flesh on the butcher's bench seemed less livid. And I heard a gunshot. I'd had enough experience to know the gun that fired it was close, but not on our street, maybe three streets farther east. The butcher and his assistant walked out onto the street to investigate. The grocer stood up and ground the cigarette with the ball of his foot. Lina M. on the first floor of the building across made an appearance on her balcony. We looked at each other across our spaces and waited. One second, two seconds, three seconds. Another shot was followed by a flurry. Machine guns were involved. The speed with which our grocer was able to unlock and lift the rolling shutters barely enough to bend over, get into the store, and lock them again was notable. The butcher and his assistant went back into the shop, closed the door, and turned off the bulb. A candle remained lit. They turned back to shadow.

I waited. We all did. We had yet to understand whether this was Gabriel blowing his trumpet or a chubby cherub playing the kazoo.

Would I be able to walk to school that morning? Probably. The gunfire had erupted from the opposite direction. I could if I walked quickly.

A few scattered shots, seemingly desultory, like an inept pigeon pecking at a seedless sidewalk—peck, silence, silence, peck. Then frightened men running down our street, out of shape and on adrenaline. Then smiling men running down our street, in shape and on serotonin. The latter group didn't seem to have any objective other than scaring the first group. One man fired into the air and kept jogging, laughing along the way. Ten minutes was all it took for Madame Taweel to conquer, adding our little neighborhood to her territory and claiming sovereignty.

I was able to leave my apartment at the usual time and have a normal day at school. Only one newspaper considered the event fit to print, and definitely not above the fold, or below the fold for that matter. Page three or four. I rarely watched television news, so I wouldn't be able to tell you whether the conquest and firefight was mentioned. I don't believe anyone said anything about it on Twitter, though I didn't follow that either. No one knew how many were killed if any. It couldn't have been many because a few of the boys who worked for the listless seal were rehired by the new padrone.

A spring sky that lacked nuance, a spotless blue that matched my mother's favorite dress and my underwear, though, obviously, no one would know that. She greeted the butcher, Abou Sami, explaining she would want half a kilo of chopped mutton for the following day and could he please make sure it was the best half kilo in the shop. He invited us in, but his flimsy mask wasn't covering his nose. We kept the prerequisite two-meter distance. Abou Sami pointed to Odette Y.'s balcony, two floors above ours, saying, "She's still doing it." Both he and my mother giggled. It seemed Odette was still washing all money that came into the house, as well as her masks, and hanging them on the laundry line for all to see. She'd been doing it for months, since the beginning of the pandemic.

A black Range Rover with tinted windows stopped before Abou Sami, who lit up as if God and all the angels were blessing him. The butcher's eyes glistened like lamb fat. Madame Taweel didn't wait for the driver to open the door for her. She stretched by the car door, her arms raised toward the heavens. She probably needed to. As big as the vehicle was, Madame Taweel probably felt cramped within it. She looked like a Valkyrie back from a day spa, tall and oddly shaped, big-breasted and big-thighed, with a ridiculously small waist, like the number eight, like eternity. Abou Sami rushed to greet her, stopped a bit short once he noticed the driver-cum-bodyguard's glare. Unlike her, both her minions wore masks. Her angular, elongated face was expressionless, as immobile as an Easter Island moai, likely recently and excessively botoxed. She wore a linen dress the same color blue as my mother's, the same as my underwear, not that she'd know. She matched that with steel-toe construction boots, incongruous, but it worked somehow. She walked toward the shop. She took big steps.

I was about to grab my mother's arm to leave, but it wasn't where it was supposed to be. She was never where I needed her to be. She'd jumped into Madame Taweel's path, startling the woman and her minion, a big thug who was about to reach behind his jacket for his gun, whose nozzle was probably cradled by the cheeks of his ass. He didn't pull it out, realizing my mother wasn't much of a threat. He seemed to be wearing an expensive suit, but made it look so ill-fitting, all the creases and seams a little off.

I moved closer to try and take my mother away. Of course, she wouldn't let me.

"Were you going to pull your gun on me?" she demanded of the defenseless bodyguard. "On me? Does your mother know you use weapons on older women?"

The bodyguard was flustered, looked as flummoxed as a puppy being trained. Madame Taweel wasn't.

"His mother died," she said.

"Probably out of disappointment."

Madame Taweel bit her lip, shattering the Easter Island effect. She was about to laugh. "His job is to protect me," she said, "and you jumped in front of me."

"Only to say hello."

I grabbed her arm this time. "We're sorry for intruding," I said. "Let's go." She weighed very little, but I couldn't budge her when she didn't wish to move.

"I'm not sorry," she said, raising her pitch and her hands. "I wanted to say good morning. Why would someone want to shoot me for that?"

"You wanted to wish me a good morning?" Madame Taweel asked.

"Yes, of course," my mother said. "I don't know who you are, so I was doing the right thing and correcting that. It's what we do."

I nudged my mother, and she elbowed me back. Madame Taweel now joined her bodyguard in bewilderment, her face a picture of stupefaction. She shook her head from side to side as if to clear it. I knew she was a terrible woman, but a part of me felt sorry for her. Deciphering my mother was a feat that would have surely flummoxed Hercules — my mother as the unthinkably impossible thirteenth task.

"You're curious about me?" Madame Taweel said. "Are you sure? You should ask your son. He seems to want to tell you something, probably that I'm a dangerous woman."

"Only in that you're not wearing a mask," my mother said, "and you should. He worries I'm not so young anymore and you might infect me."

"Well, I am dangerous," Madame Taweel said.

"You're not dangerous," my mother said. "You're just tall."

Madame Taweel's laugh was loud and disrespectful. The closest sound I could compare it to was a getaway car taking a sharp turn. I wished my mother and I were in one.

I once told Madame Taweel she was a squall that uprooted our life. She hit me with her obnoxious laugh, telling me my mother was the category-five storm that uprooted hers. Both were storms that created hurricanes and I was the bewildered tumbleweed floating every which way they blew. Later, they would endlessly rehash their fortuitous first meeting. Why, Madame Taweel never did her own shopping. She had one of her drivers do all errands. That day, she worried Abou Sami might not have meted out the best cuts to her driver, so she wanted to make an appearance, remind the butcher who he was selling to. Obviously, fate had intervened. Oh, and how long they talked that first time. Abou Sami had to get chairs for both, and then for me and her bodyguard. I tried to get them to sit apart, but they refused. Yet when my mother asked her new friend to put on a mask, Madame Taweel did. The women seemed joyous, and I was in agony. I observed the sun bathing the sides of the building before us as the old ladies talked and talked. Into intimacy they dove. My marriage was a disaster, not as bad as mine, at least you go on walks with your son, I can't bear the company of my offspring, you should meet my other son, the Buddha himself would contemplate murder in his company, Mahatma Gandhi would slap him silly.

I thought at one point that Easter Island woman was trying to seduce my mother. I made the mistake of mentioning it to her not too long after, and of course she told Madame Taweel, and I had to endure their laughter and mockery for a whole week.

They told each other everything, and for the first time in her life, my mother found a confidante with whom she could share everything. That might not be the right way to state this. I was my mother's confidante in some ways, so Madame Taweel wasn't the first, but what she offered, and I didn't, was unequivocal interest and unwavering curiosity. Everything about my mother fascinated Madame Taweel and vice versa. I listened to my mother as much as I could, but at times, when her garrulousness reached high irritation, I tuned her out. Madame Taweel didn't and never wanted to. They talked constantly, together, over each other, synchronized and asynchronized, in tune and out of tune, endlessly rehashing anything and everything. I would come out of my room to find them huddled together, pandemic be damned, whispering and giggling, even though there was no one else in our living room. Madame Taweel made the bodyguards wait outside our door. The women talked and talked, stroking each other with words. Like a cat licking another cat, they spread sonorous balm upon each other.

And when I said they told each other everything, I meant everything.

My mother told her about my brats, about Monsieur Micho, everything. One day I returned home and there was no bodyguard at the door. When I walked in, I found the two women seated on the sofa, their backs to me, and three of Madame Taweel's minions standing before them, all wearing their best suits, their hands clasped before their crotches, heads bowed as if they were students sent to see the headmistress. All of them had gun bulges in their suits (my no-guns-allowed-in-our-home rule was ignored, of course) yet they seemed terrified of me.

"Well," Madame Taweel said sternly. "What do you have to say?"

The main bodyguard seemed to be the eldest, a man in his forties. He told me he was sorry for all the things they did to me. I couldn't figure what he was talking about. All the names they called me, all the horrid innuendos. The big thug hesitated when I told him I didn't recognize any of them, let alone what they said or did. The three of them had worked for the listless seal, some of the goons who used to stand at the stronghold's lobby and entrance. They used to hurl insults and catcalls when I walked by. They felt such shame for doing all that, but they now worked for a better boss who insisted that her employees behave decently. They were so sorry.

"Can you forgive them?" Madame Taweel said.

"How can I forgive them if I can't recall them?" I asked, turning to go to my room. All neighborhood hoodlums exhibited the same sociopathic machismo with varying degrees of scintillation. How could I possibly tell them apart? They were all one blob. Should I just issue a general pardon to all men?

"Don't mind him," my mother said. "He doesn't know how to say thank you. So, thank you for apologizing. Give him a couple of days and he'll forgive you for sure. He probably already has but needs time to process things."

And when I said everything, I meant everything.

I went into the kitchen to make myself a cup of coffee. My mother was on the phone. I could tell from the timbre of her voice and its intimate intonations that Madame Taweel was on the other end. My mother hardly called anyone else anymore. "I think he has an allergy to cabbage but can't be sure yet," my mother said. "We had stuffed cabbage the night before yesterday. Yes, of course. I forgot I sent you some. Yes, they were delicious, but he woke up the next day with diarrhea. Luckily, he teaches his classes online, but still. I'm sure his students had to wonder why he had to take a break every fifteen minutes. No, I don't think it lasts more than twenty-four hours. Let me ask him. Darling, do you have to go to the bathroom this morning?" I banged my forehead against the kitchen cabinet.

And when I said everything, I meant everything.

My mother showed Madame Taweel all her photos of me: as a baby gloriously naked, as a one-year-old gloriously naked, as a four-year-old wearing my brother's hand-me-down striped top with a frayed hem and no pants or underwear.

My mother: "At that age, he was birch-thin with a butt you could sit a coffee cup on."

They examined the geisha photographs. My mother had her own — I hesitated to ask where she collected them from—and had obviously found my hidden stash, as if I needed any further proof she went through my things on a regular basis. They watched the homemade movies I made, not my originals, of course, since I didn't have a projector and they were filmed on Super 8. But someone had made copies and posted them online in the nineties. I'd sold a total of thirteen copies of the four films, to other homosexuals, of course, and one thought he would do me a favor by digitizing the Super 8 onto a DVD. I would have killed him, I should have, but he died not long after, saving me the trouble. Only one of the four became popular, *Seven Geishas*, where I recreated Kurosawa's *Seven Samurai*—an abridged version, of course—and I played all the roles. I wrote, directed, produced, and shot the whole thing in my second bedroom with my Super 8 and a stupid tripod. Costumes, makeup, fabulousness, all me. And it was a disaster, bearable only if you had a fondness for camp. Yet it kept popping up, every five years it seemed. It would disappear, die, and after a few years, it would get resurrected. Some internet personality, whatever that meant these days, would come across it, and their tiny brain would process what they were seeing as the greatest art, and bang, *Seven Geishas* would come alive once more, a revenant. And my mother and Madame Taweel watched it about a dozen times.

Madame Taweel: "Do his students know about this?"

Raja the Gullible's Tormentor: "All of them do. Apparently, they have an initiation ritual that has been going on for decades where his graduating classes have a party for his incoming students and watch the movies together. Yet Mr. Stupid still pretends no one has seen him in drag, and the kids like him so much they never bring it up. He'd probably have a heart attack if he knew that they know."

Raja the Gullible: "I'm right here, you know."

Madame Taweel: "Maybe we could get him to teach us his makeup techniques."

My mother: "Don't you think I've tried? He always wants to teach me philosophy, Nietzsche this, Kant that, whereas when I ask him to teach me something useful like how he does his insane eye shadows, he harrumphs as if that's beneath him."

Madame Taweel: "I could have one of my men tie him up in his room and not let him out until he agrees to teach us."

My mother: "Oh, let's."

Many things concerned me about their relationship, not the least was my mother letting her moral compass drop, letting it shatter into pieces. She thought all the mafioso politicians were criminals, murderers, thieves, terrible and horrible, but Madame Taweel was an older businesswoman who did what had to be done to survive in this world.

"There are rumors she killed her husband," I once told my mother.

"That's silly, obviously not true," my mother said. "Though I wish I could have murdered mine before he died."

But of course, the worst incident was the Mafia Granddaughter Affair.

I knew they were up to something when two days passed with both on their best behavior. Every now and then my mother could be nice to me, and every now and then Madame Taweel might treat me with some respect, but the two of them together, at the same time, for forty-eight hours?

Nope, no, never. Something was up.

I was reading in bed, happy, content, listening to Chopin's nocturnes, the window open, a breezy early summer afternoon, one of those glorious Beiruti days, so rare these last few years, and I heard my mother calling me.

"What do you want?" I yelled loudly enough for her to hear me through the door. She didn't always wear her hearing aid, and even though Madame Taweel was ten years younger, her hearing wasn't the best either.

"Don't be rude," my mother yelled back. "Come out here when I call. I need to tell you something."

I placed my book on the bed, pages facing down, turned the music off, and walked out of my room, finding them in the living room, their usual seats, their usual chatting, as if the world would end if they suffered more than ten seconds of silence, their nodding heads, clucking hens, Lady Kluck and Clara Cluck.

"We need your help," my mother said, finally looking up. "We put your name as a reference on an application to your school. When the acceptance committee asks, tell them how amazing the child is and make sure she gets accepted."

"What?" I always tried not to sound snippy when talking to them, but it was never easy. "How could you put my name down without asking? I don't even know who you're talking about."

"It's my granddaughter," Madame Taweel said, seemingly nonplussed by my rage. "My middle son's youngest. She's four."

"She's so smart," my mother added. "You'll love her. She'll be a great addition to your school, believe me."

"I refuse to do anything," I told them. "I don't know anything about the girl."

"Don't worry," Madame Taweel said. "I can bring her over tomorrow. You can spend quality time."

"Quality time with a four-year-old? I thought my mother is crazy, but you're so much more. I should have you both committed."

"See," my mother said. "I told you he likes you."

"Come, Raja," Madame Taweel said. She patted the sofa cushion next to her. "Sit down and let me explain the way of the world to an idealist."

I sighed. I went around and sat opposite them. You couldn't pay me enough to sit between them.

"Now," she said, "I didn't ask for your help with any of my other grandchildren. I love them dearly, but let's just say they take after their parents. They're not smart. And their parents spoil them horribly. My eldest granddaughter is getting married in a month, and I sometimes wonder whether she can string words to form a coherent sentence. She has yet to form one in my presence. This granddaughter is different. She's bright. I want to give her every advantage I can. I tried offering the same to my children and that didn't work out. I want to give her what I didn't have."

"Wonderful," I said, trying and failing to keep a neutral, non-sarcastic tone. "And what has that to do with me?"

"Quiet down," my mother said. "You talk too much."

"You know your school has changed in the last sixty years," Madame Taweel said. "Its reputation has grown, and they no longer accept people like us. Your reputation too. Your students end up in the best universities. I want that for my granddaughter. You and your brother got in when working-class children were allowed in, when it didn't cost a fortune to send your child there."

"It's probably your stupid brother's fault," my mother said. "After the school kicked him out, they decided 'never again.'"

"Don't be stupid," I said. In the sky, above the Mediterranean, I could see a jet flying toward the airport. "It's true that it costs a lot to send a brat there, but you can afford it, can't you? Aren't you wealthier now since the collapse?"

I caught the wind-borne smell of diesel, heard the pervasive low hum of engines.

Madame Taweel stared in shock, her eyes wide as porcelain saucers. "Is he being dense on purpose?" she asked my mother. Between her clenched thighs she pressed her hands, not trusting them, probably afraid she would slap me if they were unshackled.

"He's very stupid when it comes to people," my mother replied.

"You're the stupid one," I said.

"Stop it," Madame Taweel said. "I don't want this to degenerate into one of your arguments. Now, listen to me. Of course, I can afford to send my granddaughter there, but you know and I know that it takes more than that. No entry if you're not from the right families, no entry without clout or who you know."

"But that's not true," I said.

"Quiet," she snapped. "Now, tell me. How many of your students in the last twenty years have passed their baccalaureate on their first try?"

"You know the answer," I said, pointing to my mother. "She tells you everything. She can't keep her mouth shut."

"All of them," Madame Taweel said. "All on the first try. Apparently, throughout your teaching, you've never had any student fail. Some took two tries early on, but they passed."

"It's not me," I said. "The school weeds the students out. Only the best ones end up with me."

"They kicked his brother out," my mother said. "The director called me in to tell me he couldn't go on because he was going to fail troisième. Worst day of my life. Don't look at me like that. I'm not being literal."

"Every student of yours graduates," Madame Taweel said. "They go to great universities. I want that for my grandchild."

She seemed to me both vulnerable and threatening. She articulated ordinary, sincere sentences in a placid tone, but her smiling, exaggeratedly guileless face reminded me that this was a woman who knew her way around a gun, a machine gun, or even a rocket grenade launcher. I tried to explain that there was no need for any intervention on my part. The school might be doing better than most Lebanese institutions, but it was hit hard by the financial collapse. They desperately needed money, particularly since tuition was to be paid in dollars. Madame Taweel's granddaughter would be accepted easily. Not only that, but the director would probably call Madame Taweel and ask if she'd be willing to donate more money. I didn't have to do anything.

"But I want you to," Madame Taweel said. "I'll not take that risk."

"He'll do it," my mother said. "Your granddaughter will start kindergarten this fall."

"I haven't agreed to do it," I said. "It's against my principles. And you shouldn't have added me as a reference without asking me."

"All right," my mother said. "Next time, I'll tell you before we do it."

I was right, of course. The child was accepted by the middle of July, and I didn't get a phone call. Less than twenty-four hours after the acceptance, Madame Taweel received the fundraising call, and feeling generous, she agreed to pay full scholarships for ten students who would not have been able to pay tuition. That was pocket change for her. After all, the most recent calculations found that the generator mafia was a billion-dollar-a-year business, and Madame Taweel was one of its most successful padrones. She wasn't one of the billionaire politicians, but still filthy affluent.

Both she and my mother refused to believe I had nothing to do with the child's acceptance. I tried to disabuse them because I did not wish to be asked for any more favors. I wanted to be left alone. My mother demanded many favors after that, she always did, but not Madame Taweel. To the contrary, I began to receive the most exquisite of gifts, one every two weeks. At first, I wouldn't touch them, but my mother would pry open the gift, an imported jar of red miso paste, an imported jar of gochujang, a bottle of champagne, a can of Iranian caviar. I had to partake. Once my mother opened a Barolo, I couldn't let her drink an entire bottle on her own. And I also began to find Madame Taweel less objectionable. What she did for us after the explosion, the third disaster, was immeasurable. She also saved me in

America, after I made the stupid mistake of going to that place called Virginia.

You thought I'd forgotten about the email that started this tale, didn't you? I assume you probably have. A tale has many tails, and many heads, particularly if it's true. Like life, it is a river with many branches, rivulets, creeks, and distributaries. I'll get to everything, I swear. I've written about the two disasters that befell us—the financial collapse and the pandemic—but I must pause a bit before I tell of the third, the explosion. It's a bit overwhelming to write about. I'll continue the story. I just need to breathe.

III
(1960 – 1975)
Pre–Civil War

My memory is a god, and I, its servant.

I remember a scene at the military swimming club when I was five. It was the only place where I ever saw Aunt Yasmine's husband out of uniform. He was the hairiest person I'd ever seen. I found him intriguing in spite, or maybe because, of his simian attributes. I stood at the edge of the cement wharf staring into the distance, where faint cloudlets of almost human appearance gathered. And this is where I think my memory creates things. I remember wishing for nothing more than moving to the horizon and reaching the sky and climbing it. The feeling and memory are clear, but I can't imagine I would have had those kinds of thoughts at five. I was precocious, but not that much.

My father asked why I wasn't in the water with the other kids. My brother swam along the jetty, yelling that I was a coward. My cousins snickered. My mother explained to my father that I didn't know how to swim yet. My father picked me up, and before I understood what was happening, I was being flung into the Mediterranean. I heard my mother scream, and I was launched up into the sky, flying before falling into the sea. My feet broke water first, and I plunged and plunged, down and down into an underworld, and then no more plummeting, a halting. I looked up at the lighter water above me, at the skinny legs and bathing suits of my cousins, and I saw her, the face of my cousin Nahed, barely a week older than I, her cheeks more froglike than usual, holding a lot of air, her eyes wide open, staring down at me, and her limbs moving spastically in every direction to stay afloat. So I kicked my legs spastically and I waved my arms insanely and I floated up bit by bit toward the light and broke the surface. Nahed turned and paddled frantically in the direction of the metal ladder, and I paddled frantically in her wake, trying to keep her butt in my eyeline. She climbed ahead of me. When I reached the top, I saw my father enveloping my crying mother, her head on the tapestry of hair on his chest. The more she tried to push him away, the more he pulled her snug, his hand stroking her naked back between the bathing suit straps. He repeated, "I told you he'd make it, I told you, didn't I? Get a hold of yourself."

I turned into a water baby, forever desperate to go to the military club, not always able to because Aunt Yasmine's husband was the only one who could get us in. My brother and cousins would rarely leave the water, playing a never-ending game of shark. Nahed would grow to be the best swimmer of us all, the boys never wanting her to be the predator. I too wouldn't leave the water until the last minute possible, but I didn't play with them. I swam by myself, studying to be a dolphin, for that was what I wanted to be when I grew up.

My mother made us olive oil and za'atar sandwiches. I stood atop the old-fashioned stepladder to see how she made them. The sandwiches might have been plain, she explained, but science had proven what every Lebanese had known for generations: Za'atar expanded mind vessels and made you smarter. Behind her back, my brother mouthed, "Not you," while tilting his head, "not you." For the tenth time that morning, she insisted that Farouk must take care of me, just as she took care of him on his first day at school. He must hold my hand as soon as he exited the bus and lead me to Mademoiselle Saniya's class. Farouk complained about the uniform, of course. It was too long, which made it look like a dress. Did he have to button up the front all the way to the top? My mother explained that it looked the way it did because it functioned as an apron as well so we wouldn't get dirt or food on our clothes. Did it have to be red, white, and green? I knew the answer to that one, the colors of Lebanon, but I also knew not to say anything and antagonize him because he would beat me up as soon as my mother wasn't looking. I loved my uniform more than anything.

My brother would not hold my hand getting off the bus. I clutched the rail as I descended the three steps. I couldn't find him upon landing in the parking lot. I was all alone, surrounded by many. All the children on the bus had been older except for one girl, and her sister had walked her away holding her hand. I panicked for an instant. A nice old woman with suffocating perfume and stiff hair approached, bent down, asking me what my name was. She carried a clipboard. I told her my name and that I was in Mademoiselle Saniya's class.

"And right you are, Raja," she said, looking at the list. "You must be a smart boy to know what class you're in already." She straightened up, spoke to another woman in French. All I understood was the name Saniya. Both women looked around. I counted nine women in the parking lot. The teacher pointed to what must have been

Mademoiselle Saniya. She put out her hand for me to hold and led me to her.

Mademoiselle Saniya's freckled face was flush with a promise that everything would be all right. Her mouth hung in a welcoming red grin, her eyes happy to see me, happy to see anybody. Her thick, curly hair was pulled back with a skinny headband. A few unruly strands floated above her head. She explained to us, her menagerie, that we would be marching to the schoolyard with all the other students, where the headmistress would address everyone, after which we, her chosen, would move to our own special room, which of course was the best room in the whole school, probably the whole country.

My mother had instructed me to make friends because I was going to spend at least a year with these students. We wore the same uniform, but the rest of my classmates were put together better. They were like realized jigsaw puzzles, whereas my pieces didn't fit. The ironed uniforms, the combed hair, the standing straight, I had none of that. My hair was uncombable. A few of the other kids seemed to know each other from before. The rest chatted tentatively. All were making friends but not with me. One girl who looked more disheveled was being led by the hand toward us. I did not want to be her friend. I wished to belong to the jigsaw. And my cousin Nahed recognized me before I did her. She beamed, tight-lipped because of at least two missing teeth. I was scared. As soon as she was released, she ran to me, stood by me, and bumped my shoulder, almost toppling me.

All of Mademoiselle Saniya's students marched in a single file behind her, all of us facing the same direction, holding hands, left hand in front and right hand in back. Upon arriving in the vast schoolyard, we were arranged in files, straight lines, arm's-length distance. We lined up by grade. Our formation was the farthest left. Nahed poked me in the back. Look, look. She pointed at Farouk, one line between ours and his. He looked bigger than all the other children in his class. I was smaller than everybody, including the girls. At the front of the line, his teacher looked unhappy as my father in the morning. I didn't like Farouk's teacher. Mademoiselle Saniya couldn't be happier because we were her students.

The headmistress looked as old as my great-grandmother or my grandmother but dressed nicer. She walked up to the microphone, where one of the teachers had to adjust its height for her. She began to speak. Three amplified speakers formed a triangle around us. And I couldn't understand a word she was saying. I knew she was speaking French and I knew that I understood not a word of the language. Maybe merci. The students in every file listened, except for Farouk, who was snickering, whispering to a friend, and gesturing with his head in my direction. This was his third year.

I was so ashamed.

Nahed poked me in the back once again. "What's she saying?" she asked. "Why is she speaking funny?"

I didn't reply. Mademoiselle Saniya walked over, bent her knees so Nahed and I were at eye level. "Don't worry," she said. "You'll soon be speaking French like natives." She seemed to know we were the only two in her class, probably in the school, who didn't speak the language.

I was so ashamed.

The girl in front of me, with perfect pigtails and perfectly ironed uniform, turned to us and asked, "You two can't understand French?"

Before Mademoiselle Saniya was able to say anything, Nahed moved from behind me and pushed the perfect girl to the ground. The girl didn't cry. Mademoiselle Saniya was startled. The headmistress droned on as if nothing was happening.

I was so ashamed.

More than my infatuation with Barbie, it was the matchbox cars that got me in trouble with my father and his sister, Aunt Yasmine. My cousin Nahed's birthday was a week before mine. On her seventh, she received three presents, including two Barbies. She didn't care for dolls; she didn't much care for any toy. She was too busy climbing every tree in the neighborhood with her friends, teasing the chained German shepherd, and trying to steal candy from the local grocery store. I made her a proposal, asking for one of her Barbies. She didn't have use for two of them, I told her, and in exchange, she could have her choice of one of the presents I was bound to get for my seventh. She agreed. I knew even then that I should not be seen with a doll, so I hid it in the back of my closet under a hand-me-down red fire truck that I had never played with. I'd hoped I'd be able to bring Barbie out when I was sure no one, particularly not my brother, would walk in on me. I never got to play with that doll. I assumed Nahed told Aunt Yasmine about the deal she made, but I couldn't be sure. All I knew was the doll disappeared from my closet before the sun went down that day. I searched for it in every corner of the room for what seemed like hours and hours, going over every space three or four times. I was devastated. No one ever mentioned what happened, and I couldn't gather the courage to ask. The case of the missing Barbie was never solved.

For my seventh birthday, I received twenty-three matchbox cars, ten of which were new, and thirteen that once belonged to my brother or cousins. My father explained that if I liked cars and played with them often, he would get me a set of tracks that I could build myself, including—and here his voice rose a couple of notes higher to emphasize the magic of it all—a mega jump track set where I could make these tiny things on wheels fly.

I must have shown appropriate excitement, but I couldn't figure out why one would need tracks. I played nonstop with the matchbox cars for a week. I would gather them all in different groups: the garbage truck, the cattle truck, the flatbed, and the ambulance in one group; with the blue cars, the two Jaguars, the Mercedes Pontons in another. I would have one group, say, the station wagons, pay a visit to another, the sports cars. At one point, the ambulance would die, and all the other groups would have to come pay their respects to the truck family. Of course, coffee would be served to all the cars in mourning. When my father walked in on me, asking me what I was doing. I explained that the Ford and the Mercedes were visiting the English Jaguars, who would serve their guests tea, of course. I even had all the cars munching on imaginary cucumber sandwiches. Enid Blyton had taught me all about finger sandwiches with tea. My father wasn't happy. He sat on the floor next to me. He took one of the Jaguars and started driving it on the stone tile. I was to roll my cars around, he said, see how fast they could go. He held a Mercedes in his left hand and slammed it into the Jaguar. I had to get the cars into major crashes, destroy them. He made a wide circular gesture using both arms. The cars flew in the air. *Boom*, he cried out. I was supposed to make them go *boom*.

When we were back in the living room with all the family, he repeated the same advice. Matchbox cars should have accidents, not tea. I knew what he meant, knew what he wanted, but couldn't understand what was fun about destruction and mayhem.

I remember Aunt Yasmine shaking her head. So disappointed.

It was an oven-impersonating August. The room barely had any of the usual traces of my mother's scents—jasmine, cinnamon, and hairspray—even though she occupied it, sitting at the dining room table, playing a game of solitaire, a game she called double patience. All the doors in the dining room were open. All the windows in the apartment were open. A breeze that wanted to wash my face.

I asked what she was doing, knowing the answer already.

She didn't look up. I thought she looked like a queen.

I climbed on a chair next to her. Sat quietly for a bit. I pointed to where a card was supposed to go.

"Don't," she said.

I pulled my hand back and observed. I loved the look of the cards, the red and the black.

"Where's your brother?" she said, not lifting her eyes from the cards.

"I don't know," I said. "He has friends." For a moment, I was lost in her profile and her hearts and her diamonds.

We heard the disciplined clickety-clack of heels on stone. My mother stiffened before standing up and putting on a smile. Aunt Yasmine appeared, as erect and unswaying as a concrete tower. She was all upturned face and high hair and fingernails and cat-eye glasses and orange blossom perfume.

"Are you playing cards by yourself again, Zalfa?" she said, eyebrows lifted toward her hairline, toward the ceiling, toward the sky. "You mustn't do that. Do you want your husband to think you're lazy? At least pretend you're working on something. Maybe practice your desserts."

When she talked to my mother, she smiled. When she talked to me, she didn't. Not a word passed her lips that wasn't too loud.

"And you," she said, her voice rising. "Why are you always stuck to your mother's butt? Go outside and play with the boys."

"It's too hot," I said. I didn't know how to look at her.

"I don't care," she yelled. "Go downstairs now."

I moped out of the room, but not before hearing her berating my mother.

"A boy needs inspiration, and your lazing about is certainly not that. Don't you feel a shudder of disgust when you see him following you around? You're like a little girl who drags him around like her doll. You must do something about him."

"I know," my mother said. "I know. I'll do better. He's the top of his class, though. By quite a bit, it seems."

It was a Monday. Mademoiselle Marie announced that we were to return home but not in the buses we usually rode.

We had to wait for family to pick us up because we had an emergency. She wouldn't explain what that emergency was, and none of us thought to ask.

June 5, 1967.

The school parking lot was more chaotic than usual. Mademoiselle Marie couldn't keep her eyes on the kids, since all the classes were intermingling. I stayed close to her. Everyone seemed agitated. Horns honking, drivers yelling, children being shoved into cars. I tried to ask Mademoiselle Marie who was going to pick me up, but she wasn't looking my way. I got slapped in the back of my head, almost stumbled onto the pavement, which I wasn't supposed to step onto until the car that was to take me home arrived. I didn't have to turn around to know it was Farouk. I didn't even look back. He hit the back of my head once more. I yelled at him to stop it, warned him that if he did it again, I would tell my mother. We both knew that was an empty threat, since she always took his side, always. He lied to her every day, and she believed him. He hit me again, and I heard Nahed's giggle. Then she slapped the back of my head. Luckily, we all saw my mother's car turning into the parking lot at the same time. As our blue Simca approached, I saw my mother's face looking terrified. I became terrified. She strangled the steering wheel with both hands, leaning forward, her eyes scanning frantically and not calming until she saw Farouk. She inched closer, leaned, and opened the passenger door. Farouk jumped in the front, of course. My mother gestured frantically to Nahed to get in the car. Nahed started to cry. Without warning, she began to wail. I knew that for the good of everybody, I had better convince her to come with us. I asked her nicely. She yelled that she

106

wanted her father. My mother yelled through the passenger window that she was going to drive her home. I repeated the message to Nahed. She made me promise. She stopped wailing but continued to whimper and sniffle.

Once we were out of the parking lot, Farouk would not shut up. He kept wanting to know what was happening. My mother told him to calm down more than once. And as usual, she didn't use his first name when talking to him. It was always "light of my eyes" or "my life" or "my love" or the worst, "Farrou'ti." I was always Raja.

"Calm down, brazier of my heart," she said. "I will tell you, and you all have to listen."

There was a war, she explained. The bad Israelis attacked for no reason. No, not us. There would be fighting. Not here, no. She wouldn't let there be fighting anywhere near us. We had to be cautious and prepare ourselves, but everything would be fine very soon.

Farouk announced that we were going to crush the evil Israelis.

And then, out of seemingly nowhere, Nahed, next to me in the back seat, asked, "Is my father going to die?"

"No." My mother's response was loud. "Everything is going to be all right. Your father is a hero. He and his army friends will make sure nothing happens to us."

I had never seen my mother drive so clumsily. She couldn't relax. When we reached Aunt Yasmine's building, Nahed jumped out of the car. Her three brothers were wrestling in the building foyer. So many arms, so many legs, they looked like an alien octopus. Nahed didn't slow down. She jumped into the pile of limbs. My mother shouted at them to get inside but they paid no attention. We left them there.

As soon as we walked into our apartment, my brother ran to our room and my mother to the kitchen. I knew Farouk was going to lock me out of our room. That was his latest game. Still, I walked down the corridor to check. He had locked the door. If I caused a fuss, my exile would last longer. It was best to ignore him, since he got bored quickly in the room with nothing to do. He would be out of there soon enough.

My mother asked me to leave the kitchen because she didn't want me listening to the radio with her. I told her I didn't understand what the news said, which was not true. I suggested I could help her. I saw the bag of coffee on the counter. I assumed she was about to roast beans before she left to pick us up. I brought the stepladder to the far left cabinet, climbed the ladder, and picked out the roaster, a cylindrical tin pot with little doors and a handle on one side and a circular base that went over the burner. My mother sat at the table with the radio. I smelled the coffee to make sure it had cardamom seeds mixed in. I poured the gray beans in through the doors of the roaster, shut the doors, and put the pot on the gas burner. My mother didn't allow me to use matches to turn on the burners, but she wasn't paying attention, so I did. As the radio blared about betrayals and dishonor, I rotated the handle, which rotated the pot, which slowly rotated the coffee in the pot so the beans were roasted on the fire. I watched my mother's face turn sour. Oh, the humiliation. Oh, the shame. I loved the smell of coffee.

I heard my father coming through the door, grousing and grumbling. My mother ran out of the kitchen. My brother lumbered out of our room. My father was furious. Oh, the humiliation. Oh, the shame. How could this be

happening? I heard my mother try to mollify him. Everything would turn out all right.

"This is unacceptable," he yelled. "Get me a beer."

My mother returned to the kitchen and ran back out
with a beer.

High on the stepladder I remained, upon the wooden
pedestal I stood, rotating the pot, smelling the roasting beans.

I was eight years old.

I convinced my mother to let me take piano lessons
with our neighbors, the two sister spinsters, Mesdemoiselles Ghantout. A different world existed in their apartment, a world that smelled like the mountains, since they
never neglected their lavender. My mother placed sachets
between sheets, but according to her, the sisters did more.
They placed one in a pocket every morning and squeezed it
every now and then, releasing a natural perfume throughout
the day. I wondered whether our apartment had any smell,
other than when food was being cooked or served. The
sisters seemed older than their Persian carpets, which were
so worn and faded, I could barely distinguish any patterns.
I waited next to a window, my hands clasped behind my
back, watching a beam of light constraining dust motes,
which were, like my father and uncles when drunk, unable
to move in a straight line. A new world, quiet, quieter than
our apartment, no fathers yelling, no mothers complaining, no cousins running all over the place unable to settle
down before lunch. One of the sisters led me to the piano,
sat me down next to her, asked me to look away before she
played one note and then another. I was supposed to tell her

whether the second note was higher or lower. She played five notes in a row, asked me to sing or whistle them back. At that moment, I realized I had never wanted anything more than to study piano. Above the piano was a painting, but it wasn't of a mountain range or valley, not a view of a lake or a bucolic village scene; it was of two circles, red inside a blue, both off-center. I didn't understand but I wanted to.

I rushed back to our apartment, feeling as if I had drunk three full glasses of orange juice. I stood irresolute in the entryway when I heard my father chiding my mother in the living room. She should have asked him about piano lessons; I was not to take any. I was too placid as it was, what I needed was a more masculine hobby, maybe soccer, maybe metalworking, but certainly not learning to play an affected instrument from two effete spinsters. I didn't wait for the end of his speech. I returned to Mesdemoiselles Ghantout and informed them that my father didn't wish me to take any more piano lessons, that they shouldn't wait for me. I tried my best not to weep as I said that. Mademoiselle Ghantout told me not to feel too bad, that it wasn't a great loss, since I had little talent for music. I couldn't enter her world. There was a life that didn't belong to me, a world that was elsewhere, that would always be elsewhere, in another apartment, for someone else. Not for me, not for a boy like me.

The first time I wrestled didn't go well, not well at all. I didn't know what was coming — no idea. It was evening, Aunt Yasmine and her brood were over for dinner, my grandmother as well. The television was on. Black-and-white wrestling entranced me. I lay prone on the floor with my cousins, the adults on the sofas behind us. I knew I was watching the match differently from everyone else, and I should have been more wary, but I didn't know what was coming. Some nice guy was going against "The Man You Love to Hate," but I didn't hate him, no I didn't. I enjoyed both men in their underwear groping and squeezing. My father wanted the nice guy to win. Aunt Yasmine picked the mean guy, Mick McManus. They argued. My brother Farouk said that nice guys always win. Aunt Yasmine asked if I was enjoying the wrestling. The mean guy in the black trunks won. My father was upset.

Aunt Yasmine thought it was wonderful that I loved wrestling, that I should wrestle Nahed, and hopefully regain some of the honor my father had lost while backing the nice guy. I was confused. I didn't understand why they'd want me to wrestle, since I didn't know how. What honor was she talking about? Should I take off my clothes?

I was told to stand in front of Nahed, and when Aunt Yasmine said the word, I was to try and take Nahed down. I wasn't sure what *take her down* even meant, but I didn't have time to ask or think about it because Aunt Yasmine said the word and Nahed jumped on me. She sat on my chest. I felt I was being crushed. All I could do was yell no, no, no, no and begin to cry. Nahed was shocked. She got off me. And I ran to my bed. I cried and cried and cried. I thought my tears would never end, thought my sorrow would never allow me to stop crying, but I was wrong. At one point I fell asleep.

❊   ❊   ❊

I was nine years old.

I didn't count how many, but it must have been at least twenty-five family members over for fruit after lunch at Aunt Yasmine's garden: grandparents, parents, children. My grandmother yelled some encouragement to my brother Farouk as he unsuccessfully attempted to lift the giant stone mortar that she used to grind kibbeh. She slurred her words. Half the adults were drunk on arak, the other half would soon be. I figured it was time to disappear.

I closed the door to my cousins' room and looked for their comics. I found three *Asterix*, picked one, and then, like Goldilocks, I had to choose which bed suited me best. I settled on Nahed's. I was barely a few pages in when my mother opened the door without knocking. I was being called outside. She didn't specify who was calling, but I presumed it was my father doing the bidding of his sister. I told my mother I had an upset stomach. I'd eaten too much at lunch. I looked fine to her, she said, so I should go out and not make my family wait. She always wanted to accommodate my father.

Farouk hadn't been able to move the mortar, so that part of the adult entertainment was over. I knew it was my turn without having to be told.

"You're nine now," Aunt Yasmine said to me, "but are you a man yet?"

"No," I said, trying to sound resolute. I knew it was not the answer she wanted, and that I would be humiliated, but suggesting I was would only create more problems.

"But you're strong, right?"

"No." I hesitated. I had to be careful with what I was saying. I couldn't breathe right.

The family group sat in a circle. Nahed chased one of her brothers around the circumference clockwise, tagged him, and ran counterclockwise with him following her, both covered in grass and dirt. I could predict what was coming next, maybe not exactly, but in the general vicinity of humiliation.

"I think you should show us how strong you are," Aunt Yasmine said. She inhaled a dragon's breath of cigarette smoke to add portentousness to her words. "You should wrestle Nahed again."

Upon hearing her name, Nahed stopped running, jumped into the circle, chest out and a malefic grin on her face. She had yet to develop her mother's subtlety in venom. We might have been the same age, but she was quite a bit bigger.

"I'm not feeling well," I said. "I ate something at lunch that doesn't like me."

Aunt Yasmine laughed, and her mother joined her even though anyone could see neither was enjoying anything. "What's the matter?" Aunt Yasmine said. "Are you scared of wrestling a girl?"

"No," I said. I wanted to repeat that I was not feeling well, but I decided I wasn't going to wrestle again, ever. "Yes," I said. "Yes, I'm scared. Anyone would be scared of fighting her. She's not a girl, she's a tank."

Now it was my father who laughed. "You have to give him that," he said. He was talking about me but didn't look my way. "She looks more like a short Bulgarian weightlifter."

"She does not," Aunt Yasmine said. "She's a good girl. This is just a phase she's going through."

113

Nahed's face turned into an amalgam of queries, unsure of what was happening around her. What were they saying about her? Why was I not wrestling her?

"The boy is just afraid, always afraid," Aunt Yasmine said. "Farouk isn't. Come here, Farouk. Come wrestle my daughter. Show us what a good wrestler you are."

Nahed was back in her element now. She faced Farouk, smiling and eager. My brother stood up, walked over to her, and punched her in the face. Nahed collapsed onto the hard ground, clutching her mouth. My father yelled at Farouk. What was he thinking? Aunt Yasmine cradled her daughter. He was supposed to wrestle, not box, the fool. My grandmother laughed, since she was at the not-making-sense stage of drunk. Everyone was in an uproar. Farouk was confused. Nahed was crying. I walked back to the room, lay back on her bed, and read *Asterix*.

My Japanese adventure began one day in April, not that I'd visited Japan or anything. I guess I should call it my Japanese infatuation. I was fifteen. I walked all the way home from school because the weather was a delight that day and there was no fighting. Everyone assured everyone that there would be no war, no more shootings or bombs. Everyone had had enough. Everything would go back to normal. Except my parents didn't believe everyone. Just that morning as I sat for breakfast, they were discussing whether they could afford to send Farouk to study in France, avoiding an interruption of his education in case of a war flare-up. No one asked me, but I would think that interrupting his education could be a good thing. My parents still believed he could become a doctor or an engineer or something even though he'd had to change schools because he couldn't keep up. I was offended. Granted, I didn't study half as much as I should, had no clue what I wanted to do when I grew up, and I smoked a little hash every now and then. Still, my grades were higher than his by quite a bit. I might not want to be a doctor, but if I did, I'd be a better one. I was smarter, everyone was. Yet it was always Farouk this and Farouk that. We all knew they loved him more, but did they always have to be so blatant about it? So I interrupted my parents, asking my father if he was going to send me to France too. I received the usual: He'd figure out Farouk's situation first and then get to me. He always assumed I was a child, as if I couldn't understand they'd barely be able to cover Farouk's expenses if that, so there was no way I was going anywhere but my bedroom, the bedroom I shared with my boring brother.

That afternoon, upon returning home, I saw Mrs. Murata struggling to get her shopping bags out of the trunk of her car. The building's caretaker, who would've usually helped, wasn't there. She gratefully accepted my neighborly offer to carry a bag or two. The Muratas lived on the second floor while we were on the fifth floor. They had it better than us when the power went out. I didn't know much about them, except that Mr. Murata worked at the Japanese embassy. Everyone thought he was a spy, but I couldn't fathom why Japan or anyone would send a spy to Lebanon. What Lebanese secret would any country want, a hummus recipe? My father explained that after the fiasco at the Israeli airport a few years back, Mr. Murata was probably in Beirut to keep tabs on Japanese citizens who might be members of the infamous Red Army. All I knew about that incident was that three Japanese men shot other passengers at Lod Airport, killing about thirty people, including seventeen Christian pilgrims from Puerto Rico, along with one of their own. I could imagine the one who was shot by his fellow Japanese saying, "We're freedom fighters trying to liberate . . . hey, you shot me . . . blegh . . ."

The Muratas' apartment might have been the exact same size as ours, but it looked gigantic. Mrs. Murata probably was the only adult in the building who wasn't bigger than me and she looked so tiny in her cavernous living room. I realized our apartments seemed so unalike because the Muratas used space differently. We were four living at home and they a childless couple, but that alone didn't account for the discrepancy. They had fewer things in the living room, fewer unnecessary things. I loved that. You could see where everything was. There was nowhere for a mouse to hide. My family was partial to excess in almost every form. We had so much stuff, a ton and a half of history, and squeezed much of it into every room. The damaged sixteen-seat dining table. The hanging tapestries stitched and sewn by two of my aunts. The six Persians in the living room, all of them stained in different spots, were inherited by my mother. The Muratas had a carpet, but it certainly wasn't Persian, just a smallish white one with a black line that looked like it was painted across it. Everything seemed brand-new, so modern. I told Mrs. Murata that I thought her home lovely. Her face was pale, so when she blushed, her skin seemed to jump to life. I asked if she decorated everything in black and white to give the impression of a capacious room. Oh, no, she replied. The placement of the two mirrors was what did that. The color scheme was only because her husband was colorblind; the black and white made things easier for him to see.

I wondered what it would be like to live in a world with no colors. I wondered what it would be like to be from a culture that wasn't chaotic, where things were orderly and served a purpose. I grew up in a city where everything was unmoored.

There were spills of color on the white coffee table, a couple of rectangular art books as well as a juniper bonsai that twisted and turned as if the air-conditioning unit across the way produced a panoply of gales and hurricanes. I dropped to my knees to examine it, the first bonsai I'd ever seen. I thought it a glorious contradiction, imprisoned and tortured yet regal and utterly gorgeous. I had this inexplicable urge to pet it. Its grace ravished reason.

Mrs. Murata handed me one of the three books that were on the coffee table. If I liked design, I should peruse this tome. So much allure, so many enchantments. She suggested I borrow it, but that I should be careful with it as it would be difficult to replace. She understood that I wanted to rush up to my room to study it, but she'd made tea. She insisted I sit with her so she could thank me properly, even if only for a few minutes. I drank the tea from a small porcelain cup without a handle. I tried to be polite with my conversation, but I screwed it up as usual. She didn't wear a kimono, she replied, because Japan was a modern land: no samurais, and no geishas. She explained that her country was highly retentive of its traditions but was trying to unshackle itself to move forward. I should think of a kimono as more of a costume these days, and the costumes she liked to wear were Chanel suits. I felt more at ease when she asked me questions, how I was doing in school, how come she never saw me playing outside with the other boys of the neighborhood. She was surprised when she found out I was fifteen. I said everyone thought I was younger, and it wasn't my fault. When Farouk was my age, he was taller and hairier. Not me. Just bad luck. Could I please be excused so I could look at the book?

In my room, spread open upon my bed, the book transported me to a new world. Whereas the Murata apartment was hueless, almost every photograph in the book was a wondrous explosion of color. The gardens in green, the gardens of pebbles in stone and gray, the various shades of wood. I would have been able to teach geometry by showing the symmetrical lines of one living room. A banishing of the random, a celebration of order.

I'd never seen anything of the world outside of this land, but I was sure that Japan would be the one country that would be the direct opposite of Lebanon in every way I could imagine.

I wanted to be Japanese, which was not going to be easy.

I must have shocked Mrs. Murata when I rang her doorbell barely half an hour later. I told her I wanted to learn Japanese. Did she know of any teacher or school who could help me? She explained that there were a couple of teachers and at least one school, but none of them were available at the present time because of the troubling political situation. Many Japanese had returned home or left for another country at the beginning of the troubles. This damned country wasn't going to allow me to fulfill any of my dreams. "Wait a second," Mrs. Murata said. She had something that might help me begin. She disappeared into the back rooms, returning with a book, *Genki: An Integrated Course in Elementary Japanese*. I was elated. I babbled a million thank-yous.

Genki means having energy or pep, she said. That was me for sure.

I would teach myself Japanese. The book seemed easy enough. For the next month, I studied this life-changing manual for half an hour before dinner. Each chapter took me about two weeks. I didn't have to speed up because I realized I had time. I asked my father if I could go to Japan for the summer and he didn't stop laughing for days. He said he was happy I could still make him laugh during these tough times. I was going to show him. I was going to speak so fluently that Japan would welcome me as its long-lost son. Come back home, all of Japan would say, a chorus just for me.

I was able to say good morning and hello to Mrs. Murata in her language every time I saw her. I learned to say simple things like the weather was nice today. Mrs. Murata loved it. I knew I wasn't saying everything correctly, my pronunciation surely atrocious, but I knew I would improve. I worked hard for a month before I had to interrupt my Japanese for the dance. Once I got involved with Micheline, everything changed. And Mrs. Murata went back to Japan when the war started. I never saw her again.

IV
(1975)
Civil War

I shouldn't have been in the car. I should have kept my mouth shut. I should have said no to Micheline. I should not have tried to move up in the world, should have been satisfied with being the friendless loser I always was. The boys I was with in the car, Joe and Yves, were older, probably the most popular boys in my high school. They were men; I was technically a teenager, but still in the stammer of adolescence. Joe, the handsome driver, the richest boy in his class, was the son of a member of parliament, and more important, was dating Micheline, the hottest girl in our school. She was the catalyst for our meeting, the catalyst for his acknowledging my existence, the catalyst for so many things. Every boy in school desperately wanted her to notice him, yet she picked me. It was perhaps inevitable that as soon as she acknowledged me, I would tumble right down to hell, plunge headlong into its pit. Mere mortals should be wary of gifts from the gods. Micheline was my apple. "Here," the serpent said. "This exquisite girl noticed you. Do everything she says, and everyone will begin to like you."

She needed a partner for the end-of-term school talent show. She wanted to ballroom dance, and none of the more appropriate boys, not Joe or anyone in her class, could keep a beat. All the boys practiced macho-sauntering before their mirrors but they all had two left hoofs. I wasn't sure how Micheline figured out I'd be able to do it. She intuited that

I was the one boy who would not spend the entire tango staring at her breasts.

I would not stare at her breasts because I knew early on I wouldn't have a chance with her, or with any other girl for that matter. Girls wanted to be taken places in a car, to have the freedom of being driven. I mean, it wasn't a coincidence that Micheline, the most beautiful girl in school, was dating Joe, who had the best car. I understood I wouldn't have a chance to date a girl until I was eighteen with a license and access to a car. While all the boys around me were talking endlessly about girls, hopelessly fantasizing about which one they were going to have sex with, I thought it was quite okay not to think about girls at all until I could drive, and I didn't.

About a month before the talent show, every kid in the school heard Micheline yell to me across the yard, "Hey you, yes, you, Obélix, do you want to *cha cha cha* with me?" I nodded of course, even though I hated being called Obélix since I wasn't fat, maybe a little over, maybe plumpish. I did have red hair, but mine was curly and unruly, and I obviously did not keep it in braids like the Gaul. But was I going to tell her not to call me Obélix? Of course not.

Micheline and I were going to dance together, to spend quite a bit of time in each other's company. I felt my school status rising like warm mercury every second I was around her. We made a strange couple: she seventeen, I barely fifteen; she lovely, me not. Barefoot, she was taller than me, yet she insisted on wearing designer high heels. She towered over me, and I would've found it comical like everyone else were I not her partner. We practiced every day until the dance. She machine-gunned orders constantly—keep your back straight, don't fidget, look at me not your feet — but I didn't mind. As the youngest in my family, I was used to being told what to do. I practiced with her as well as on my own in my room, door shut, in front of the mirror atop my dresser, one, two *cha cha cha*, one, two *cha cha cha*, one, two *cha cha cha*. I kept at it until my father would yell for me in his deep voice to stop the racket. Every night, Farouk, who usually ignored me when not mocking me, watched surreptitiously from his bed, probably imagining himself dancing with the gorgeous Micheline.

She and I might not have made a perfect pair onstage, but I didn't make a mistake, not one. Yet everyone could tell she barely tolerated me. Once our dance was over, I turned into a ghost again. An abrupt transition: without a thank-you, without an it-was-nice-to-dance-with-you. At the final dip — she was so tall that her head looked smaller, like a Henry Moore sculpture — we heard the applause and took our bows. She then exited left with a cynical smile on her face and never acknowledged me again.

Her boyfriend couldn't, though. You see, Joe's father was not just a parliamentarian, but a gunrunner who owned two huge hashish farms. He thought the sun shone out of Joe's ass, spoiled him rotten, buying him anything he wanted, including the bright orange BMW 2002. Now, he might have been willing to grant Joe any wish, but he wouldn't allow him to smoke hash, and made sure to warn everyone who worked on his farms not to give his son any. The parliamentarian's threats were to be taken seriously, particularly since the times were chaotic. I didn't know it then, but the civil war had started. I just thought, you know, that it was the usual skirmishes.

Here was where I became useful to Joe. An older cousin on my mother's side was the manager at one of his father's farms, and he allowed me to steal from his hidden stash every now and then when we visited them. I'd be at his place, I would pretend to go to the bathroom, sneak into the master bedroom, and open his varnished dresser drawer. There would be five sandwich bags between his BVD underwear, each containing twenty grams of hash, premium pollen too. I'd stuff one into my pocket. It took my cousin a while to figure out it wasn't my brother who was taking the bags. He assumed I was too young to do so, and once he realized I wasn't, he began to wink each time I left his house. Now, you make sure to behave, he'd tell me as his wife kissed all of us goodbye. My parents thought he managed a tea and tobacco farm.

You smoked hash by rolling the pollen mixed with tobacco into a cigarette or by using a pipe, or maybe a hookah. I had neither of those and I didn't smoke. What did I do? I figured it all out by myself. I'd stick a pin into cardstock so it could remain upright. I would then press the resinous pollen into a small piece that I could stick on the pin. I'd have a glass ready, and when I lit the hash, I'd cover it with said glass, and then lift one side to inhale all the delicious smoke. I wouldn't waste a single atom of the glassed-in fog. I did all this in bathrooms, of course, and I would have to run to a window and exhale so that no one could smell the hash.

I was stupid enough to explain my method to Micheline while we practiced, and sure enough, the following day Joe and his best friend Yves waited for me outside the school gate. In no uncertain terms they informed me that I was to hand over all my hash, which they might allow me to share every now and then if they felt like it. Yves lifted me by the shirtfront so he could threaten me at eye level. He was the asshole of the pair. I mean, how could you not be an asshole if your mother named you after her favorite designer? For a month or so, until the car ride, I became Joe and Yves's drug supplier, or as Yves preferred to call me, their little doggie. Joe refused to pay for the hash because he insisted it wasn't mine but belonged to his father. He would die owing me, I don't know, maybe like two or three hundred dollars, maybe a thousand.

Joe, like most boys in our school, was not awed by the mystery of death, or the mystery of life either. He was too stupid to be awed by anything. He drove his car as if he was challenging death around every corner, BMW versus sickle. When Yves figured I came close to peeing my pants at every turn, he'd encourage Joe to go faster. The only thing that would make me feel calmer in the car was to get as high as possible, and I was so, so high that night.

The BMW drove fast, but all was slow. Evening noise hit me in waves, *whoosh, whoosh, whoosh*, a tide of sound advancing and receding. Soft, loud, soft, loud. Beirut registered in squares and rectangles as if drawn on a dark writing pad. Big squares eating little squares and small rectangles eating big ones, every shape contained in another. I wished to draw the map of it, but dark spots attempted to form crop circles at a point between my eyes. *Whoosh, whoosh, screech*, and a big black monster of a car swerved in front of the BMW, forcing Joe to pound the brakes quickly. I didn't shriek. Luckily, I was strapped in with the seat belt. Up front, Yves hit his bulky head on the dashboard. He yelled multiple curses at the offending car, was joined by Joe. I wanted to say something, anything, but my tongue felt furry and lazy. The dark spots moved with somnambular vagueness. Yves tried to open the door a couple of times before succeeding, but he didn't get a chance to get out of the car. I wondered whether he saw what I saw. Out of the gyrating spots, out of the other car, four masked men emerged, three carrying Kalashnikovs, and one a mere gun. Yves had one leg out of the car, and his head had barely peaked above the car door before he slumped. His body emitted a dull groan and dropped onto the pavement. It seemed I heard the thud of the fall before the bang of the bullet, which didn't make sense. And then the *whoosh, whoosh* again. It took Joe a second, maybe more, but it seemed like an eternity before he screamed, and not a manly scream. I didn't. My mouth and tongue refused to behave. The man who shot Yves with a gun reached Joe's side, opened the door, and pulled Joe out like he was a sack of feathers. Joe stopped screaming when the gunman slapped him. Even from a distance, even in the greenish evening light, I could see blue veins etch Joe's neck. The guy who came for me had his face covered not with a ski mask, but with a red-and-white bandana. He was one of the Kalashnikov guys. He stepped over the corpse that was once Yves, yelled to no one in particular that he thought there would be only two of them. I tried to get the seat belt off, but my hands were too clammy. I still couldn't scream. I saw Joe get his head covered in what looked like a burlap sack. All I could think was *That must itch*. The guy with the gun guffawed, an exaggerated laugh, and mocked Joe for peeing his pants. My guy ordered me out of the car. Get the fuck out now, he said, out, out. His voice sounded familiar, very familiar. I assumed I was hallucinating. I tried to unsnap the belt once more. I couldn't, I told him, I swore that I couldn't. What, bandana guy said, I can't believe I have to do this, why couldn't Joe's fat father buy him a four-door car? He might have been complaining but he knew exactly where the thingamajig that moved the front seat was. He asked if I was the only boy in Beirut who wore a seat belt. Just his luck. He bent into the car, somehow maneuvered himself halfway into the back seat. Big guy, another one who towered over me. He reached over and unsnapped the belt, grabbed me by the shirtfront, but hesitated.

"Hey Obélix," he said, sounding excited.

Was I going to tell him not to call me Obélix? Of course not. "Hi, Boodie," I said.

"Don't call me that," he said, "I use Hulk when I'm on the job, what are you doing with these two assholes?"

I wanted to tell him I wasn't meant to be there, that they forced me to get into the car with them, that they always forced me to go with them, to do things I didn't want to. "Boodie," I said, "I'm so scared."

"Shh," he said, "just come out of the car."

I tried to sober up, succeeded up to a point. I couldn't remain stoned having to step over Yves's body, which seemed to be emanating a weirdly chemical odor. Yet I couldn't have been clearheaded because Boodie seemed to be holding me up by the back of my shirt collar. My limbs lacked solidity. I felt like a marionette — a terrified, horrified marionette that could collapse upon itself at any moment.

"Yves is dead," I said.

"That's what usually happens when you get shot in the head," Boodie replied.

The guy with the gun told Joe to move forward. Joe mumbled over and over, asking where he was being taken, that he couldn't see anything. The guy put the gun to Joe's head. Joe started moving. He stumbled on something, maybe a rock, a branch, maybe his own feet, and the guy shot him in the head. *Boom*, and blood exploded, spurted out of the bag. Joe collapsed. My heart dropped all the way down to my balls, metallic fireworks lit up my tongue.

"Why the hell did you do that?"

"I didn't. The gun went off."

"What do you mean it went off? You pulled the trigger."

"I didn't mean to. It just went off."

"Fuck him," Boodie, who wasn't part of the garrulous argument, said, and then softly, just for me, "I hated that guy."

"Don't shoot me," I said. "Please don't."

The other three continued arguing. They wouldn't be able to collect the ransom. Killing daddy's boy was not good. You're an amateur. No, you're an amateur. How were they going to explain Joe's death? They would take the car, which should get them some pocket change if not the grand return of a ransom. They should leave before anybody showed up. They were taking too long. What should they do with me? No one had told them about a third boy. What should they do? "Shoot him," the guy with the gun said.

My soul stuttered. "No," I said, my tongue unleashed, "no, don't shoot me, I'm not worth killing—"

Boodie told me to shut up, said I talked too much, told the others he was keeping me. The mean guy with the

130

gun wanted to know what he meant by keeping. Boodie explained that he'd store me in the garage apartment they had set up for Joe now that Joe wasn't alive enough to use it. I need him, he said. The three others looked confused but didn't seem willing to argue. I felt some hope. Mean guy asked what Boodie needed me for. I was going to teach him to dance. One of the guys shook his head in disbelief; mean guy shrugged his shoulders.

I was going to teach Boodie to dance. Little did I know he was serious.

I woke up in encompassing darkness, an enveloping absence of light. I didn't know how long I'd slept. It felt like a long time, but I had no way of knowing. As usual, I'd forgotten to wear my watch when I left home last night, and had I not, I still wouldn't have been able to see the hands, since my father refused to buy me a luminous watch for my birthday. I didn't think I'd be able to sleep, thought my terror and worry would keep me up all night. It wasn't every day you saw two people shot dead, had guns pointed at you, or had your head covered in a burlap sack that smelled of potatoes while being driven to who knows where.

And I needed to pee desperately, but I didn't know where either the bathroom or the light switch was. I assured myself I'd be able to figure things out. I was resourceful. There was a light. I was certain of that. I remembered it from last night. An unadorned lightbulb dangling from an incompetently painted ceiling. I should remember where the door was, next to which would surely be the light switch. I was good at pointing myself in the right direction. Everyone always told me that. My feet, sockless and shoeless, felt concrete, not carpet, not stone tile, not wood. I'd gone to bed in my clothes from yesterday sans windbreaker. I stood up, felt a bit woozy, put my arms in front of me and traipsed in one direction, to my right, one step, two steps, and my hand touched a wall, then I sidled sideways, one step, two steps, three, four, eight, nine, no door, corner. One more step, and my foot touched dirt, not cement. Yuck. Whoever had poured the concrete must have run out of it. I needed to pee. And then, stupid me, I remembered I had a packet of matches. Was it in my windbreaker? No, in my pants. Eureka! I struck the match, the tip flared on the second try. Door was on the opposite side of the room. I caught a glimpse of the light switch before the flame almost burned my fingers. I walked toward the door, stumbled on what I thought were my sneakers. I didn't fall. My hands touched wall. My right hand felt door, then doorhandle, my left hand went up and down, searching, landed on the light switch. Let there be light, I said. Hideous, nasty room. The far corner had a naked quadrant of brown dirt and pebbles. I'd slept on a mattress without sheets, a pillow without a cover. I hated this. I opened the door to another room, sofa, small television, smaller kitchen. No windows anywhere. Bathroom to the left. I rushed in. No, no, no, no. The toilet was an old-fashioned squatting one. And no bidet. I unzipped, unfurled my dick, and peed.

The bathroom was tiled, though, unlike the bedroom. The living room, badly lit with one bare lightbulb as well, was horrible; it looked as if it was decorated by someone with terrible taste who got bored and left with the job half done. The midsize sofa, the only place to sit, was a repulsive green color, and still covered in its plastic. It was new, but the small coffee table that leaned to one side wasn't. Numerous cup rings bit one another upon its varnish. I walked to the door; a metal gate protected it from the inside. I asked myself why anyone would want to put a gate indoors, and that was when I realized, stupid me again, that it might not be to protect but to imprison, not to keep out but to keep in. I began to panic again, and it was a whole new kind of panic because now I was sober.

I tried to open the metal gate, but it didn't even have a knob. I shook it and it barely budged. I needed a key. As coppery bile left its mark in my mouth, I noticed that I'd have to put my hand and a key through the grate to open the gate, and since it swung outward, I'd have to open the outer door at the same time. I screamed. Help! Help!

No answer, no window, no noise but mine.

I needed to get out of here. My parents were probably freaking out. I was freaking out.

I could be calm and rational. I surveyed my surroundings. One bedroom, one living room, a small bathroom, a small kitchen.

I decided to sit on the couch's plastic and consider my options.

His actual name was Abdallah or something like that. Probably named after his paternal grandfather as was the tradition, and he probably hated his old-fashioned name, or maybe his mother did, and the nickname Boodie stuck. The cool name fit him, like his colorful shirts, like his ubiquitous smile. He was one year ahead of me in school, in the same class as

Micheline, Joe, and Yves. He was seventeen, like Micheline, one year younger than Joe and Yves, who were probably held back at some point. I felt bad for Joe and Yves, but I'd say academia was not mourning their death. I didn't know Boodie well. There was no reason for me to. I did know of him, of course. I noticed him a lot because he was always around. All the students did. He played on the school's soccer team, probably the best player. Someone described him as both athletic and game-smart, whatever that meant. All I could tell was that for a big guy—tall, broad-shouldered, not lean—he was fast. I didn't know if he had a girlfriend. I would think not because he didn't have a car yet.

Before the crazy killings, I liked Boodie. Almost all the kids did. He was nice, never bullied anyone, always said hello and smiled when he saw me. How could I not like him when he knew I existed? Why he'd want to associate with the masked hooligans was beyond me.

I heard the anthracite door being unlocked, then opened. I jumped up. Boodie appeared behind the gate, his white teeth brightening a disarming smile. He cocked his left eyebrow as he swung the gate open. In one arm, he carried a largish brown shopping bag, misshapen and slightly soggy. He didn't need to lock the gate behind him, since I wouldn't be able to open it without a key.

"Why didn't you remove the plastic from the couch?"

"Why would I do that? I need to go home. You must let me go."

"I can't. We talked about that. You're staying here for a while, which is why you should have removed the plastic.

You need to make this place more comfortable for you, more like home."

"I can't stay here."

"We talked about that."

"No, we didn't."

"Last night. We talked. You shouldn't use drugs. They're not good for you. You kept going in and out of making sense. It was difficult to keep up. We agreed it's best if you stay here for a while."

"I didn't agree to that. There's no way I'd agree to that."

He remained standing, a smile dancing upward along his face. As if he was talking to an underdeveloped child. I wanted to slap him. He moved toward the kitchen, delicately placing the bag on the small counter. He then walked to the bedroom, looked in. He shook his head in mild consternation. His left eyebrow shot up once more before he spoke.

"We did agree. You didn't put on the sheets. Did you sleep in your clothes? I told you not to. It might be a couple of days before I can get you some other things to wear. And I can't get a washing machine, so you have to wash everything by hand."

"What are you talking about? Washing? I'm not staying here."

"We agreed."

"No, no, we did not. And even if I did, I take it back now. I wasn't in full mental capacity to agree last night. I am now and I don't want to be here."

"You know I don't need your agreement, right? Full mental or whatever. You can't leave. That's all there is to it. I saved your life on the condition that I won't let you go. If you leave, the boys will hunt you down and kill you. You know too much."

"I know nothing. I know you but I would never tell on you. You know that. I swear, I won't tell on you."

"You know who killed Joe."

"No, I don't. He was wearing a mask."

"Oh, come on. You figured out it was Michel, you know, Micho."

"No, I didn't. I didn't. I barely know Micho and he was going incognito. I recognized you because you said hello, but I didn't know who shot Joe."

"Well, now you do. Wasn't that the strangest thing? I knew things might go wrong but not like that. Micho is the best shooter of all of us. He always has the highest marks during training. It's as if he was born with a gun in his hand. Did you see how he took out Yves? How far was he, seven meters, eight? Bang. Yves was down. Now, that was professional. But then with Joe, it was walk this way, and then oops, bang. There goes the money."

"You killed them."

"I didn't."

"Two people. They were your friends. They were in your class."

"Yes, but they were such assholes. They thought they were better than everyone else. Why would you hang out with them? Get up. Let's take the plastic off the couch."

I stood up. I wanted to tell him that maybe I was hanging out with assholes—through no fault of my own—but he was hanging out with criminals, murderers even.

"We bought this couch so whoever was guarding Joe would be able to sleep. We spent three weeks planning this abduction. We cleaned this place up. We got some kitchen-ware and filled the pantry. We even brought in the small fridge. We got the money from command, who thought it was a good investment. But then oops, *poof.* Now you get the benefit of the investment."

"Benefit? What are you talking about? How is this a benefit?"

"You still don't get it. The only reason you're alive is because of me. Micho wants me to kill you. Command wants me to kill you. Everybody thinks it would be easier if I killed you."

"You can't kill me. You know me. You'd feel guilty."

"Not if you keep mouthing off. I won't feel guilty at all. I've been nice to you. I saved your life. But all you do is talk back and argue. This can't work. We must set some rules. I'm the man. You're my prisoner. You always do what I say. I'm always the man. Do we understand each other?"

"Well, what does being a prisoner mean? Do I have to stay—"

"Shut up and look at me. I said look at me. Do you understand?"

"Yes."

"I am the man. Say it."

"You're the man."

"Are you hungry? I am."

He opened the brown bag, on which grease had oozed darker patterns. The delicious smell unfurled toward my nose, and my stomach lion-growled in anticipation. He took out two plates from a stack inside the cabinet, placed two manoushehs on each. He was the one who had to set up the apartment for hostages, he said. He had to surreptitiously find out from his mother what was needed, particularly when it came to the quantities of dry goods, or olive oil, just as an example. He thought he did a good job. He was sure that as time went on, we would find out he missed some things, but that could be corrected since he still had some discretionary funding from the original command money. The stove was old but refurbished, and he installed the gas cannister himself. He was sure it wouldn't explode on us or anything like that. I should teach myself how to cook because he obviously couldn't afford to bring in meals all the time. Every now and then he could buy fresh vegetables and dairy products, and I'd have to make do with that. He must have realized I wasn't engaged in this conversation, but that didn't seem to bother him. The only interruptions to his monologue were when he took bites of his manousheh.

He made one mistake, he said. He brought down a television, but he was unable to get a reception this far underground, so that was a waste. He wouldn't have worried about it had Joe been the hostage because he didn't care whether Joe was entertained or not. He didn't want me to be bored all the time, so I had to figure out ways to entertain myself for the duration of my stay, which unfortunately was going to be a while. Maybe I could do push-ups and sit-ups to build muscle. That would be a good use of my time. When we're not dancing, that is, he said. We should start the lessons soon.

❋   ❋   ❋

"My parents are probably awfully worried."

"I know. Not much we can do about that. But at least they'll see you again one day. Think about Yves's parents. They probably found the body by now. Joe's shitty dad is probably screaming at people, threatening everybody."

"But my parents haven't done anything to you. They don't deserve to worry."

"I know, but you're alive. So there's that. Did you tell them you were with Joe and Yves?"

"No, of course not. I told you. They forced me to go with them because they enjoyed making fun of me. I couldn't tell people they treated me like that."

"So, no one knew you were in that car. Maybe your parents will think you ran away. Okay, that's not likely. And they won't think you'd join a militia either."

"Can we tell my mother?"

"We can't."

"Please."

"We can't."

I lay on cotton sheets, staring at the lightbulb. Boodie helped me dress the bed. He was surprised I didn't know how. I make my bed every day but I never had to do it from scratch. My mom always changed the sheets. I tried not to think of her, but that proved difficult. I kept pressing Boodie, insisting that she should know I was alive, until he finally snapped. Fuck your mother, he said, and told me that if she cared about me, she would have shown up to the school talent show to watch me dance, that someone in my family should have. He said all I kept doing was making things difficult for him.

My mother would have shown up if my father hadn't told her not to. He didn't want her to see my hips moving from side to side onstage or something like that.

I should tell Boodie to get me some candles. As soon as I turned off the light, I wouldn't be able to see anything. No windows. How was I to get back to bed? What would happen when the power went out?

Candles and some books.

He'd left four hours earlier and I had absolutely nothing to do. No one to talk to, no reading, no television, no David Bowie. I masturbated twice, which took a total of maybe fifteen minutes. When Boodie left, he told me he had to go for training at five in the afternoon, so I was able to estimate the time.

Maybe he could get me a clock. And mirrors to make the space feel less constrictive.

What if the electricity went out and I needed to use the bathroom? When I complained that I probably wouldn't be able to have a bowel movement while squatting, he told me I was being silly. Men had been shitting in that position for thousands of years, and it was supposed to be better because the spine would be straight, which allowed the bowels to evacuate easier. I hated him. And I had to do it and there was no bidet, so I had to wash my butt using the hose right next to the toilet.

I couldn't live like this. I needed to figure a way to get out.

I was sure my mother was worried sick. Whenever she was concerned about something, she would get into bed. I used to make fun of her, calling what she did the sleeping cure. I wondered whether she was in bed already.

My sleep wasn't curative. Feverish dreams. I must have died at least three times in whatever little sleep I had. Shot once by who knows who, lifted off the ground and strangled by Yves, and so on. I woke up once to a scream and realized it was my own. Only I heard it. Alone in a stupid bed, in a stupid underground apartment, in some part of town.

Faint light crept into the bedroom from the lightbulb in the so-called living room through the door I'd left ajar. I sat up, my feet loathing the feel of concrete. Why tile the apartment but quit before doing the bedroom? Why pour concrete in the bedroom but leave a corner undone? I stood up to slide on my underwear and hurried to the bathroom. As soon as I came out, I heard the jangling of the keys and Boodie opening the gate. He beamed when he noticed me.

"Did you just wake up?"

"What time is it? I can't tell the time."

"It's seven in the morning. I'd tell you to go back to sleep, but I only have a few hours before I need to head back to training."

He placed a sizeable cardboard box on the floor next to the gate. Sweat bubbled on his face, one drop streaking down along his unshaven cheek and dropping onto the floor. When he stood back up again, I noticed the gun. He wore new camouflage fatigues, army boots, a ridiculous-looking olive-green beret, and attached to his belt a webbing pouch with a plastic water bottle, another with a magazine of bullets, and a brown leather holster with a goddamn gun in it. How did he keep his pants up?

"Don't I look good?"

"I don't know. I don't like it."

"Oh, come on. Doesn't it make me look manly?"

"It makes you look scary."

"But that's good."

"But you're not in the army."

"Our army is shit. We need a new one. We're patriotic fighters. Our mission is to restore integrity and pride and peace to our country."

"With guns? You're going to restore peace with guns?"

"Of course. There are way too many armed, lawless guys out there. We must reclaim the streets. Make them Lebanese again."

He tapped the badge stitched above his heart, a flag of Lebanon supposedly rippling and fluttering, but so poorly designed that it managed to make the cedar look like a sick tree that had been discarded on a winding road. What was not winding was the left-side part in his black hair, always straight. Not once had I seen him with a crooked part or a single strand out of place.

"Should we start the lesson now or do you want breakfast first?"

I must have given him somewhat of a quizzical look, because he let out a solitary, raspy "Ha" before taking a cassette player with two small speakers out of the box. He glanced toward the coffee table, then at the kitchen counter, placing the machine on the latter, plugging it into the wall socket.

"The sound will probably be better if it doesn't come from too far below us, don't you think? Don't look so confused. You're going to teach me to dance."

"What are you talking about? I don't know how."

"Yes, you do. I saw you or did you forget?"

"I did one dance with Micheline. That's all I know. That one dance is the only one she taught me."

"That's what I want you to teach me. That one song. You're going to help me. I want to learn so I can dance with Micheline and then fuck her."

Boodie turned around before pressing the play button on the cassette player, a portable, metallic-colored number that had seen better days. The ever-familiar acoustic guitar opening flowed out of the speakers. He grinned rapturously, a peacock in outsize army fatigues. He asked how he was supposed to stand.

I repeated that I only knew this one dance, and not very well at that. I couldn't teach him anything more.

"That's all I want. I'm going to dance with her. I don't need to dance for anything else. Show me."

I stood in front of him, still in my underwear, still shoeless—toes, heel, and ball pressed onto tile. I held my right arm out as if I were a school guard about to tell the little kids to move along. My left encircled an imaginary waist. Back straight, top of my head horizontal, an imaginary book atop my crown, eyes straight ahead until the first step, when I'd look at my partner.

He mimicked my movement, but we weren't mirror-imaging. Boodie took one step back, hesitated for a moment before moving forward.

"Remember, I'm me and you're Micheline," he said.

"I'd need high heels and higher breasts."

"You'll do until the real thing."

"I don't know how to dance the girl's part."

"Well, we're practicing, aren't we?"

His right hand took my left, his left pressed onto my lower back, warming my skin. My hand felt uncomfortable on the coarse material of his fatigues.

"I should put on my clothes."

When marimba rhythms start to play. I hated Dean Martin, loathed him even. *Dance with me, make me sway.* When Micheline finished with me, I'd thought I would never hear that damn song again. He was one of my mother's favorite singers, not sure why, but it was Dean along with Johnny Mathis and the one with the stupidest name ever, Engelbert Humperdinck. Not Tom Jones, though, because he swayed his hips too much for my mom. She'd always play one of these three crooners' albums while she cooked. My father and I would always tell her to turn it off, but she'd only lower the volume. One of the few things my father and I could agree on was that my mother's musical taste was horrendous. Of course, I hated his favorite music as well. My mother wouldn't just play her music while cooking, she sang along with her men: "Chances Are" with Johnny; *Please release me, let me go,* with her Humperdinck, *for I don't love you anymore.* My father used to accuse her of not being able to hit the correct note to save her life.

The whole month when I was practicing for the dance, when I played Dean Martin's song in my room, my father would yell at me to turn off the racket and my mother would yell at me to turn it up. I was surprised when she didn't show up for the dance. I thought she would in spite of everything.

❁ ❁ ❁

Boodie's underwear did not fit me. He wanted me to try it on because he wasn't sure where else he could get me some. I went into the bedroom to change. I heard him ask from behind the closed door whether it fit. Of course it didn't. I could fit two of me in his underwear. I could wear his old T-shirt as a dress, the hem falling just above my knees. Loudly, so he could hear me, I complained that his sister's sweatpants didn't have a drawstring. I should try them on, he said. Without a drawstring they no longer fit his sister, since she had a flat butt.

It took me a second to get mad, but get mad I did. I forcefully opened the door, almost tearing it off its rusty hinges. I stood in the doorway, arms akimbo, screaming at him.

"Do you think my ass is too fat?"

"No, no, I didn't say that. Your ass is nice. I said my sister's ass is flat. Yours is curvier, that's all. It will be able to keep the sweatpants from dropping and that's a good thing. Your ass isn't fat. It's shapely. I'm talking about the fit of the sweatpants. Just try them on."

I realized I was wearing his pineapple-print T-shirt, no pants and no underwear. He couldn't see a thing, of course, since his T-shirt covered everything above my knees.

"I can't wear them. They're for girls."

I couldn't imagine how sweatpants could be more girlish, neon fuchsia with dazzlingly bright sequins in the shape of a kitten sewed onto the thigh. I hated them.

"No one will see you in them. Come on. Don't be difficult. I don't know where I can get more clothes. Please try them on."

I turned around and walked back into the room. I picked the sweatpants up off the bed and tried them on. He was right, and I hated him for it.

I was awakened by a feathery movement on my upper thigh, not too far from my crotch. I opened my eyes in perfect darkness once again, no light seeping from the next room. The electricity must have gone out again. Boodie promised he'd get me at least one flashlight and some candles, although both were hard to find because of the continued skirmishes. I thought I must have dreamed the touch on my thigh. The room was quiet enough that I would have heard if someone was nearby and breathing. But then, under the sheet, I felt it again, same place. My left hand traveled down to scratch, and I felt some creature skitter away. I snapped. I jumped off the bed, screamed, jumped up and down rubbing my hands all over my body. I screamed again. I was sure it was an ugly cockroach. I stopped moving because I didn't want to step on it by accident. Naked and barefoot, I wasn't sure what to do. I couldn't be certain where the bed was. I wasn't going to get back into it—no, I most certainly wasn't. Which way was the door? I walked in the direction I thought it would be, steps cautious and gentle just in case. I did find the door. I went into the living room, shutting the door behind me, knowing full well that it was a futile gesture because the cockroach would have been able to follow me by scuttling beneath the doorsill. I felt my way to the couch. I wished we hadn't removed the plastic because I felt so grimy. Clouds of anxiety drenched my heart as I waited for the power to come back on.

I heard the dry howls of at least two dogs in the distance. I wondered how far underground I was, most likely in some building's garage, most likely one or two floors down. The dogs quieted, and within a few seconds a muffled explosion allowed my lungs to join my heart in its anxiety. My stomach was churning like a pot of boiling water. I began to inhale air in earnest. How would I be able to measure the distance of sound? Was the explosion close? What if I was buried alive here, rubble and shrapnel covering all the exits? How many floors were in the building above? The darkness turned darker. I was too naked. I felt about to faint.

As soon as I heard the jingling of the door's handle, the power returned as if by magic, the living room bulb came on, and the room sprang at me like a predatory cat. Boodie appeared behind the gate, all toothy smile once again, a canvas bag across his shoulder, a flashlight in his hand. "I guess I won't need this right now," he singsonged. I stood up. He turned the flashlight off before opening the gate. "The explosion couldn't have been too far," he said. "You must have heard it."

"There's a cockroach in the room," I screamed. I realized I was naked and jumping up and down again but couldn't stop myself. "It was on me," I said. "It crawled on me, there are cockroaches in this place, and you left me alone with cockroaches and I hate you."

Framed by the doorway, he shook his head, languorously, from side to side. He bit his lower lip. Even a blind man could feel the effort he exerted in suppressing a laugh.

I hated him even more. All the new light in the living room seem to contract and swirl about him.

"I called your mother. I told her you're okay, so you can stop pestering me."

"You talked to her? What did she say?"

"Nothing."

"What do you mean nothing?"

"She didn't say anything. I called and your mother answered. I said you wanted her to know that you were not dead but couldn't come home right now and I hung up."

"You hung up on my mother?"

"I promised I would tell your mother you're okay. I wasn't going to chat about the weather with her."

"She's probably more worried now."

"You keep this up and I'll make sure her worrying was for good reason."

"You're inconsiderate."

"You're ungrateful."

"I hate you so much."

"You keep saying that. Let's dance."

A geisha dances and you might think it's a simple thing: languid, discrete movements that seem easy to replicate. You would be wrong, of course. The beat is slow, unlike, say, Tahitian or African dance. A Lebanese belly dancer is somewhere in between, relying primarily on hip movements, similar to the Tahitian. The Lebanese Dabkeh, a dance for both men and women, relies on staccato feet movement. There's a Côte d'Ivoire traditional dance called the Zaouli, which is the craziest thing you'll ever see, insanely fast as well as glorious. I point these out to say there are many forms of dancing, but all require a minimum of two things: an elementary understanding of beat and grace. Boodie had neither.

"Don't worry," he said. "Everything is going to be all right."

He was sure he was going to be able to dance with Micheline, and I knew he wasn't. He thought he would be able to for about a week or so.

I would say the seconds tick-tocked, but I still had no reasonable way of measuring time or anything really. Boodie had brought an ormolu desk clock he must have stolen from somewhere, not realizing that it was no longer working. It was of no use whatsoever. I was alone in a lousy apartment in hell. No breeze, no sun, no fresh air. I could hear myself breathe, except when the echoed sounds of gunfire reached me, an explosion every now and then. And the barking dogs, and the howling dogs, and the wailing dogs. And I had nothing to do but listen.

A dog had been wailing for a long time. It was joined by others every now and then, but this one was in pain. The sound arrived muffled, but I could still distinguish between each dog's bark or wail. And the dog continued to wail on and on. And then I heard a shot, and the dog no longer wailed.

I began to hyperventilate, a squall of sips and gasps and stuttered inhales. I lay down on the ugly green sofa.

I hated this. I hated the apartment. I hated everything. And I hated myself because I desperately wanted him to come back. I hated myself because I preferred dancing with him to being alone.

And he couldn't dance. One, two, *cha cha cha*, and he couldn't even manage that.

On the first day of my captivity, my jailer brought to me a manousheh.

On the second day of my captivity, my jailer brought to me his underwear and his sister's sweatpants.

On the third day of my captivity, my jailer brought to me a flashlight and thick candles.

On the fourth day of my captivity, my jailer brought to me his sister's slippers and four oranges.

On the fifth day of my captivity, my jailer brought to me a bottle of hair conditioner (I'd asked for that) and a stupid magazine called *Monday Morning* that was three years old (I certainly didn't ask for that).

On the sixth day of my captivity, my jailer brought to me a sack of rice, a can of tuna, and three bottles of Pepsi Cola, and I hated cola, so I screamed at him for thirty minutes that just because he liked cola didn't mean I did.

On the seventh day of my captivity, my jailer brought to me Mr. Cat.

When Boodie appeared behind the gate, I yelled at him that I needed a watch. I was going crazy being alone all the time; I was going crazy not being able to talk to my family; I was going crazy not having anything to do, I shouldn't be going crazy trying to figure out whether it was day or night. The desk clock didn't work but I didn't want another one. I needed a watch, an automatic, not one I must wind every day. He asked that I stop complaining until he crossed the threshold at least. He was still smiling, showing teeth. I hadn't noticed the moustache the day before. He hadn't shaved in two days and must have kept the moustache last time he did. His army fatigues were extra rumpled, in contrast to his hair, of course. Still had his gun in its holster, but today also a strapped Kalashnikov and a knapsack on his back. I waited until he laid his assault rifle next to the gate and his knapsack on the kitchen counter before I started yelling again.

"You can't keep me here," I said. "It's not right. Even real prisoners get to see the sun every now and then, but not me. They get books and watch television, but not me. I'm all alone. This is so wrong. You're a monster."

A faint meow echoed from somewhere within him. Ever smiling, he loosened the top two buttons of his uniform, slid his right hand inside through inchoate chest hair, and pulled out a small orange kitten, with a face that could launch a thousand rocket-propelled grenades.

"I think he has fleas," he said. "I could feel them biting my belly."

I was speechless.

"He's for you," he said, approaching me. He blinked, extending a tentative, kitten-holding hand. "I thought he might keep you company when I'm not around. I found him hiding under a crate. Had to chase out a pack of dogs trying to get to him. He was terrified."

The emaciated kitten looked unsure. I took him gently. He was so small he could easily fit into a soup bowl, so light

I worried about him floating up to the ceiling. He made my hands feel large and solid.

"I saved him," Boodie said, "just like I did you. You two are my rescues."

"Shut up," I said, holding the kitten with both hands. "He's so scared."

"We should wash him now to get rid of the fleas," he said. "I should wash myself and my clothes as well. Let's do it before we have an infestation."

I went into the bathroom, and he followed at my heels, his smells engulfing me—sweat, ash, and olive oil. How was I going to feed this kitten? How old must he be? A couple of months, six? I was not sure even a vet could have guessed his age since he was so malnourished.

"We need a baby bottle," I said. "Maybe with a tiny nipple. Do nipples come in different sizes?"

"How would I know?" He snickered. "I haven't sucked on a baby bottle in more than sixteen years."

Once in the bathroom, I tried to close the door, but Boodie was right there, surprising me. He squeezed in and shut the door. The bathroom was barely enough for one person. The kitten still trembled in my hand. Boodie began to unbutton his uniform.

"What are you doing?" I asked.

"I told you," he said as he lifted his T-shirt over his head, standing shirtless before me. "I have to shower and then we have to wash my clothes to get rid of the fleas."

"You're not going to shower with me and the kitten in here. Get out. Let me wash the poor kitten and then you can do whatever."

"Stop being childish," he said. "We can't have fleas jumping all over the place." He began to take off his pants, which, because of the cramped space and my crouching, meant he bumped me with his knees at least three times, on my head and twice on my back. "Okay, just because you're a baby, I'll wait to shower until after you wash the kitten."

I wanted to kill him.

"Put your pants back on," I said. "You're traumatizing the kitten."

"Don't get too excited." He laughed. "You have to control your urges."

"You're so boringly vain," I said. "I hate you."

I filled the green washtub with water. The plastic circular tub might have been small, but the kitten could easily drown in it. I decided not to use soap because I had no idea how it would affect the poor thing. I sat on the tiles, the tub between my legs atop the floor toilet, and Boodie stood spread-eagled, his large feet the quotation marks around my calves. If he leaned a bit, his underwear would press into my forehead. I refused to look at it. The water wasn't exactly warm—it never was in this hellhole—but it wasn't cold either because of the hot summer weather. Riotous light spilled out of the naked bulb. The tight space smelled of him, the heat and damp underscoring his odors.

The kitten didn't enjoy the water but was too weak to struggle. He bit the bay of flesh between my thumb and forefinger, but I hardly registered it. My wet fingers sliced through his fur, making temporary furrows that quickly disappeared. Only one flea slid into the water. I caught it between my fingers and squeezed it dead. I saw no larvae or eggs on him, but on his skin were a number of red welts, probably scratches from fights. I held him close to my chest, hoping to calm him. That didn't seem to help.

I was unable to stand up while holding him. The space was too constricted. Boodie held out his hand and helped me up. His giant thighs were so hairy. I wrapped the kitten in our one small towel.

"Take your clothes off," Boodie said.

"Are you serious?"

"We don't want an infestation in the apartment. Stop whining and undress."

I had on one of his sister's T-shirts and a pair of her shorts. I dropped the shorts but couldn't take off the T-shirt with the kitten in my hands. Boodie held him while I pulled the T-shirt over my head. He handed the kitten back, his fingers looking gigantic. The skin at the base of his nails was slightly reddened, a brighter hue than the tiny cat's orange fur. I turned away.

"And your underwear, silly."

"You're doing this to make fun of me."

"I don't need to see you naked to make fun of you. Take off your underwear before you go back into the living room."

"Shut your eyes."

"Stop being such a child. I've already seen everything twice."

"Please shut your eyes."

He did. I took my underwear off and I was sure he peeked. He was probably going to make fun of me for the rest of the day.

As soon as I shut the door behind me, I heard him say, "Are you coming back to help wash our clothes?"

I ignored him.

I hoped the kitten would use the patch of soil in the bedroom to do his business, but we would need more dirt. What was I going to feed him? We had a can of tuna, but Boodie hadn't brought a can opener yet. Would he eat rice, the only thing we had plenty of? We had a tin of powdered milk. I walked to the pantry, took it out, placed it on the counter, took out the smallest plate, a saucer, but I couldn't manage pouring the powder. I laid the kitten and his towel on the floor, turned back toward the counter, only to notice, out of the corner of my eye, an orange blur rushing out from the towel to the ugly green sofa. Where did he find that energy? I made the milk and placed the saucer on the floor before the sofa. I should have known he wouldn't come out. I prostrated myself, knees and elbows on the floor, head down, ass up, saw him trying to make himself smaller under the couch. A crumpled tissue lay next to him, and dust, a lot of dust. I decided I needed to clean house better. I pushed the saucer of milk toward him, but he wouldn't move.

"Eat," I told him, using my gentlest voice. "You have to eat."

He stared with golden eyes, would not look away. I was his danger. I was his threat.

Boodie exited the bathroom not covered by a single thread except for the towel drying his hair. His body was the opposite of mine.

"You're naked," I said. "Put your clothes on."

"You're naked too. At least I'm not praying with my ass pointing toward God. What will the almighty think when he looks down and sees that big white thing?"

I tried to stand up, wanting to do it dramatically, walk to the bedroom in a huff, but nothing worked. My springs and coils had lost their elasticity that morning. I used the sofa as support and walked to the room without looking his way.

I didn't have many choices in what to wear, so I put on his sister's besequinned fuchsia sweatpants, rolled up the hem because Boodie's sister was taller, and walked back out to check on the kitten. Boodie, in clean BVD underwear, was removing a second uniform out of his knapsack.

"I have to leave soon," he said.

"But you just got here."

"I know. I'm sorry. But I'll be back this evening and can stay until tomorrow morning."

I crouched, looked under the sofa. The kitten was in the same place, still staring wide-eyed, but the saucer had been licked clean. I pulled the plate out. "Do you want more?" I asked.

"Do I want more what?" replied the big lug. His fatigues looked as rumpled as the ones he'd taken off. He leaned back on the kitchen counter, lifted his foot, and slid on the thickest socks.

"I was talking to the kitten. We need to get him food and some dirt or a litter box if you can find one and maybe some cat toys and treats."

He laughed.

"What?"

"Everyone is trying to kill each other out there and you want me to look for cat toys?"

"Yes."

"You're something."

156

"He'll get bored if he's stuck with me here. Oh, and bring a can opener. I want to feed him the tuna but can't without an opener."

He theatrically raised his eyes toward the opalescent ceiling bulb and its cold light.

"The tuna is for us."

"He needs it more."

I walked toward him, toward the kitchen counter, to make another saucer of milk, but Boodie inserted his hand into the knapsack and came out with a scary knife as big as my forearm. I stopped, stood rigid.

"Oh, come on," he said. "If I wanted to hurt you, I wouldn't use this knife. It'd be too messy."

He opened the cabinet, took out the tuna can, and stabbed it with the knife. It took him less than a couple of seconds to take the top completely off. He placed the tuna on a small plate and handed it to me. I headed back to the couch, bent down, and slid the plate closer to the kitten. Boodie crouched in front of me, top of my head to top of his head, both of us watching the kitten watching us.

"Do you think he eats solid food?" Boodie asked.

"We'll soon find out."

"He's not moving."

"I don't think he likes his dinner as a social event. He'll probably eat if we stop talking and looking at him."

"He looks so raggedy even after the bath, as if he's waiting for new fur. We should call him Shabby."

"Absolutely not," I said. "We should give him a respectable name, something for him to aspire to."

"Colonel. That would be a good name."

"No!"

The kitten wouldn't move. Boodie helped me up again.

"I need to leave. Do we have time for one dance?"

"No, of course not."

"We'll have a full lesson tonight then. And please wash my clothes. I might need them when I come back."

"You said you were going to wash them."

"Wash my clothes," he said. "You have nothing to do, so wash."

"Just because you're busy killing people doesn't mean I should do your laundry."

"I'll bring out the knife again."

"I hate you."

"You love me."

He packed his knapsack, strung the assault rifle across his back, holstered his gun.

"I'll bring food. Okay?"

I refused to say anything. A dog wailed somewhere out there, the sound clearer with the door open, yet Boodie was still smiling.

When he left, I bent down again to check on the kitten. He was in the same place, still staring wide-eyed, but the tuna had vanished. He must have scarfed it in a couple of bites.

"I will call you Mr. Cat," I said.

He didn't come. I waited, but he didn't come. And Mr. Cat wouldn't budge from under the couch. I spent so much time bent over on my knees, my head almost entirely under the couch trying to entice him to come out. I finally figured I was probably scaring him. I boiled some rice for dinner, but then added some powdered milk so he could share my meal. I sat on the couch, having placed his saucer under it.

I talked to Mr. Cat as I ate. I didn't berate myself for doing so. I always thought of myself as being able to be on my own a lot. Most of the time back at home I would wish for everyone to get out of our apartment so I didn't have to talk or listen to my parents or brother go on and on about the most trivial thing ever. But now I realized I needed some people in my life. Being on my own might have been more bearable had Boodie brought me some books. He kept saying he'd bring some, but all I ever got were magazines, most of them tattered, all of them stupid. Talking to Mr. Cat was my only option.

I was in hell, and he didn't come.

No stupid dance lesson for now.

The food tasted terrible, but Mr. Cat massacred that plate as well.

I was in hell, and I was eating cat food.

I washed the pot and the plates. I'd already washed Boodie's stupid fatigues and his underwear. I'd asked him to bring a washboard so I could remove stains better, but he mocked me as usual, asking where I thought he'd be able to steal a washboard from. I put everything away. Luckily, the power hadn't gone out yet, but I picked up the flashlight just in case.

"I'm going to bed now," I told Mr. Cat.

I should wash the sheets when I woke up, but I wasn't sure where to hang them. And I doubted they would dry in time without sun. I wondered if they would dry at all without air and without sun. My mother would probably know things like that.

I undressed, turned on the flashlight, turned off the bulb, and got in bed. I pushed the flashlight into the tucking of the bed. I'd be able to reach it even if half asleep. Must have been a few hours later when I felt a light movement next to my head, opened my eyes but couldn't see in the dark. I did feel Mr. Cat's breath on my nose, then my eyelids, then back down to my lips. I didn't move, so he kept going, moving around the bed exploring, and I plunged back into a deep sleep.

I felt Mr. Cat jump off my pillow. I opened my eyes to see the light in the living room come on and the orange blur disappear behind the doorjamb.

"I must have scared him," Boodie said. "The kitten just ran back under the couch."

I heard the clatter of his laying belongings down. I slipped on my underwear quickly. He appeared at the doorway but didn't cross the threshold. He looked different, but I couldn't pinpoint what had changed. The moustache couldn't have gotten thicker in less than twenty-four hours. Same uniform only more crumpled. Ever smiling. He leaned against the jamb, holding a burlap sack in his arms.

"Why have you slept so late?" he asked.

"I wouldn't know, since you haven't brought me a watch," I said. "I waited for you, and you didn't come." I hated myself for sounding so whiny.

"We were called in."

"Called in to what? You never tell me anything."

"Do you really want to know?" He scratched the stubble beneath his chin, which drew my eyes to his bobbing Adam's apple.

"No, definitely not, but you shouldn't have kept me waiting."

He laughed, walked into the room toward the patch of earth in the corner. "It doesn't look like he pooped here. Do you think he did it somewhere else?" He opened the sack and poured some dirt, then placed it on the ground. "I brought a lot of goodies this morning. You should say thank you."

I put on my shorts but not a T-shirt. It was already hot. "What did you get?"

"Say thank you."

"But I don't even know what you brought yet."

"Say thank you."

"Thank you."

He walked by me, his head nodding for me to follow. On the kitchen counter were two knapsacks. He opened the newer-looking one, taking out a couple of grayish, milky jars. I knew what they were before he said anything, and my heart leapt.

"Preserved lamb fat," he announced. "Am I great or what? And more. I found fresh eggs, sausages, tomatoes, some lemons. And I pilfered one of my mother's bottles of pomegranate molasses."

I took one of the jars from him and tried to twist open the top, but it wouldn't budge. He took it back and with the slightest turn handed it to me, open. I tried to ignore his smirk. I spooned a bit of the fat onto a saucer and walked back to the couch. I pushed it toward Mr. Cat, who I thought regarded me less warily, but he wouldn't go near the saucer.

"But this is for us," Boodie said.

"Mr. Cat is also us."

It seemed Mr. Cat would not eat if he was being observed.

My mother didn't like to eat alone. She would always say that if no one was there, she'd have trouble eating.

"Let's make breakfast," Boodie said. "Fried eggs."

"We don't have butter, only olive oil."

"Which is better for eggs with pomegranate molasses. Wait till you taste my mother's pomegranate. It's divine."

I knew we shouldn't have had a dance lesson. Although he still pretended otherwise, Boodie was beginning to grasp what was blatantly apparent. He was such an atrocious dancer that it might take at least a year for him to move one foot correctly, let alone two. The situation was hopeless, but he soldiered on.

During the last couple of days, my cue that it was time for the lesson would be his standing rigid in the middle of the living room, holding his right arm out. This, his ability to hold his arm out horizontally, was the only advantage he had as a dancer over a Ken doll. Boodie did the pose before turning on the Dean Martin cassette. A full smile, waiting eyes, arched eyebrows. I wondered if he wanted me to pretend to swoon when he did that.

"Take off your boots," I said, before moving toward him.

"Do I have to? I promise I won't step on your foot again," he said, ever the optimist.

With my left hand, I reached for his right. He quickly grasped it and pulled me by my waist, plastering me to him.

"Too close," I said. "That's too much. You need to hold me close when we come to the dip, not before."

"I know that. I was having fun. Where's your sense of humor?"

"It deserted me after you kidnapped me."

"Oh, no. Are we going to go through this again? Let's dance."

He might have been a terrible dancer, but I discovered that I'm a worse teacher. I lost patience after the first mistake, which unsurprisingly happened with the first step. Every time. He was supposed to lead with his right foot, I with my left. He didn't. I berated him, and for some reason, he glared at me as if I were the reason he was not remembering to start with his right foot. We began again, and this time his mistake arrived with the fifth step. One, two, *cha cha cha*. How he couldn't or wouldn't remember the third *cha* was beyond me. I shouldn't have said anything. He obviously knew when he made the mistake, so I shouldn't have mentioned it. I shouldn't have. I could see his eyes contracting, his face reddening. A little vein bulged on the right side of his forehead.

"Enough," he said.

This was our shortest lesson so far.

"This isn't working," he said, "and you're not helping."

"I'm sorry," I said. "Dancing isn't easy, and neither is teaching. Maybe I'd be better if I was less anxious. If you didn't wear your gun while dancing or if you took off your boots, I'd be able to concentrate better and not think about other things."

"I don't like this at all. I need to figure something out."

"Don't go," I said.

He didn't wait, didn't hesitate. He turned around, picked up his knapsack, his Kalashnikov, and left. He didn't slam either the gate or the door. He didn't have to. He was angry. He forgot his other knapsack.

A muffled gloom fell over the living room and me. I wanted to return to bed. I checked on Mr. Cat. He'd eaten all the lamb fat.

I woke up to the sound of an explosion not too far away. That was disturbing, but more so was the horrid odor. I wondered whether a sewage pipe had burst. I reached for the flashlight under the pillow, turned it on, and came face-to-face with Mr. Cat. On the bed, next to my head, on all fours, ready to jump away if need be. No sudden movements. We stared at each other. I knew not to try and touch him yet, not to move, but I couldn't keep lying down. The smell was debilitating, would probably kill the canary, maybe even a pigeon. I sat up. Mr. Cat jumped off the bed and ran to the doorway. He turned around and watched me.

"Did you do this?" I asked. "Did you cause this smell?"

He didn't reply. I got up, flashlight leading my way to the light switch. We had electricity. I went to the bathroom, both to pee and to see if the smell was coming from there. I hoped not because I'd cleaned it the day before. Mr. Cat watched me pee. The smell must have been in the bedroom, since the bathroom was nowhere near as bad. As soon as I was back in the bedroom, my nose figured the odor was coming from the dirt patch cum litter box.

"You did it," I said. "It was Mr. Cat in the corner after all."

He watched me, sitting on haunches no more than a couple of steps away. And I realized that he might have been skinny, he might not have been fully healthy yet, but he was surely the most beautiful cat in the universe.

The mound of dirt looked innocent. Mr. Cat had buried the evidence and the crime. He followed me to the kitchen. I returned with the one thing the apartment had in overabundance, a soup spoon, as well as a plastic bag. On my knees, I stuck the spoon in the dirt and had to desperately control my retching.

"No more lamb fat for you," I said. I could have sworn he was grinning.

Boodie hated taking the garbage out, but it wasn't as if he'd let me do it. I tightened the knot on the bag to imprison the odor. I washed my hands when I got to the kitchen. Mr. Cat followed me, keeping a distance, but watching. I gathered he must have been hungry. I scooped half of the can of tuna onto his saucer. I had to save some just in case Boodie was late. I placed his food on the floor, next to the counter, but he wouldn't come near it. He approached as soon as I walked away. He put his face into the saucer and swallowed everything in less than ten seconds.

I sat on the couch and waited. I never knew when Boodie would arrive. I guess killing people wouldn't fit into a regular schedule. I didn't want to think about what he was doing out there. I waited and waited, and he didn't show up. Mr. Cat refused to let me pet him, but he didn't run under the sofa either. He lay down where he could watch me, under the counter, near the door. I walked to the kitchen, gentle steps so as not to scare him, and came back with a rag, dropping it on the floor not too far from him. He explored the rag, smelling every nook of it for a minute or so, and sat on it. I watched his drowsiness overtake him.

The room grew warmer. It must have reached one thousand degrees or more. It was probably afternoon. I considered washing myself but wasn't sure I could afford to waste water. What I would give for an air conditioner.

My father refused to buy us a unit, always complained that it cost a fortune and our electric bill would skyrocket. I didn't mind. Insufferable heat was rare, and summer breezes were refreshing. I slept with open windows for almost nine months of the year. What I would give for a window.

I made dinner, rice with lamb fat for me and rice with powdered milk for Mr. Cat. He finished his plate, I didn't. I went to bed. Mr. Cat joined me, settling near my feet. That was the first day Boodie hadn't shown up at all.

Two cycles, two days—probably, since I couldn't be sure. I slept, woke up, slept, woke up, slept, and still no Boodie. I understood that panicking was not helpful, but I couldn't stop myself. I woke up with a start, sat up in bed. Surprised Mr. Cat, who was sleeping on my pillow. He was no longer afraid of me. I was afraid for me. I could feel my quickened heartbeat in my eardrums as I began the morning ritual: flashlight until I reached the light switch, available electricity so lights go on, bathroom to pee, kitchen to feed Mr. Cat, back to bedroom to clean litter.

If Boodie didn't come back, what would I do with the litter? If Boodie didn't come back, who would bring me food? If Boodie didn't come back, I would die. Not any death, but a horrible one, a never-ending one where I would waste away and Mr. Cat would get so hungry that he would eat me.

I freaked. Rapid, shallow breaths. I sat on the couch. Mr. Cat stopped eating to watch me rev up into panic mode, then went back at it. I was sure I was having a heart attack. If Boodie was killed, would anyone know I was here? Was he dead? Did I do something wrong, which made him decide I deserved to die all alone? It wasn't my fault he couldn't dance. My right quadricep began to spasm violently as if I'd run a marathon.

Mr. Cat finished his plate, looked up, then his ears perked, each twitching separately and in a different direction, and he ran under the sofa. I heard the jangle of keys, and Boodie, in full if tired regalia, appeared behind the gate. Smiling as usual, he unlocked the gate and swung it out.

"Where have you been?" I yelled. I hated myself for sounding like Elizabeth Taylor in so many of her films.

"Can I at least cross the threshold before you start yelling?"

He dragged in quite a bit of stuff that he'd probably had to lay down to open the gate. Like Santa Claus, he brought in cloth bags, plastic garbage bags, knapsacks.

"You left me alone."

"You missed me?"

"That's not the point. I could have died. I thought maybe you died."

"I'm not going to die. I couldn't find the time. I had to work."

"You're not working. You're killing people."

"Just shut up or I swear, I'll kill you right here and now."

"You can't threaten me while smiling," I said. "If you want me to take your threat seriously, you have to make a menacing face or something, maybe like Dracula before he sucks your blood, not the way you do it, like a happy Mickey Mouse."

"It's a good thing I like you, because you're so unlikable."

"You left me alone for three days. That's inhumane."

"You seem to forget there's a war going on. Come help me put away this stuff."

Part of the stuff was fresh bread, which must have come out of an oven less than an hour ago because as soon as I opened the clear plastic the enchanting aroma triggered a longing for home that almost caused me to tear up.

"I haven't been able to wash up in three days," he said. "Not since I was here last. Let me shower. We'll both feel better after I do."

He sat on the sofa and took his boots off. He smelled his socks and made a face, smelled his boots and made a crinklier face. Mr. Cat's orange tail appeared from under the sofa, from the left side, all the way at the back. It swept the floor back and forth a couple of times before disappearing again.

"How's the cat?" Boodie asked as he took off his green T-shirt with its almost black underarm half-moons. I could see beads of sweat in the ridges of his muscles, congealing around a whorl of sprouting body hair.

"I was able to find a case of tuna cans," he said. "That should last for a while. Do you think he would eat baby food? Some of the guys are hoarding baby food, hoping to make some money when we have a shortage."

"He's eating everything so far," I said. "He swallows whatever I put in front of him."

"That's a good boy." He got up, dropped his pants, then his underwear. He took a step to the bathroom before turning around. "Can you make breakfast, please?" he said, standing naked and unadorned in the middle of the living room. He went into the bathroom. He began to sing "Hey Jude" loud enough to be heard from behind the door and above the twanging tune of running water.

Mr. Cat came out from under the sofa, inspected Boodie's pile of clothes on the floor. He walked over everything, smelling, discovering. He stopped at one of the socks, began to knead it, then bite it, ending up on his back fighting against the sock demon. He then attacked the underwear, which was three times his size. He bit into it and clumsily carried it under the sofa.

I gathered up the rest of the discarded clothing. The pants felt more like plastic than cotton, rind stiff with dust and muck that held Boodie's shape almost perfectly. The last time I mentioned that he should try to keep his fatigues a bit cleaner, he said that war was a dirty business and laughed at his own joke. The gun was right there, still in its holster. The Kalashnikov in its usual place, on the ground next to the gate. I could shoot him while he washed. I could point the gun and threaten to shoot him if he didn't let me go. That wouldn't work. He wouldn't believe for a second that I could or would do it. Where were the keys? I looked in his pants pockets. I took out a wallet, a gold chain with a cross, another with a gold cedar tree, a good-sized ring with a black onyx stone, various scraps of paper. I put everything on the coffee table. Where did he put the keys? Probably in his knapsack. I hesitated before going toward it and that was when I heard the singing and the water stop.

I picked up his dirty clothes and laid the pile next to the bathroom door for later washing.

❊ ❊ ❊

We needed a breakfast or a dining table. We could eat standing up at the kitchen counter or sitting on the sofa, the latter uncomfortable since the coffee table was too low for plates, but that's where we were, eating eggs. He had nothing on but a new pair of gray sweatpants, no shirt, no socks, no underwear (the dirty ones still under the sofa with Mr. Cat). Even though the sofa was too small for both of us to sit comfortably, he was more comfortable than I was, his knees spread wide, one hand holding the plate between them, and the other dipping the bread in the egg yolk. I balanced my plate on my knees, which were angled to the right yet still pressed to his cottoned thigh.

"You're leaving me no space to sit," I said.

"Oh, come on. That's not fair. I'm a big guy. You're a small guy."

I tried not to look at the bulge between his legs but couldn't help sneaking peeks. I'd last seen him naked only a few minutes earlier, yet even though I'd seen that his dick was larger than mine, it seemed the sweatpants made it look quite a bit bigger and heavier.

"Can't you get me a pair of regular sweatpants like the ones you're wearing?" I'd had to finally crop his sister's pants because they were so long. Everyone was taller than me.

"Actually, there's something I wanted to talk to you about," he said, "but I wanted to wait till after we finished breakfast. Sorry, but I was starving."

"What?"

"Are you done?" he asked. "Let's do the dishes." He stood up, held out his hand to help me up.

"You mean, I'll wash the dishes while you watch."

He laughed. "That works for me."

I washed. He dried. But he wouldn't tell me what he wanted to talk about until he was back on the sofa, patting the seat next to him for me to sit down.

"Now, don't get upset until I've said what I have to say. Don't interrupt me. Just listen for a change."

"I don't interrupt," I said. "I always—"

"You always do. Shh. I want to discuss why my dancing is not improving. Shh. Not one word. Listen to what I have to say. I understand I might not ever be the greatest dancer, but both of us can see I'm not getting better at all. I've been thinking about why. I'm a good athlete. I can play any sport, but I can't seem to be able to move my feet while dancing. Why is that? Shh. Don't say anything. I've been thinking and thinking and I finally figured it out. You're the problem."

"I'm not. I've been—"

"Can you not interrupt? Can you just once do what you're told?"

"But you said I'm the problem. That's—"

His hand seemed to appear out of nowhere, smothering my mouth. His head moved closer to mine, eyes glaring into me.

"Let me finish," he said. "Just let me finish. Okay?"

I nodded. I was stuck at the end of the sofa, couldn't move any farther.

"You're the problem, but it's not your fault."

I wanted to tell him that didn't make any sense, but I knew better, since his hand hadn't moved from my mouth.

"I can't dance with you because you're a boy. Every time I get ready to dance, I look at you and see a boy. It's not working. I can't get over it. I know I keep saying I'm me and you must be Micheline, but I can't seem to be able to imagine that. That's my fault. I've tried and it doesn't work. I keep seeing you as a boy. That's why I say it's not your fault but mine. Do you understand me so far? Nod your head."

I did.

"So, we have a problem."

I wanted to say that we didn't have a problem, he did.

"We have a problem and we need to find a solution. You are a boy and that's not going to change. I'm a man and I can't dance with a boy. I'm a man and I haven't been able to imagine you as a girl so that I can dance with you. Do you follow? Nod your head again."

I did.

"I need your help," he said. "I can't do it without you. Are you willing to help me? Nod your head again."

I did.

"Good. I'm glad you understand. You must help me imagine you as a girl. This will work. Trust me. I've thought about it for a long time. Okay, I'm going to move my hand now. Don't go crazy on me."

"Why would I go crazy?" I asked. "I'll try to help you imagine, but I don't see how. Maybe you can shut your eyes. I don't know."

"No, no," he said. "I brought some dresses."

"Are you fucking crazy?"

❧   ❧   ❧

The dress I wore was his sister's and it certainly didn't fit
well. The hem reached my shins. It was a scoop neck, but I
had difficulty keeping it on when both my shoulders would
slip through if I wiggled. Boodie insisted I looked fine, but it
was all wrong. It was wrong because I was in a dress and it
was also wrong because the dress was wrong — wrong size,
wrong cut, wrong colors. I couldn't imagine any woman
looking good in it. His giant of a sister had gotten rid of it,
but how could she have worn such a bizarre disaster in the
first place?

"You look all right," he said. "I promise."

"No, I don't. You're blind."

"Let's dance. You'll feel better. I'm sure of it."

He took up the usual pose, his hand out for me to
hold. He hadn't changed, still barefoot, only sweatpants. I
too was barefoot. Luckily, his sister's heels were too big for
me. He had wanted me to put on pantyhose, but I refused.
Not in this heat.

He pressed the play button on the cassette player. Surprisingly, he didn't make a mistake on the first step. We
moved together faultlessly if terribly for fifteen beats before
he stepped on my foot. One, two *cha cha cha*; one, two *cha
cha cha*; one, two *cha cha cha*, ouch.

"That was so good," he yelled. "I told you it would
work."

"It was better, but it wasn't good."

"Yes, it was. You're always the pessimist. You're amazing. I'm amazing. Let's start from the beginning again."

He rewound the cassette, and the stupid acoustic guitar began again. I took his hand, and he pulled me too close to him. Dean Martin crooned.

"You're pulling me too close," I said.

"I know," he said, "I'm happy. Just follow my lead."

"But you don't know how to lead."

"Shut up and enjoy this."

One, two *cha cha cha*; one, two *cha cha cha*; one, two *cha cha cha*, and we almost stumbled into the kitchen counter. He wouldn't stop though, moving through one mistake after another. I couldn't help giggling when he laughed. But then his left hand dropped from my lower back and grabbed my ass. I stopped. He laughed, squeezing my butt again.

"Why did you do that?"

"Because I'm happy," he said, with a mischievous lilt in his voice. "Don't ruin it. Follow my lead. Let's dance, Micheline."

We moved again. He squeezed my ass again and again. Weirdly, his butt-squeezing kept a better beat than he did. One, two *cha cha* squeeze; one, two *cha cha* squeeze. Our dancing was terrible, but he was having fun. He pulled me even closer, and his erection poked me in my lower belly. I tried to stop again, but he was having none of it. He kept moving. I looked down. His dick was so hard, so large. The head began to peek from under the waistband. I glanced back up at him and he was smiling, beaming. I stopped and he did as well.

"I can't dance like this," I said.

"Then help me."

"What do you mean?"

The hand that held mine moved to his waistband. Both hands pulled it down. His dick, almost bigger than my arm, sprang up like a jack-in-the-box. He placed my hand on it and held it there. It was warmer than the bread.

"Help me," he said.

I wasn't sure what to do but I couldn't move my hand. I held it. Some nerve in my belly snapped. My dick was hard. I put both my hands on his erection. His smells overwhelmed me. He had showered, but his aroma was still all Boodie.

"Help me," he said again.

He gently nudged me on the shoulder, and I found myself on my knees. Luckily, the dress was long enough that it offered protection from the tiles. I inhaled deeply. Some nerve in my brain snapped. And I put his dick in my mouth. And I was lost.

I was lost that night. He made me suck him once more before he left. I didn't want to do it. Not that I didn't like doing it. I did, very much so. I didn't want him to think that I would anytime he wanted. He was at the gate, about to leave. He said please, I said no, he said please, I said no, he said please, I said I wouldn't do it if he was still wearing his gun and his Kalashnikov strapped to his back. I realized that was a mistake when he beamed. He grabbed my hand once again and placed it on his groin. I felt his dick throb under his fatigues and that was all it took. I found myself on my knees again, in the ugly dress, sucking him off while he still wore his gun. And I swallowed him.

And then he left.

And I was lost.

And I was consumed with tremors of shame and joy.

I had figured out I was not like other boys. I knew I didn't like girls the way other boys did. I knew in every cell in my body. As soon as I started developing sexual fantasies, I began to gather that I liked men in that way. But I didn't know I would like them this much. I knew I was different. I hadn't known I was that different.

I sucked him off, and it was lurid, fetid, and childish, yet also a slap in the face—a slap that made me realize that I might one day have a driver's license, might one day drive a Ferrari, a Ducati, or a donkey cart, but I would never be dating a girl.

I sucked him off. I hated him, yet I desperately wanted him to kiss me. And he didn't. This wasn't fair. He probably didn't worry about what we had done, whereas I had to figure out why I did what I did. I decided I didn't want to feel guilty. What happened was not my fault. I refused to feel shame.

Mr. Cat meowed. So loud for such a little guy. Hunger is an ungrateful mistress, and brutal as well. He followed me into the kitchen, where I opened another can of tuna. I noticed a paper bag that we'd forgotten to unpack. In it I found a baby-blue nightgown, a pair of pantyhose, no, five of them. Why would he bring so many? I took them out and found some batteries for the flashlight, more candles, and cassette tapes. Finally, some music. A Frank Sinatra mix. Why would he bring that? Bob Dylan's *Highway 61*, the original, not a copy. Bleh. Deep Purple's *Machine Head*. Not bad but come on. Sly and the Family Stone. Yay! And a copy of Bowie's *Hunky Dory*. Yes, yes, yes. I can listen to music.

I ended up in bed, listening to Bowie on a continuous loop, while Mr. Cat played catch with my hair. The music would go on until the electricity didn't.

I felt Mr. Cat jump off the pillow. How could I not? He was sleeping on my hair. But I didn't wake up. I heard him scamper away. It was hellish dark, probably no power. I slept on. I woke up when Boodie slipped into bed.

"Go back to sleep," he said. "It's still too early. I'm exhausted."

"How can I? This bed isn't big enough for a couple."

"Shh."

"Don't shush me."

He slid in closer to me, spooning. His right arm slid under me, and his left hand covered my mouth. His chest hair soft on my back.

"Go back to sleep," he said.

I wanted to bite his hand, but he kissed the top of my head.

"I found you some books," he said. "I'm sorry it took so long."

I moved to get up and see what he got me, but he wouldn't let go, pulled me in closer. I was naked. He was naked. I felt his erection where I didn't want to.

"I wish you'd worn the nightgown," he said.

His hand fell away from my mouth. His penis grew harder and he softer.

"You are not going to fuck me," I said, softly.

I wanted to say it more emphatically, but he had already gone to sleep. His heart thrummed a lullaby on the back of my neck.

I woke up drenched in perspiration, unsure whether it was mine or his. Insufferable heat in a windowless space. Boodie snored, softly, unlike my brother, who snored like a donkey. I moved from under his arm and got out of bed. I needed to pee. I turned on the flashlight to find Mr. Cat on the floor on my side of the bed staring at me. I rushed to the bathroom with him following me. He would follow me until I fed him.

He didn't get to finish his meal. As soon as he heard Boodie yawning, he scampered under the sofa. I was moving his plate to his hiding place when I saw Boodie's dick enter the room before he did.

"Put your underwear on," I said. "You're scaring Mr. Cat."

He yawned again, stretched his back, lifted his arms to the ceiling, making sure I got to see every inch of his body. "He will get used to me," he said. "He'll love me just like you do."

"Put your dick away."

"You love my dick," he said, ambling to the bathroom.

"Make sure not to spray everywhere," I yelled.

He didn't close the door.

"Maybe you can help me get it down before I pee."

"Fuck your mother. I hate you."

I looked through the bags he'd brought. Another dress, this one nicer, red with white dahlias, summer cotton with exquisitely thin shoulder straps. I put it back in the bag. A book. *The Little Prince*.

"I should have thought of bringing in a table and chairs," he said, walking into the kitchen, standing next to me. "I didn't think about it when I was getting this place ready. We could have been able to sit down for breakfast like normal people." He took *The Little Prince* from my hands. "This is my favorite book."

"It's not mine," I said. "I want books that engage me, not some childish book that pretends to know anything about anything. And don't get me *The Prophet* either. I bet that's your favorite book too. And the Bible too, I'm sure."

He sighed. "One of these days I'm going to smack you and have you flying all the way to the moon." He took out seven other books from the bag. All novels. He handed them to me one by one. Those in French first: *Crime and Punishment*, *Memoirs of Hadrian*, and then *Story of O*. "This one to give you some ideas." Then the ones in English: *A Tale of Two Cities*, *Love Story*, *Valley of the Dolls*, and with a big flourish, *War and Peace*. "This one should, what was it, engage you for a while."

Treasure. These were gallons of water after spending so much time in a desert. I wanted to hide them under the bed to keep them safe.

He took the red dress out of the bag.

"Put this on," he said.

"Now? Can't I look at the books first?"

"I want you in this dress."

I unfolded it and began to slip it on.

"No," he said. "Take everything off first."

I took off the T-shirt. He was standing too close. I pulled down my underwear. I could see blood flow to his

179

dick. I slipped on the dress. It seemed to fit well, but I would have to check the mirror in the bathroom to make sure. It must have looked good, though, because he was looking at me funny. His eyes had a prurient sheen.

"You look amazing," he said. "I did good. The dress matches your hair."

From the other bag on the counter, he pulled out one of the pantyhose.

"Put this on."

"It's too hot," I said.

"Put it on."

"Without underwear?"

"Put it on."

I did. I pulled it up to my waist, and much to my embarrassment and chagrin, I was erect, just like him. He looked me up and down, moved closer, jammed us together, and kissed me. I tried to resist, but who was I kidding? His tongue explored mine, his hand explored my butt. As soon as he began to lift me, my legs hung on to his waist, not wanting to let go. He carried me all the way to the bed that was not meant for two people.

We slid into the furrows of routine. He would arrive in the evening, sometimes late, sometimes not, most often starving, so I would make him dinner, which he would gulp down faster than Mr. Cat ate his. When I would pick up the plates to wash, his hand would maneuver its way under my dress or my skirt, whatever I was wearing. Sometimes I was able to do the dishes while he dried before he fucked me senseless, and sometimes he wanted it so urgently that he fucked me on the kitchen counter. We'd talk some, though he didn't want us to bring up anything that mattered—never about what he did outside, how the now-raging war was going, when he was going to let me go, nothing like that. He wanted to leave all that outside. He would ask about the book I was reading, how many times did the power go off, why Mr. Cat still hid whenever he was around. He was frustrated by Mr. Cat. He brought him food. He made cat toys by tying feathers on yarn, but Mr. Cat wouldn't come out from under the sofa. I could make Mr. Cat run after the feathers all day long, but never when Boodie was around. He couldn't understand how he was unable to make Mr. Cat fall in love with him.

He spent the night—every night—for two weeks. He fucked me before going to bed, and again in the morning. Three times each day. He was obsessed with pantyhose. We ran out of them in a few days because he would tear them in the back when we started. And then he couldn't find any more.

The dancing? He forgot about it for a few days, then suddenly remembered that technically that was my purpose for being there. We tried once again, one, two *cha cha cha* and we were fucking on the sofa. He no longer needed to pretend after that.

"I like that your hair is growing long, so soft and loopy," he said. "You're so beautiful like this."

I missed my mother terribly.

Every day the same thing. I was now better able to figure out what time it was, when the day began, when it ended.

"I'm bored."

"Do you want me to teach you how to make a bomb?"

"Of course not."

I had to get ready for him. I took two eggs out of the fridge, started boiling rice. We had been out of butter for a few days. Mr. Cat meowed, a request for me to pick him up and deposit him on the counter so he could smell everything. He was getting bigger but still not big enough to jump that high. I warned him the burner was too hot. I knew he was smart enough not to get close, but I still worried. I picked him up again and placed him on the floor. He followed me to the bedroom, to the pile of clothing on the floor. How could I keep things neat if I didn't have a closet? Boodie always said he thought of everything when putting the place together, but he obviously missed so much. How could you not think of a closet or a dresser or something? No vanity, no mirror except in the bathroom, a mirror that never fogged up because we never had hot water. I took off my underwear. Mr. Cat watched me put on the green dress, which had a hip-side tear the size and shape of Greenland. Boodie must have gone shopping in a dumpster for this one. He loved it, though. Matched my eyes, he said, and the tear was strategic.

Time to wait.

I couldn't abide *Love Story*, but *Valley of the Dolls* was delicious. I lay on the uncomfortable sofa, my head on its unforgiving arm, my feet pulled up, my body folded in the form of a *Z*, and began to read. Mr. Cat jumped up, settled next to my stomach, waiting for me to scratch him everywhere. For a couple of hours, I was engrossed with the

Hollywood actresses, high on their drugs and sex drive, and Mr. Cat was lost in the ecstasy of belly rubs. And then he jumped up and ran under the sofa. His hearing is keener than mine. Boodie was home.

He looked more tousled than usual, but he still wore his smile.

"What's that?" I said, standing and pointing to a dark stain on his cheek.

"Don't worry," he said. "It's not mine."

"Is it blood? Are you wounded?"

"We're not going to talk about it. Don't even try."

"But—"

"Shh," he said, as he walked to me. "We're going to have a quiet evening, and you are going to be so grateful."

"What do you mean?"

"I got you something. You're going to love me."

"Never."

"Ta-da!"

"No! I don't believe this. Are these Japanese conversation tutorials?"

"Twenty cassettes no less, for both beginners and then intermediate."

"God, where did you find them?"

"An abandoned bookstore. I got more books too."

"Did you hurt anybody?"

"No, why would I? I told you I only hurt those who deserve it."

"Why was the bookstore abandoned, then?"

"You seem to constantly forget we have a war out there."

"These cassettes are amazing."

"Told you you're going to love me."

I kissed him. I couldn't help it. I ignored the bloodstains on his face. I jumped on him and kissed him and smelled the outside air on him and we fell back onto the sofa and he was inside me so quickly and the sofa kept sliding toward the door and poor Mr. Cat must have had so much trouble staying under it.

The dogs were wailing again. I still couldn't tell how far away they were. Even though I'd heard many guns going off the whole day, at least no one was shooting at them. They stopped barking for a minute before starting up again. The sound grew louder and more plaintive when Boodie opened the door. He was his usually happy self, but his grin seemed somewhat crooked. I couldn't tell what was off exactly. It was him but disjointed. He deposited a case of Perrier onto the counter. He walked over, without unshackling himself from the Kalashnikov, and kissed me before I had a chance to object. I pushed him away.

"You smell like cigarettes, and you taste even worse. Why did you smoke?"

"I had to," he said. "Everybody was smoking. I'm the only one in our troop who doesn't smoke and I had to do it."

"No, you didn't. You don't have to be like everybody else. You can't bring cigarette smells in here. We don't have any windows. I'll suffocate. And I'm not kissing you with that kind of breath."

"Okay, I'll brush my teeth."

"We ran out of toothpaste, remember? I told you to bring some, but you forgot."

"I didn't forget. No one can find toothpaste anywhere in town."

"Have you been drinking?"

"Just a little. Look, everybody was tense. We needed to let loose a little. We took a little break."

"I don't get to take a break. I sit here all the time, and you're out there having parties. I won't have it."

He moved in and kissed me once more. Pushing him away was more difficult. He stopped kissing me but didn't let me pull away.

"I'm not bad," he said. "I had a lot of cigarettes and a few drinks, but it was one time. I'm not taking pills to stay awake or anything like that even though everyone thinks I should. I've been good. Kiss me."

"Promise me you won't smoke again."

"I promise."

"And you'll find toothpaste."

After a few seconds, I got used to the taste of his tongue.

Mr. Cat ran out of the bathroom. Boodie was home. I heard the swinging gate. I was filling all our containers with water: both jerricans, the green washtub, the thirteen bottles. It was proving more difficult to bathe or do laundry, as the frequency of water cutoffs had dramatically increased. I was shampooing my hair in the morning when the water stopped. I had to traipse wet into the kitchen, bring back a half-drunk bottle of Perrier, and use it to rinse my hair. This would not happen again.

He peeked into the bathroom, looking even more chipper than usual.

"What's for dinner?" he asked.

"Same as yesterday, I'm afraid. Were you able to get bread?"

"I sure did."

"Vegetables? I would kill for a good tomato."

"Couldn't find any. It's getting desperate out there."

I made him carry the jerricans to the kitchen. I brought in some of the bottles. He kissed me in the kitchen. I thought I detected a different smell, a lingering cologne of some sort. He removed the dinner leftovers from the fridge, placing them on the counter. I began to reheat.

"How was your day?" he asked.

"Nothing changes."

"Well, I had a great day."

I gathered he wanted me to ask why, but I wasn't going to, since he wouldn't tell me about what was happening outside, always keeping me in the dark as if what he did was so important, as if I could telephone whomever he was going to kill next and warn them. I took out two plates from the cabinet, filled them with the rice. He grasped my arm, pulled me to him, and kissed me again, deeper this time. I was unable to resist.

He looked so happy. His smile felt uncontrolled, like it could fly up to the ceiling. His face was barely a centimeter apart from mine. How could I not smile back?

"I fucked Micheline," he said. "I finally did it. I didn't need to dance. I just fucked her."

"You did what?"

I tried to push him away, but he was obliviously ecstatic, wouldn't let me go.

"I fucked Micheline. Can you believe it? In her own bed. It was meant to be, you know."

I was finally able to push him away. I turned my back, couldn't look at him. I so wanted to grab a knife and stab him a hundred times. In his heart, in his stupid heart. One hundred times.

"You could say it was luck," he went on, "but not really. Command wanted someone to send a package to her father, and as soon as I realized who it was for, I volunteered. I went to her house, but her father wasn't there, and I told her I was sorry for her loss, and she started crying, and then we started kissing, and then I fucked her, but we didn't even take our clothes off, since her mother was in the next room."

He stopped. I assumed he wanted me to say something, but I couldn't. I thought the best course of action was to ignore him. I would go into the bedroom without talking to him and he would leave.

"I'm starving," he said.

"Eat shit," I screamed, the loudest I'd ever screamed. "Eat shit and die right now."

"What's the matter?"

"You're a dog—a mangy mongrel. You should leave right now and spend your time with the wailing dogs outside. But no, the dogs wouldn't let you because they're more decent than you. They won't let a cur like you into their pack. Go back to your command and stay with your stupid friends because you're all worse than dogs. You're rats. That's what you all are."

"Take a breath. Please put the knife down. You'll hurt yourself."

"I want to hurt you."

"No, you don't. Come on. Why are you upset?"

"Why are you so stupid? That's what I want to know. I spend all this time alone and you are busy having sex with Micheline. How could you?"

He moved closer but I ducked and walked out of the kitchen.

"Wait, please," he said. "I try to come over as much as I can, but it's not always easy. I had to go to Micheline's. You know how much I've wanted to fuck her. I had to do it. I ran over here as soon as I was done."

"I'm sure I have a medal here somewhere. Let me look for it. You're so considerate and sensitive to other people's feelings."

"Please, stop. Tell me what's going on and we can work it out. I'll apologize, I swear. Just talk to me."

"I'm not talking to you ever again. Go talk to Micheline."

"It's not like that," he said. "It was just sex. That's all."

"You're a selfish rat. Did you even stop to think about her? She's grieving. Her boyfriend had been killed. You killed him. She's sad and lonely. Not only that but she was crying, and you decide to fuck her. What a gentleman."

"It wasn't like that at all. She wanted to. I wanted to."

"Don't come near me."

"Are you crying?"

"No, I'm not. I hate you."

He stopped moving. I couldn't. I turned my back. The power went off again. Pitch-black.

"I'm sorry," he said softly. "I am. I wasn't thinking. It just happened. It didn't mean anything. Not like that. It's this thing I thought I had to do and then I didn't think. She was my Mount Everest."

"She's a person, you rat. And what am I? An anthill you can shove your dick into whenever you like."

I hated myself for saying that. He was on me before I could take another breath. In the dark, he was always quick when he wanted to be. I tried to shove him away but couldn't budge him. He was always stronger when he wanted to be. He lifted me easily, my back on one forearm and the back of my knees on the other.

"Take out the flashlight from my right pocket," he said.

"I don't want to touch you."

"Come on. Please fish it out. I don't want to bang your head trying to go through the bedroom door."

"Then put me down. I know how to find my way in this dark now."

He sighed, dropped my legs while holding my shoulder, took out his flashlight, and swooped me up again.

"You're grinning," I yelled in his face. "You think this is funny? Put me down. I hate you."

"No, you don't."

He carried me across the threshold into the bedroom, laid me down on the bed.

"Get off me," I said. "You're too heavy. You're suffocating me."

He didn't move. The flashlight on the bed lit his face strangely, all soft shadows and angles. I couldn't hold his gaze.

"I'm sorry," he said.

"No, you're not. Don't kiss me. No. You smell of her."

"I'm sorry," he said. "I'll wash, I swear."

"That's not enough," I said. And as much as I didn't want to, I started weeping again. "It's not enough."

"I know it isn't and I'm sorry."

"It's not enough. I'm sure you didn't even think to wash your dick after you were with her. You just came over. Tell me I'm wrong. You can't, can you?"

"You're not wrong," he said. "I've been a fool. I'm sorry."

"Get off me."

"It won't happen again. I'm sorry."

"I don't care. It happened and you can't make it unhappen."

"I can make it up to you and I will. You'll forget this happened. I will make you forget everything bad. That's how we make it unhappen."

"Get off me."

In the stygian dark, when I heard the indelicate clanking of the gate being opened, when he finally showed up after three days of abandonment, I rushed to berate him, but something felt wrong. I shone my flashlight. The soft light settled on him like ochre morning dew. His tiny torch pointed toward the lock. I saw him in the dim light and all words got stuck. He looked terrible, no smile, his eyes not glittering, swatches of his black hair pointing in different directions. His sad, gray face looked nothing like him. He smelled of sweat, dirt, and sulfurous smoke. He carried humidity in with him, and the smell of the sea, of ozone, of fish, and the weight of it all overwhelmed him. He shut the gate, pausing to gather his breath.

"Are you okay?" I asked.

"I'm fine," he said unconvincingly. He tried on a fake smile but couldn't go through with it. The skin under his eyes dark as a peach pit. "I'm tired, haven't slept in two days. I was going to go home because I badly need a bath, but I thought I should check in on you first."

I helped him unstrap his Kalashnikov. I helped him move while holding the flashlight. I wasn't sure whether I should guide him to the sofa or to the bed, the two functional pieces of furniture in this hellhole. The first was closer. He sat on the sofa. I moved the coffee table and knelt before him. I unlaced his boots, but it took me quite a while to get them off his feet. I unsocked him. He was most certainly right: definitely needed a bath. I looked up at him to make fun of his stink, but he was out. I considered leaving him there, since he obviously needed the rest, but I knew he wouldn't be comfortable. I began to undress him. So many unnecessary layers for this heat. Why would he wear camouflage fatigues all the time? It wasn't as if it camouflaged much in urban warfare. It didn't blend with anything. I unbuckled him, unbuttoned, unzipped, but couldn't pull down his pants at first. I tried to lift his butt, but he was in no state to help. I kept tugging and tugging until I was able to get his pants and underwear off. His crotch smelled worse than his feet, sour and tangy like moldy onions. I unclasped his watch, a new one, luminous like I always wanted. I tried it on, but there was no way I could wear it without it sliding off my wrist. It was almost ten at night. I worked on his shirt, and as soon as I tried to lift one arm, he woke up, grimacing. Ouch, ouch.

"Don't," he said.

"I'm sorry," I said. "I was trying to make you comfortable."

He moved forward, pulled his fatigue shirt over his shoulders. I helped pull it off, and only when it was completely off did I notice the blood. His left side, under the arm I tried to lift, had a layer of rust-colored stain, not a heavy flow but still prominent.

"What's that?"

"I tried to match it to your hair, but it tricked me and went darker."

"That's not funny," I said. "You're hurt. What happened?"

He gave me an amused you're-misbehaving-again look. He raised his right arm above his head. "Help with this," he said, "but slowly."

I lifted the T-shirt, pulling it over his head and off his left arm without him having to move it. A roll of bandage circled his chest a few times. He pointed toward his knapsack. I brought it to him. He took out an aluminum lunch box with an image of Superman flying over a tall building, a makeshift first aid kit that included only bandage rolls, bandage clips, a bottle of Hibiclens, and a large tube of Fucidin, which I assumed was an antibiotic. I helped him unroll the bandage, and then, at his direction, removed the gauze covering the wound.

"It's not bad," he said, after I gasped but before I had the chance to speak. "It looks worse than it is."

A sutured cut, above his bottom rib and below heart level. I wasn't a physician, but whoever stitched it must have been an amateur.

"Are you going to tell me whether you've been shot or what?"

"I'm not going to tell you anything, you know that. I must clean myself now."

"You can't do that by yourself. And it's a good thing you didn't go home for a bath. Soaking the wound would have been stupid and dangerous."

I helped him stand up. Our only light was my flashlight, and still, I noticed a dark, multihued bruise the size of a tennis ball below his left shoulder blade.

"When did you get that?"

"A couple of days ago. Everything is better now."

"This is better?"

He was so exhausted he could barely walk. I led him to the bathroom, had him sit on the floor facing the door, which I left open. He leaned against the wall, his legs spread around the sinkhole that was our toilet, his testicles and the head of his penis dangling above it. While the green washtub was filling with soap and water, I left him to get a candle. I lit it, turned the flashlight off to save battery life, but kept it close to the candle in case it got wet and flickered out. A shimmering fan of light appeared on the wall above his head.

I poured the pink Hibiclens liquid onto our washcloth.

"I hope this doesn't hurt," I said.

"Just be gentle. It'll be fine."

He flinched when I washed the sutured cut but didn't say anything. I ran the cloth over the wound three, four times, and the washcloth turned pinker. I made sure there was no blood crust left. He didn't bleed. I dunked the washcloth back in the tub, turned to him, and he was out again, his head leaning to the right, his eyelashes fluttering. He was so filthy I didn't know where to start. Should I begin with his feet and move up or with his hair and go down? I sat cross-legged like a yogi, lifted his left leg onto my knee, and began to wash. I did his legs. His humongous thighs were knotted. I washed his groin. He didn't wake. Worked on his torso. He was putting on muscle. His chest was beginning to look like the two halves of a cantaloupe sprinkled with a dusting of fur. I washed his hair, his face. He didn't wake. I noticed Mr. Cat observing us from the living room. I stood up. My dress soaking wet, I moved Boodie slightly forward, soaped and rinsed every part of his back, making sure to be more tender around the bruise. I had to figure out how I could get to his butt. I pushed his torso to one side, his head and shoulder reaching the side wall, and I was able to reach one globe. I repeated for the other side. I stood above him, triumphant. Unconscious, he looked goofy, and adequately clean.

I dried him, then hung up my dress and dried myself. I couldn't leave him there and couldn't move him. I shook his right shoulder three times before he woke up. I helped him stand up, walked him to bed. I sat him down and warned him not to fall asleep because we had to put the bandage on. I covered his wound with antibiotic. I leaned against him to wrap the bandage around his torso.

"You can't keep your hands off me," he said, "can you?"

"Fuck your mother."

He ended up on my side of the bed because he couldn't lie on the wound. I wanted to let him sleep but he wouldn't let go of my arm. He didn't say anything, just pulled me onto the bed and spooned me. As soon as he fell asleep, Mr. Cat jumped on my side of the bed and maneuvered his way into my arms.

❊　❊　❊

He wouldn't wake up for twelve hours. I was on the sofa, my feet up on the coffee table, repeating infantile Japanese phrases back to the cassette recorder. "Yukio wa hahaoya ni wakare o tsugeta." Whenever I spoke, Mr. Cat's ears would perk up. He must have found the Japanese language as exotic as I did. He didn't mind when the machine spoke it, but seemed perturbed when I did.

But then he slid off my lap into his comfort space under the sofa. Boodie had woken up. He paused at the bedroom's doorway, rubbing his eyes, looking healthier. Naked, of course. He asked what time it was. It took me a minute to register his saying something. Why did he have to be so goddamn beautiful?

He walked to the bathroom; I to the kitchen counter, where I had left his watch.

"It's quarter past twelve," I said, but he didn't hear over the cacophony of his peeing. I waited until I heard the flush before repeating.

"You mean noon?" he yelled. "That can't be." He rushed out of the bathroom, now moving as if he'd never been hurt. "Why didn't you wake me?"

"I thought you needed the rest."

"I'm going to be in so much trouble."

He snatched his watch from my hands, walked into the bedroom, I on his heels.

"Why would you be in trouble? You're injured. What's going to happen? Will the teacher send a note to your parents?"

He riffled through the clean clothes pile on the floor, picking out his underwear, socks, pants, and T-shirt.

"Where's my shirt?" he asked.

195

"I washed everything this morning. Didn't you notice them in the bathroom? Nothing is dry yet. You didn't bring an extra shirt?"

"Then you shouldn't have washed it."

"What? It had blood on it. Took me forever to clean it out."

He raced through everything, getting dressed, running to the bathroom to brush his teeth. Combing his hair, which usually took forever, he did in three seconds.

"Slow down," I said. "You'll hurt yourself."

"I have to go."

The knapsack over one shoulder, the gun holstered, the Kalashnikov returned to his back.

"But you haven't eaten anything," I said. "I saved us some rice and meat for lunch. You need sustenance to heal."

He was at the gate when he stopped, turned around, and with his finger asked me to come to him. He grabbed my butt, pulled me to him, and kissed me, a deep, passionate kiss that made me forget where I was, and then he was gone, leaving me staring at the stupid gate.

I was deep in the land of sleep and didn't hear him come in. I woke up when he pulled me to him in bed. How could I not with the giant thing poking me in my lower back? I wanted to turn around to see if he was okay, but he wouldn't let me move.

"Go back to sleep," he whispered into my ear. "I got you a present to make up for not being able to come over."

"What?"

"Sexy panties. Now go back to sleep."

I wanted to hit him. I spent two days worrying if he was okay, whether his wound would heal, whether he was even alive, and he brings me underwear—a gift for him, not for me.

"I should try them on."

"We'll do that in the morning. Go to sleep."

"I want to see how they fit."

He no longer wanted to wash himself. I was to do it. I called him a baby, but that bothered him not at all. In the tiny bathroom, I had to scrub him, shampoo him, make sure his toenails were trimmed. He returned the favor when he felt like it.

He scoured my back with a loofah, unlayering dead skin, as I faced the mirror.

"I look dreadful," I said.

"No, you look great."

"I don't think so. Everything is wrong."

"Would you like me to get you some lipstick?"

"No, of course not."

"You might like it."

"No, I won't."

"You might like the way it looks on you. These lips were made for lipstick."

"You'd probably get me the wrong color anyway."

Maybe I wouldn't have gotten so upset had he not fucked me before telling me. Maybe if he hadn't spent so much time, almost an hour, pleasuring me before fucking me. He made me scream in ecstasy so often I ended up hoarse. By the time we had moved back to the living room, I couldn't unglue myself from him. I sat on his lap, my head on his chest, hoping to melt into him.

"We have to talk," he said ominously. His voice was almost a whole register lower than usual. He moved me aside, lifted his knapsack from the floor, and produced a gun. "This is for you."

I didn't grasp what he was saying, not at first.

"I will teach you how to use it," he said. "You can't practice shooting, not in here, but you'll be able to protect yourself if you need to."

"Why would I need a gun? That's silly."

"There's a war going on. I can't always be here to protect you. You'll need this."

"No, I won't. I can't shoot anyone."

"You might have to. If anyone other than me comes here, you shoot them. Do you understand?"

"What are you talking about?"

I could see he was frustrated. I could see that he was holding something back.

"You seem to regularly forget that there are people who want you dead," he said. "You saw things you shouldn't have."

"But I told you I won't say anything. You know that."

"It doesn't matter. You're a threat."

"Me? I would hardly call myself a threat to anybody."

And that was when he raised his voice.

"You're not taking this seriously enough. Command said I should kill you."

"You can't kill me," I said. "Wait, your bosses ask you to kill me, and you give me a gun?"

"Micho said that if I couldn't kill you, then he was going to come down here and do it himself."

"You can't let him kill me. You can't. Does he have a key? Why don't you let me go? I'll hide, I swear, and I won't tell anyone."

"You're better off here. I can deal with Micho. He's been acting erratic ever since he started taking those diet pills."

"Is he fat?"

He gave me one of those you're-such-a-child looks, which I hated. I couldn't remain still. I got off the couch and began pacing.

"You can't keep me here forever," I said. "You know that. At some point, you'll have to let me go. Why not now?"

"Maybe at some point when things calm down a bit. It's worse now than it was six weeks ago."

"Why is it worse?"

I couldn't tell whether blood began to rush to his cheeks, or it drained from the rest of his face. He might have been blushing or scared. Boodie the imperturbable was flustered.

"I can't tell you. It's bad right now."

"Are you losing the war or something?"

"Drop it. I'm not going to tell you."

"I won't. It's my life. If your people want to kill me, I want to know why."

"It's your mother. Okay? She's causing so many problems."

I had to stop. I couldn't believe what came out of his mouth. His hand supported his head as he stared at the stupid tiles on the floor.

"I shouldn't have said anything."

"What do you mean my mother is causing problems? How is that possible?"

"Your mother is insane."

"No, she's not. You don't even know her."

"I don't have to. Everyone at command talks about her all the time. She has been looking for you. She's running around the city, crossing demarcation lines, sometimes with an army driver, sometimes alone, trying to find out who has you. She's not right in the head."

"You're not right in the head."

"She's threatening people. She now comes into command yelling at everyone. Today they refused to open the door for her, and she broke a window. She threw a huge rock through the window. She could have hurt somebody."

"That can't be my mother. She wouldn't do anything like that. My father would never allow her to do anything, let alone something like that. She's the most timid human in the universe. She's terrified of my father and his family. I can't see her doing this."

"It's your mother, and it's all your fault. You made me call her. She knows you're alive and she went on a rampage. She knows someone is keeping you somewhere. The good thing is she doesn't know who has you. She goes around from one militia to the next, from one part of the city to another, threatening everybody. It takes her a while to come back around to command."

"Threatening with what? I mean, she's tiny."

"How the hell should I know? I haven't been there when she's shown up. All I can tell you is everybody at command is terrified of her. Only a few people know you're here. If more knew, she'd likely break someone, and they'd tell her. Most of the men are probably more afraid of her than of their superiors. She told this guy, Imad, that if he knew where you were and he didn't tell her, she'd make sure God would cover his body with boils, and he believes her. She made him swear on his grandmother's grave. Micho says he's going to kill her, but I was told he hid in the bathroom the last time she showed up. He now wants to kill you. I had to lie to command and tell them I wasn't stupid enough to call her and tell her you were alive, but I'm not sure anyone believes me. It's a mess and it's all your fault."

"Then let me go home."

"You're not listening. Command wants you dead. If you show up at home, then they will know I let you go. They'll probably kill me. I know Micho wants to kill both you and your mother. We can't do anything now. We must wait till things are calm again."

"They're never going to be calm. There's a war going on."

"Come here," he said. "Sit down and let's not think about things. Your mother makes the rounds of all the armies. She won't return for seven or eight days. We don't have to worry for now. Come, let's relax."

"I can't relax."

"Come."

I lost track of time. The days felt thick and viscous. I couldn't tell if he had been away for five days or for six, maybe a week.

The dogs were quiet, the guns were not. The fighting had moved closer, every shot more intimate. So much shooting, it felt as if they were trying to kill each other outside the door. What if he couldn't come back for me? I had drinking water for four days, maybe more if I rationed better. I only had rice left. Mr. Cat and I had to share a can of tuna in the morning. I hated tuna. My panic had been building steadily for the last five, six, or seven days. When I heard the loudest explosion and concrete dust descended upon Mr. Cat and me and the whole apartment, I went full-fledged berserk. Mr. Cat rushed into his hiding place. I rushed into nowhere. I ran around the tiny apartment, doing nothing other than screaming. More gunfire erupted, and more, and more. Another blast and the floor danced. I thought of hiding in the bathroom. Decided against it. It was probably the worst place to be if the roof caved in. How many floors would fall on me and Mr. Cat? Would the walls buckle? I ended up in what was probably the most unsafe of places, on my bed, under the sheet. Another explosion, the ceiling shimmied, the walls jiggled, but no dust. The lights went out again. I began to count from one to a hundred, tried to figure out how much time passed between each explosion. I worried about Mr. Cat. I went back to the living room with my flashlight, kneeled before the sofa, and called to him. He stared at me but wouldn't come out. I had to call him twice more and stretch my arm toward him before he did. I carried him to bed, and we both slid under the sheet. I felt better. I would have liked him to purr. He usually did in my arms.

Time passed, probably an hour, but how would I be able to tell? Two months — I had asked him for a clock for two months and he kept forgetting. The gunfire slowed, then stopped; every corn kernel had popped until the next batch. A few seconds of quiet before the muffled sound of men shouting. Mr. Cat's ears perked up.

It had always been difficult to assess a sound's distance or direction from within the apartment. I was within an enclosed womb within an enclosed womb. Echoes thrived. Yet the men sounded as if they were in the garage, behind the dark door. I carried Mr. Cat toward it and listened. Couldn't decipher much. Lots of movement and running around. One man yelled at someone to check what was in that room. Another guy replied that the only things inside were cement bags and lots of trash. What about that other room? Someone moved closer to the door, jiggled the knob.

"It's locked," the man said. "I bet that's where they kept their weapons."

Mr. Cat's kitten claws were digging into my left forearm. I held him closer.

"Hello," I said to the door, but what came out sounded more like the chirp of a chick. The knob jerked as if it were having an epileptic fit.

"Hello," I said, louder, more forceful, more desperate. "Can you help me?"

The knob stopped moving. A moment's hesitation before the man yelled, "There's someone in here." I heard more men rushing to the door.

"Who's there?" someone asked. The accent was strange, not Lebanese, nor Levantine for that matter, probably North African. "Tell us who you are, or we'll shoot you."

"I'm nobody," I said. "My name is Raja."

"What do you mean nobody? Who are you with? What are you?"

"I'm not with anybody," I said. "I swear. I'm just a boy."

I heard more shuffling feet. A man with a harsher voice, someone who probably smoked two or three packs of cigarettes a day, yelled, "Who do you belong to?"

"I'm not sure how to answer that," I said. "My mother? Yes, I'm my mother's boy. I was kidnapped. I didn't do anything. Please let me out."

"Are there any guns in there?"

"There's one gun," I said. "It's not loaded."

"What about loot? Did they store anything in there."

"I have rice, that's all. And some books."

"Books?" the man yelled. "Who wants books? I'm talking about valuables. Everything here belongs to us now."

"This land is ours," another said. "We've conquered it."

"We're the new kings in town," the hoarse-voiced man said. "We're the Almoravids."

"The what?" I said, and I knew I shouldn't have said it as soon as I did.

"You don't know your history? Open this door and let me teach this boy a lesson. Shoot the lock or something."

Gunfire erupted before I had a chance to move, and my heart dropped to my ankles. I stepped back even as I realized the shot didn't seem to have been aimed at the door. Then more gunfire. Then the men shouting, then cursing, then running around, then more gunfire, then screaming, then more gunfire, then I was in bed under the sheet with Mr. Cat.

The heat swelled and time seemed endless. In catatonic silence, I sat in the lightless black of the apartment with a

T-shirt wrapped around my nose because dust had again settled everywhere, on the sheets, on the sofa, on the floor, on me. I couldn't wash or mop because I was out of water. Mr. Cat hated everything. He spent most of the time cleaning himself over and over. A repulsive smell seeped into the apartment, and I couldn't figure out the source. Dogs had been wailing nonstop. Electricity had not returned for two days, or more precisely, two sleep cycles, since I had my bizarre encounter with the idiotic militia. One flashlight died, and I wasn't sure how long the second would last. I tried to keep it turned off as much as I could to conserve the batteries, but also because when the light was on, I noticed that the walls were sweating in unnatural places, drops of water appearing near the ceiling and sliding down, furrowing into the dust, forming what looked like slug trails.

I had two candles left, barely a liter of drinking water, and no food for Mr. Cat. If Boodie did not return soon, we would starve to death in grimy darkness, unless the ceiling collapsed on us first. And the ceiling suddenly groaned, a new sound, frightening and disconcerting. I turned on the flashlight, stood up, and ran to the gate. I shook it for the hundredth time. I yelled three times in a row. Nothing happened, of course. I was alone. I leaned my forehead against the gate, the metal bars pressing right above my eye sockets. I sighed, took a deep breath, and that was when I saw the keys on the ground, in the in-between space. They had been slid under the door. How long had they been there? I sneaked my hand between the bars and grabbed them. I put my hand through the gate again, this time next to the lock. I couldn't see the slot, but luck seemed to be on my side, the first key slid in. And the gate opened. I had to unlock the door before being able to swing the gate open. The second key worked. I hesitated before opening both. I ran to my room, put on my sneakers, picked up Mr. Cat. I wanted nothing else from this goddamn place, not even the Japanese cassettes. I returned to the gate and slowly swung it open. Clutching Mr. Cat to my bosom, I peeked from behind the door. No movement, dark enough—the garage ramp at the far end, meagre light descended from the entrance. The stench assailed my nose. Excrement for sure, and more, rotting cabbage, mothballs, and something else sour and sulfurous.

I stepped out. My eyes adjusted and I wished they hadn't. The first corpse was a dog. I walked quickly to the exit, not looking at the two men piled atop each other on my right. Mr. Cat's claws dug into my forearm. I ascended the ramp into the morning light. The air was windless and warm, with a faint tang of burning, but it was still fresh. I took a deep breath.

I wasn't sure what I expected. A leveled neighborhood, collapsed buildings? Not so. All the buildings were standing, the damage cosmetic, bullet holes like a map of stars. What made the scene strange was the absence of life—that and a mountainous heap of garbage. I had no idea where I was. I was certain I was in Beirut, but it felt not. I had to decide how to proceed. I knew, like every Beiruti, that I would be able to find my way if I were to reach the sea. The smell and feel of salt in the air, the undulant pulse of the sea, would lead me to the Mediterranean, and the perpetuity that is the Mediterranean would lead me home. The first step was a slight right, westward, I presumed.

I walked in a ghost town, still not recognizing much. I stuck to a straight line in the middle of the trafficless street. Parked cars and rubble blocked the pavements. A shuttered grocery store, a pharmacy that looked to have been looted. Some apartments had windows with broken glass, but all windows were opaque, either their shutters closed or their drapes drawn. A curtain on the third floor of a building to my right shimmered after I looked up. The neighborhood wasn't empty, its residents were hiding. I was an alien in what once was my home.

I reached an intersection, the third since I left the garage. The buildings ahead of me seemed in better shape. I continued but felt Mr. Cat's claws dig in. One more step and a bullet struck not a meter ahead. I froze. Mr. Cat wanted to jump but I held him tighter. I thought of running for cover but I was too scared. Was the bullet meant for me and missed? Would I be shot if I moved? I remained immobile, feeling like a mole that had found a rock in its path. On which side should I continue to burrow my tunnel? I looked up to the building I believed the shot came from but couldn't see anything. I pointed at the spot where the bullet hit. I inhaled deeply and ever so slowly began to move my foot forward. Bang, a second bullet hit the same spot. And it hadn't come from where I thought it had. The shooter was in the three-story building to the left. I pointed to the right, a useless gesture most likely, but if the shooter wanted me dead, I would have been already. Nothing happened. I took a step to the right, then another, then another. I was no longer in the shooter's eyesight. I walked two blocks, looked up at the buildings wondering if snipers were embedded there, but all I saw were window boxes overflowing with geraniums, the blue enamel street name. I turned left, toward the sea, and no one shot at me.

I had barely crossed another street when I arrived at a neighborhood that seemed familiar, probably because the properties had fewer bullet perforations, less wreckage littering the street, less quiet, a few voices cascading down from an apartment. Every step I took became lighter. A long-haired young man seated in an ornate wicker chair at a building's entrance talked to three younger men standing before him, a college student lecturing high school kids on the philosophy of being cool. One of the younger ones noticed me, and his face froze in shock, as if I were an ambling extraterrestrial with thirteen eyes. He pointed at me, yelling, "Look, look." The lecturer turned around and jumped up. It was then that I noticed the guns, his and his sidekicks'. They rushed at me. Mr. Cat hissed when they came close and that seemed to confuse them. They stopped a few paces away, the younger boys a step behind. One wouldn't remove his eyes from Mr. Cat, smiling questioningly. He was probably older than me but not by much. His acne-filled face made the gun and its holster look incongruous. Mr. Cat had a different effect on the college-aged guy, who looked like a dimwitted hippie—unkempt hair way past his shoulder, a paisley-print shirt with saddlebag sweat blotches, faded jeans, a crochet belt, and a mouth that was lifted, open, and pale pink. He carried a faint yeasty scent.

"Where do you think you're going?" he said, trying and failing to sound threatening.

"Home," I said. I noticed the tendons in his neck repeatedly tensing and relaxing, danger and no danger, danger and no danger.

"Why didn't the sniper shoot you?"

I wasn't sure how to answer such a question. I wondered if he was high on hash, but none of the giveaways were present. Just vacant eyes, probably a preternatural imbecile.

"The sniper is shooting anyone crossing from one neighborhood to another," the hippie guy said. "He should have shot you."

"Maybe he didn't want to hurt the cat," the boy with acne maculating his face said.

"Maybe it's because he's wearing a dress," a boy with feathered ducktail hair said.

And I looked down, noting that I was indeed wearing a dress, having forgotten all about it—a nice dress, too, the red one. It didn't go well with my sneakers, though.

"Why are you wearing a dress?" asked the hippie guy.

That question I could answer. "Everything else I had was dirty. I hadn't been able to do the laundry because I ran out of water."

"Why should we let you pass?"

"Because I need to get home to see my mother."

Hippie guy took a cigarette out of a pack, lit it. He inhaled deeply. I was sure he had studied the mannerisms of Alain Delon in *Borsalino*. He flicked his head westward. The boys spread out, making a path for me. I walked away.

With each step I took, the heat of August made the air change color: sky blue, rosy, scarlet, white, transparent.

One could ladle the humidity. Every cell in my body seemed to be sweating. Blocking the street to my right was a triple-strand barbed wire. And I knew where I was. Our apartment was a thirty-minute walk at most, down this shortcut alley whose edges were lined with litter. The summer must have been exceptionally hot and humid, oppressive enough that the bougainvillea that was only huge last summer bloomed dragon-sized, spilling friendly fire. Just as I began to feel more comfortable, more at home in the city I grew up in — the roasted-looking grocer sitting on a stool outside his store beneath the rubber tree, the expensive furniture shop that never seemed to have any customers — a jeep with a mounted DShK passed by. The standing guy manning the gun, layered in a keffiyeh, a horseshoe moustache, and an archipelago of acne glared at me, at the world. He swiveled the machine gun and vibrated himself, pretending to shoot me. And then they were gone.

I wondered if I should call my mother so that she would know I was coming. I reached the University Hospital. I decided I should stop there first, call home, and maybe a nurse could give me something for my headache. I walked into the emergency room, which didn't seem too busy, or not as busy as the last time we were there, when my father tripped on a piece of loose pavement right outside our building and my mother and I had to jump into the car and drive him to the ER. We had to wait for an hour and a half with him complaining nonstop before he was seen by someone. The nurse receptionist at the triage desk looked up and seemed shocked to find me standing before her. She asked if she could help me. She had kind eyes.

"I was kidnapped," I found myself saying. "I was locked in a garage for more than two months and I need to call my mother to tell her I'm safe and I have a headache."

I did not know who uttered those detached words. He didn't sound like me. I didn't know why I told her all that. And the look that appeared on her face told me what I said was the last thing she had expected. She stood up, walked around the desk, and placed both hands on my shoulders. She'd wanted to hug me, but Mr. Cat was in the way. I did not feel awkward.

"I'm okay," I said.

"Are you sure?" she asked. "Why are you holding on to the kitten?"

"He's okay too. We both are."

She led me down a corridor following a rainbow of straight lines, both pairs of sneakers squeaking noisily on the linoleum. We entered a small, bare room, with only a desk, a chair, and a small fridge lonely in the corner. Handbags hanging from hooks were the sole interruption of white on the walls. A pair of heels camped below them. She pointed to the gray-green rotary phone on the table.

"Do you want me to talk to your mother?"

I told her I would do it. I expected her to allow me my privacy by leaving the room, but she remained standing there, waiting for me to do something. I sat. I moved the phone closer and cradled the receiver between my cheek and shoulder. I only had one free hand because Mr. Cat was restless. I pushed my index finger into the number six slot, but it wouldn't move any farther, as if it had forgotten how to dial. I tried to push again, but my finger disobeyed. It would not move. I couldn't figure out what was happening.

The nurse suggested she dial my home number. I heard the ringing. And it was picked up. My mother's voice came through the receiver. "Hello. Hello? Hello!"

"It's me, mama," I said. "It's me."

And I didn't know what came over me. I couldn't say anything else. I started crying like I had never cried before, crying like mourners at a beloved's funeral. I couldn't stop. My mother was talking, but I couldn't understand anything. I held the receiver tightly, bawled into it. My mother kept talking and nothing made sense.

The nurse took over. She took the receiver. "Yes, he's all right, seems healthy . . . we'll wait here for you . . . he showed up with a kitten . . . make sure to bring some clothes for him to wear . . . we'll wait here, don't worry . . . yes, of course I'll tell him."

She sat on the table facing me. She petted Mr. Cat first, then me, her hand caressing my neck. "Your mother will be here in five minutes or less," she said. My tears began to dry as hers fell. "She said you'll understand. She asked me to tell you she would break the world for you."

And the world was broken, and all the king's horses and all the king's men couldn't put Humpty together again. You could say a civil war that would last for fifteen years crumpled everything, but truly, it was the dress that did. The fact that I reentered the world above wearing a simple summer dress and sneakers, and carrying a cat no less, was a devastation. I didn't think. I left the garage apartment. Someone had left keys for me to get out and I had no idea how long they were there. The door opened and I walked out. Not many people saw me in the dress, but it seemed to have been enough. Everyone around me scattered like quail. People talked, and talked, and wouldn't stop talking about me in a dress. My father couldn't bring himself to speak to me directly for about six months after I returned, and then, slowly, he resumed being his usual stupid self, engaging with me only when he needed to. His sister was worse. If you assumed every horrible rumor about me began with her, you wouldn't be wrong. Did I run away from home to become a dancing boy for all the militiamen? Of course I did. Did I play Russian roulette where if I didn't shoot myself after a roll, I would sexually service whoever wanted me to in front of all the other men? Yes, I did. Even if it didn't make any sense, even if I couldn't physically have done it, I did it. Why did the infamous sniper who killed every person who tried to cross his street not shoot me? He'd never missed a shot during the entire war. Obviously, he called to me, and I climbed the stairs to the roof, where I bent over, and he fucked me while sniping innocent passersby. When I was sixteen or seventeen, I was told by a student in my class, and for the life of me I can't remember why he did, that the image of me twirling continuously like a dervish with a rising skirt before seated men with machine guns resting between their legs was imprinted in his memory.

My life was never the same, but you knew that, right?

My relationship with my brother was bad before and became irredeemable after. He accompanied my mother when she showed up at the hospital and ended up having to hold Mr. Cat while I was being examined by the attending resident. And he lost him. Farouk claimed Mr. Cat scratched him and he had to throw him away. Luckily, Mr. Cat hid in a bush not far from the ER entrance and came to me when I called him. That was when everything turned between my brother and me. I didn't exactly threaten him, but I told the cretin that if he ever touched Mr. Cat again, or harmed him in any way, I would kill him. I was calm, emotionless, and I meant it. It seemed I terrified him. He would never hit me or taunt me again. But then he insisted that he refused to share a room with vermin. My mother tried to mollify him, but my father took his side. Farouk shouldn't be required to sleep in the same room as an animal if he did not wish to. I suggested that I sleep on the balcony with Mr. Cat. We would manage with bad weather and with bullets. My mother solved the problem. She would move into my room, and Farouk the imbecile would share my father's bed. They both objected; they both wanted Mr. Cat to be returned to the streets, or at least to another home. Mr. Cat and I were inseparable; I stood firm. My mother put her foot down, the first time she contradicted either of the men in her family. She moved into my room and would not move out, not when Farouk the imbecile was sent to Baghdad because he kept failing the baccalaureate, not when I moved out after I graduated, not even when my father died, not until my brother the asshole conned her into selling the apartment and giving him all her money. Mr. Cat wasn't able to leave my room until I moved into my own apartment, where he was crowned king of the realm.

Aunt Yasmine would accuse me of ruining my parents' marriage. By that time, I'd stopped giving a shit.

And Boodie? I refused to think of him ever again. I cut him out of my memory. I forbade my mother to bring him up. I wouldn't allow him any life in my life. He wasn't just dead to me — he never existed.

V
(1975 – 2021)
The Port Explosion

Now, where was I? Oh, yes, the blast. The third in the concatenation of calamities.

The fear that bad luck or disasters happen in threes, triskaphobia or triophobia, is said to have started during the First World War with what was called third light: the unlucky third person to light a cigarette from the same match. (A sniper sees the first light, takes aim on the second, and fires on the third.) I wasn't religious or superstitious, and I didn't believe the nonsense that disasters occurred in threes, but my mother did, as did Madame Taweel. Before the financial collapse and the pandemic, if I said something innocuous, like "It's going to rain so much today I'm going to drown," my mother wouldn't be bothered, but after the two catastrophes she would admonish me for calling misfortune upon us. If I mentioned that fewer people were wearing masks and it was highly likely more people would die, my mother would demand I apologize. She was expecting a disaster, I wasn't, and none of us were expecting one of such magnitude.

On August 4, 2020, Beirut exploded.

It was a tad after six in the evening. The summer's heat had been building, layer upon layer of humid smothering, and reached its crescendo now that August had started. I was on the balcony drinking Japanese green tea, studying the buildings' shadows as they leaned eastward. My mother, to my right sans tea, our woven rattan chairs almost touching, on her mobile, chatted with who else but Madame Taweel. It was one of those rare occasions when she had her hearing aid on without my having to pester her. She waved at someone on the street below. I saw Madame Taweel waving back. They would not interrupt their conversation even though they would be interacting face-to-face in a matter of seconds. Blah, blah, blah. We were outside to give our air conditioner a break. It had been running nonstop since seemingly forever, which we could do despite the diesel shortage because Madame Taweel was our drug dealer. That evening the heat had pinned the air down in a choke hold and wouldn't let up no matter how much the air and everyone else in the city tapped the mat. My mother told me to turn down the volume of my stupid opera if I knew what was best for me because she couldn't hear herself talk and did I want all the neighbors to throw rotten tomatoes at us? I replied with something like who cared whether she could hear herself talk since she repeated the same stupid things over and over and why did she have to crowd me by sitting so close? Our usual inanities.

And everything went surreal, or unreal would probably be a better word, or Wonderland insane.

If I told you things happened so fast neither my mother nor I had any idea of what we were doing, and neither had any recollection of what we did during that minuscule segment of time when our world and the city turned upside down, I would be telling you the truth. If I told you time stood still, that we knew what was going to happen one millisecond before it did and reacted with the deftness and precision of combat veterans, I would be telling you the truth. Nothing made sense.

She felt it first, the heaviness of the air and its vanishing. She stopped talking, still holding her phone to her ear, looked at me, surprised, an instant before I felt a weight on my chest, like a millstone was crushing my lungs. A hiss, and I couldn't breathe. Even though I hadn't felt anything like it before, my Lebanese body remembered. My right arm reached to stop my mother's rattan from falling backward, which it was because my mother, dismissing senescence and reclaiming agility she'd lost no less than forty years earlier, had jumped off her chair and placed her body between the world and me.

It arrived. And what an explosion it was, a great, discordant blow from Gabriel's horn.

My mother and I, my Japanese tea, and my chair jumped at least two hands off the balcony's floor. My mother's chair, now empty, flew a bit higher than that. My hand, still holding her chairback, raised above my head. The mini speaker singing Montserrat Caballé arias jumped off the balcony to its death, *Tosca*-style. As if the loudest-ever blast wasn't already weird enough, its sound kept coming, arriving in incessant undulating waves, even though it couldn't have lasted more than a second or two. And then the queer cloud, which appeared above the building across the street, above all three buildings across the street, yes, a mushroom cloud but shaped more like percolating evil mud that would soon sprout the monster from the deep. And it was pink, cotton candy pink against a perfectly blue sky—perfectly blue until it was bruised and the slim layers of dust and colorless muck covered my mother and me and everything around us. And the pink cloud sparkled as if it were calling for a unicorn to fly through it, but no, it was only fireworks going off inside it. Nothing made sense.

The fact that I could think nothing made sense meant I was still alive. I was capturing images fast and my thoughts ran faster. Did Israel finally drop a nuclear bomb on us? The Israelis hated us enough to include celebratory fireworks with our annihilation by radiation. Were we already dead?

I heard the absence of birds, the stillness of it.

My mother moved first. She lifted herself off me, asking if I was all right. "What was that?" I had no idea.

"Oh, no!" She stood up and scrambled to the door, cursing, and praying that Madame Taweel had survived. I moved in the opposite direction, to my room to check on Monet and Manet, who were wide-eyed terrified under my bed. My mother screamed. I ran to her, just as a bloodied Madame Taweel stumbled into the living room, slapping the hands of her bodyguard, who was trying to help her walk. She wasn't terribly hurt. She'd gotten off the elevator when she was thrown backward into her well-stuffed bodyguard and the sconce attacked her. It was just a forehead cut. I looked out our door. Both the sconce and the ceiling light fixture were shattered on the ground. My mother asked for the first aid kit. In the bathroom, the kit had fallen out of the cabinet onto the sink. While my mother fussed over Madame Taweel, the latter was spewing out orders to her bodyguard. Tell this one to come over, tell that one to check everything in her house, tell that other one to call the minister and find out what the hell happened.

I went around the apartment checking for damage. One kitchen cabinet had disgorged its drinking glasses, all seven shattered. Nothing major in my mother's bedroom or mine. The Japanese lintel had jumped from my chiffoniere, and every single painting in the apartment was tilted. One of the windows that looked out onto the balcony was on the floor. We were lucky. We were protected by the buildings across the street and our windows were open. The apartment above us had all theirs shatter because they had their air-conditioning working. The one below had only two windows left standing. You could say that Madame Taweel's providing the building's generator with lower-cost diesel ended up costing more.

We gathered in the living room, my mother, Madame Taweel, two of her minions, and I, stoic and resolute, watching television news hoping to find out what happened. Madame Taweel received phone reports every few minutes. All of us dazed. We had all been through a civil war, shootings, car bombs, wanton destruction, Syrian shelling, unabating Israeli missiles. Those had not prepared us for this.

If you're reading this book, you know what happened. Unless, of course, you get all your news from watching videos of adorable kittens, a lucky prerogative.

The largest nonnuclear explosion in history.

At the port of Beirut, 2,750 tons of ammonium nitrate that had been stored in a warehouse finally kaboomed, causing hundreds of deaths, thousands of horrific injuries, hundreds of thousands displaced, billions in property damage, and scars that would never heal. The blast was felt in Turkey, Syria, Palestine, Jordan, and Israel, as well as parts of Europe. Oh, and for some reason, the ammonium nitrate was not only unsafely stored for years but shared the warehouse with fireworks. A fire had ignited both into a pretty, if fatal, *boom*.

You could also say that the city was fortunate. The port's humongous grain silos, all concrete, absorbed most of the shock of the explosion, shielding most of the city, though not all of it, from more severe harm.

Of course, there would be no investigation and no consequence for the ineptitude and malice of anyone in charge. Just as with the banking collapse, the assassination of presidents and prime ministers, the gangsters would not allow any inquiries into these matters. Follow the stench of shit and you run into a member of parliament.

Both my mother and Madame Taweel would call the explosion evil, which it wasn't, of course. An event cannot be so. The people causing said event might be. No, you have to understand, one of the worst things the non-evil event caused was the reentry into my life of the evil of evils, the wickedest witch of the Middle East, Aunt Yasmine.

I had to ask after my colleagues. One had lost his home, and another had it worse. Nisrine's house killed her brother-in-law, who lived with her. It collapsed on him while she and her sister were driving home. She was one of our Arabic teachers, and weirdly enough, the other Arabic teacher had her home destroyed earlier when an Israeli missile brought down an entire building in the 2006 violation. Nisrine was a great teacher and colleague, and I liked her, but we weren't very close. Still, I ended up speaking with her for half an hour or so. She needed to talk. I was somewhat surprised, wondering why she didn't want to leave her line open so her worried friends and family would be able to reach her. And then I realized it was almost ten at night and I hadn't heard my mother or Madame Taweel in quite a while. I left my bedroom to find no one in the apartment. I ended the call with my colleague and called my mother. She picked up, a bit harried. I asked where she was.

"I didn't want to pick up," my mother said, "because I knew you wanted to harass me, but I did because I didn't want you to worry and that's because I care about you, but I'm busy now and can't talk and I'm having some food delivered to the apartment just for you, and goodbye now."

That was enigmatic even by mother's standards. I called her again, but she didn't pick up. The doorbell rang. One of Madame Taweel's thugs, the big bodyguard, face-masked and overloaded with heavy pots and plates, asked to come in. He joked as he crossed the threshold that he wouldn't be able to remove his gun before entering, since his hands were busy. He went into the living room and placed his aromatic burden on the dining room table. He wouldn't have been able to slide easily into the kitchen. It took a few seconds before I noticed the diminutive woman accompanying him. Silent, she glided by and squeezed into the kitchen. She was of peasant stock, headscarf-covered, had one of those indeterminate-age faces, could have been in her forties or older than me. She began moving the pots to the counter. The thug stood next to me, hands on hips, smiling and admiring.

"What's going on?" I said, somewhat gruffly. "Who are you and why are you in my kitchen?"

She didn't pause. She didn't even glance my way. I thought at first she might have been shy or maybe adhering to some religious dogma about talking to strange men. But no, she looked more earnest than shy, moved around my kitchen as if she owned it, as if she'd been cooking here for generations.

"Your mother thought you might be hungry, and Madame Taweel suggested that Mounira cook for you," the big thug said, his voice filled with nothing if not high admiration. "She began working for the boss last week."

"But I don't want a stranger in my kitchen, or in my house for that matter," I said. "I don't want you to cook for me."

Mounira stopped, turned in my direction, acknowledging my existence for the first time. She still wouldn't look at me. "I do what I'm told," she said softly. Heavy accent from the south. "Dinner will be ready in five minutes. Please wash your hands and sit down."

"Far be it for me to tell someone like you what to do, professor," the big thug said, "but I suggest you sit down to eat and say thank you."

"But I'm not hungry. We had the explosion. I just finished picking up the broken glass in the apartment and you want me to think about food?" I was griping again, and I noticed that I was directing my mewling to the big thug, not the cook. "And anyway, if I eat now, I won't be able to sleep until two in the morning. And my mother shouldn't be making these decisions for me. If I'm hungry, I can make myself a sandwich."

"I'm not going to say anything," the big thug said, and the little cook floated in her own world, paying little if any attention to either one of us. She turned on the burner, scooped up what looked like rice from one pot into a pan, and the aroma overwhelmed every other sense in my body. I ran to the bathroom to wash my hands. I returned, slid my butt and me into the kitchen—the thug snickered, the cook didn't—and sat down like a good boy.

I had to invite both to join for dinner (manners, tradition, whatever), but they had already eaten. The thug was waiting for the cook to finish to drive her back, and it seemed he wanted to watch me eat. I assumed it was to be some joke at my expense, that the meal would be so good I'd have to eat my words. Mounira told me she was going to serve one dish and store everything else and that we needed a bigger fridge. Two kinds of soups, a lentil dish, and a whole chicken. She placed the one dish before me and started putting things away.

I assume I don't have to tell you it was incredible. Leg of lamb with rice and sauteed nuts and spices that could penetrate any cell. Mounira would have been surprised if you called her a chef. She would have never thought what she did was art. She cooked. That was it. She cooked the same meals her mother taught her, the ones her grandmother taught her mother, and her great-grandmother, a hundred generations of mothers if not more. Mounira blessed me that evening. That first dish quite literally brought me to tears.

"Thank you," I said.

I thought it was the greatest meal I'd ever had, and I knew, deep in my bones, that my mother was going to make me pay for it.

You figured that out, right? That was how my mother worked.

I was right on both counts. I couldn't sleep before two in the morning, and my mother made me pay. I was about to be visited by Hypnos when the lights in my room turned on, banishing the poor god of sleep. I opened my eyes to find at the foot of my bed both my mother and Madame Taweel standing like justices if missing their scales and swords — no blindfolds either, though replaced with face masks, which was unusual since they no longer masked around each other or me.

"Get up," my mother said. "We need to talk."

I asked what time it was, complained about them coming into my room while I was naked under the covers, yelled at them for being out and about in the middle of the night when our city had exploded. They refused to engage as was their wont. The only concession they allowed me was leaving the room so I could get somewhat dressed and join them in the salon.

I entered the living room to find my mother telling her friend that she should go home, that my mother could handle everything henceforth. Madame Taweel pooh-poohed the suggestion. They'd spent most of the night dealing with this, she wasn't about to leave now that it was almost done. What was almost done?

"Your aunt Yasmine's apartment was destroyed. It was a miracle she wasn't killed, not a scratch on her. Her daughter Nahed had two cuts on her right arm from broken glass, but she's fine now. You know, she had been taking care of her mother, such a good girl."

It didn't take a genius to figure out where this was going. This was why I was given such a magnificent meal.

"No," I said. "Absolutely not. Never ever. There's no way that evil woman is coming into my home. I can't believe you would stoop so low to ask this. You're an awful person.

Even with all the dreadful things you've done to me, this must be the most appalling."

"Stop being so melodramatic," she said. "It's late. We don't have many options."

"Who's we? I have options galore. She's not setting foot in my house."

"Okay. She's the one who doesn't have any options. If we don't take her in, she's out on the street. I won't have that. We take care of family."

"She's not my family. She has her own. She has three hateful sons. Have them take care of her. It's not going to be me."

"Her two eldest are working in Saudi. Her third is in jail in Egypt. You know that. None of them have homes here. We're her only family."

"She's not coming here. Why would I let the devil into my own house? I'm not that stupid. After everything she did to me, after all the things she said about me, you want me to help her?"

"Yes," my mother said.

I expected her to add something to her curt response. She waited for me to come up with another argument. We glared at each other for a bit. Well, I glared. She wouldn't look away.

Madame Taweel intervened. "You know, she's a harmless old woman now," she said. "She's ninety-two and frail, a wisp of who she was. I would have put her up, but both my sons are with me right now. She needs your compassion. You shouldn't be afraid of her."

"I'm not afraid of her. I hate her. And she hates me. Isn't it convenient that she went out of her way for years to make my life hell, she would insult me and avoid me, but now that she needs a place to stay, she thinks we're family. If she weren't two-faced, she'd choose to be homeless over sharing space with me."

"She probably doesn't remember who you are," my mother said. "She doesn't remember much of anything. She's been having memory trouble."

"Think about this," Madame Taweel said. "You can curse her every day, call her all kinds of names, and she won't remember, and you can do it again and again. Therapeutic, if you ask me."

"I can't tell which of you is worse than the other," I said. "You're like two butts in the same pair of knickers. Why are you helping my mother with this? Don't you have other people to worry about or annoy?"

"Listen, darling," my mother said. "I need to go to bed at some point, so I can't keep doing this. I'm asking you to agree because Nahed insisted it be so. She won't come inside this apartment if she and her mother wouldn't be welcome. I told her you'd welcome them once they were here, but for some reason, she thinks I'm offering her the place against your wishes. So, I'm asking you to agree, and we can bring them here. They'll stay in my room, and I'll move to the small room."

"You can't move to the small room," I said. "You can't even fit a closet in there, and how can you live without your vanity? That's stupid."

"Funny," my mother said. "That's exactly what Nahed said. I guess you're right. They can stay in the small room. I'll text her and tell her to come up."

"No, you won't. What do you mean *come up*?"

"They're downstairs. Nahed is just waiting for your approval. She wouldn't come up otherwise. Isn't she sweet? Such a nice girl."

She lied. They were not waiting downstairs, but right outside the door. Madame Taweel opened the door, and four people entered: two of her thugs, one carrying a suitcase and the other pushing a wheelchair bearing Aunt Yasmine, who was knocking at death's door, oxygen cannister and all; and Nahed, who looked like she could easily take down both thugs without breaking a sweat. Nahed, carrying a backpack and sleeping bag as if she was going camping, thanked me, and promised that we would talk later, after she put her mother to bed. Weirdly, they all wore not just face masks, but plastic face shields and latex gloves. Madame Taweel directed them to the small room, behaving as if this was her apartment. I noticed she wore latex gloves as well. The two thugs rushed out the door. Nahed and her mother couldn't possibly sleep together in that small bed.

"Don't worry about that," my mother said. "We decided this is the best solution, until Yasmine gets better, or is no longer contagious." She fished around in her purse. "Oh, I forgot to tell you," she added, handing me a mask. "Yasmine has Covid."

Aunt Yasmine didn't start out hating me. After all, she loved my father more than anything, more than she ever did her husband, probably more than her children. She was the eldest and felt responsible for her two brothers, and my father was the youngest, her baby. My grandmother, a drunk whom Aunt Yasmine idolized, channeled most of her love to my father. Aunt Yasmine followed suit—in adoring my father, and in drinking. I always thought their love for him bordered on the obsessive romantic, though platonic, of course. When he married, both women found his young bride wanting and outright naïve. To ensure she would fit into their family, they instituted an indoctrination program that would have made Mao proud: how to dress, what to cook, whom she could have as friends, whom to like, whom to hate. My mother was the intruder in this menage.

I found my mother's early timidity unnatural and irrational. Even as a child, I couldn't make sense of it. She allowed my father and his stupid family to douse any flame of life in her, hardly ever fighting back, nor did she seem to want to. My mother claimed both her mother-in-law and sister-in-law treated her with no little disdain until she did what every traditional wife had to do to gain respect. She provided my father with his first son, my brother. Once the ever-venerated Farouk arrived on the scene, Aunt Yasmine eased off my mother a bit, but not for very long, mind you. *Oh, Farouk is so magnificent. Oh, Farouk is so wonderful, so strong, so manly for a young boy, isn't he?*

My mother followed every direction my father pointed to, walked behind him on every path. *You shouldn't watch your son's dance recital. Dancing onstage leads to degeneracy.* Farouk didn't take long to begin to boss her around just like his father. *How many times do I have to tell you I don't like okra?* Or, *Sell everything you own and give me all your money because I got caught embezzling from the dental group I belonged to and was stupid enough not to know that I should cover my tracks, no, no, I meant to say because I borrowed money from loan sharks.*

Yes, irrational. How could the woman who terror-
ized the terrorizers looking for me return to being a dutiful
housewife the instant my father or his evil sister demanded
anything?

Aunt Yasmine used to tell this story of how she and
my mother bonded when they were pregnant together, she
with her fourth child—her first daughter, Nahed—and my
mother with me. Their due dates were only days apart.
Yasmine once told the story at a large family gathering when
I was twelve. "As the more experienced mother," she said
loudly, holding her usual court, "I taught my sister-in-law
everything about her pregnancy." She then added while
pointedly looking at me, "But maybe she didn't follow every
instruction."

When I was a boy, I believed Aunt Yasmine could turn
a green fruit ripe just by looking at it. I hated that woman,
hated her, hated her, hated her, hated her, hated her, hated
her, hated her, hated her, hated her, hated her, hated her,
hated her, hated her, hated her.

And that awful woman returned to my life. I must admit
here that I wasn't proud of my behavior—actually, not my
behavior so much as my thinking. I'll come out and say it:
I wished her dead. Now, you might think that's not surprising knowing what she had done to me, but it was for me. I
know, you think I'm being childish because I always mention
I want to kill my mother, but that's metaphorical. I mean, I
want to kill my mother but I don't want to hurt her. That's
just silly. My mother is my muse of matricide. I didn't want
to kill or hurt my aunt. I just wanted her dead. Truly, I did.

She was ninety-two. She had Covid, her second bout in five months. There was no hospital bed for her because of both the pandemic and the explosion, no space. In other words, she was dying soon. I simply thought it wasn't soon enough and hoped she would hurry it up a bit. She would not accommodate. No one thought she would survive the first bout of Covid at her age, but she did. What I didn't know was that she'd also survived two bouts of breast cancer (double mastectomy), and she had been diagnosed with non–small cell lung cancer two years earlier (tumor, parts of a lung and lymph node removed). She ran most if not all the highest risks of dying from Covid, let alone getting it twice. She had the highest odds of not surviving for another day, yet she did. There wasn't much left of her, she weighed so little, she should die for the good of all of us. Her daughter had to be sequestered in the same room (hadn't gotten ill yet), only leaving momentarily to use the bathroom (bedpans for auntie). I worried for my mother. I couldn't believe she would let Covid into our home. I worried for me. I wished Auntie Yasmine dead. I guess she was waiting for the birth of a suckling baby with a 666 brand to relieve her.

Of course, I was unable to go back to sleep the night the evil one crashed into my world. I lay in bed tossing and cursing my aunt, God, Satan, the deities, and my mother most of all. I swore I would throw all of them out of my apartment in the morning, starting with my mother. I got out of bed at six thirty red-eyed and exhausted. Everyone else was asleep. I heard my mother snoring, the deep sleep of the blithe. The little room's door was closed as well.

I brewed tea and went out to the balcony. The dust that covered the city made it seem like I was the first to wake after a national bacchanalia. This would not do. I brought out the broom and dustpan and began sweeping the balcony. I considered using the vacuum in the living room but didn't want to wake anyone. I swept and mopped the living room, the tiny foyer. I brought out the feather duster and realized it wouldn't be enough. I wiped every surface with a wet rag. Went back outside and cleaned the balcony's railing, I even ran the rag over the laundry lines — somewhat of a useless gesture, but I was on a roll. It was eight fifteen by the time I was done, and still no one was up. Good thing, I thought. I was feeling better but I wasn't yet ready to face people or my mother.

I carried the heavy broom, the small dustpan, and two plastic bags down the stairs and onto the street. The city, the government, no one would clean up if I didn't. Lina M., from the building across from ours, must have had the same thought. She was sweeping the entrance. I began with the pavement in front of my building, sweeping up dust and muck and shattered glass. By the time I reached the pavement of the building next door, closer to Lina M., I had half a bag full. Thirty minutes later, I began to sweep the street. Odette Y., my neighbor on the fifth floor, suddenly appeared at the other end of the street as if by magic, with her own broom and her plastic bags, though no dustpan. She yelled across the street, asking if we were all right, asking about my mother. She then went quiet, concentrating on cleaning. Within minutes, more of my neighbors showed up with brooms, and lots and lots of garbage bags. The butcher Abou Sami had a huge dustpan, thankfully. The grocer; the three concierges; my neighbors from the second floor, the husband, the wife, and their two daughters; the neighbors from across the street. We all swept. No one talked much, or even said hello—a silent, synchronized cleaning. Odette Y., on her knees, scoured the tiles with a steel-wool scrubber and an oven cleaner of all things. We would walk on sparkling ground.

The entire group turned the corner, working on another street. There were now more people than would be needed to clean our neighborhood. Children running, weaving around and between us, parents cautioning them to avoid shards of glass, and for some reason, one neighbor decided to sing a patriotic song. I walked away, back toward my building, before anybody thought it would be a good idea to join her.

A truck was parked in front of the building—well, next to the cars already parked, leaving barely enough space for another car to squeeze through. A short, stubby man exited the truck, a cigarette drooping precariously from his lips. He lifted his pants up at the waist. Odette Y. noticed the truck logo, a glass-door-and-window repair, and told the guy she needed him to fix the five windows in her apartment that were blown out. Could he come up to her apartment? She could pay him right away.

"You couldn't afford my windows," he said. "Maybe in a month or two."

I watched Odette Y. recoil, which surprised me. I would have thought she'd expect such a response. So many people in the city were going to need new windows. He was going to charge a fortune. Yay, capitalism. I watched her look disgusted as the guy spit his cigarette onto her clean tiles and didn't even bother to stamp it out. He picked up a paper-wrapped rectangle of glass from the back of his truck and walked right past her. I knew where he was going.

"The man is here to fix our window," I told Odette Y. "Talk to my mother. She'll get him to fix yours for the normal price, I'm sure."

"Your mother can do that?"

I looked across the street at the parked but idling black Range Rover, a Lebanese criminal's favorite car, tinted windows, of course. I always thought of these cars as youngsters that would one day grow up to be hearses.

"Oh," Odette Y. said. "Of course she can." She turned around, began walking to the building. "Are you coming?"

No, I didn't want to see Madame Taweel, my mother, or either of our interlopers. I still wasn't ready. I walked away, walked toward the site of the explosion. I shouldn't have. I don't mind walking in August, but this month was warmer than usual, loaded white-hot air in the middle of the day. I dripped sweat. I wished I could wear shorts and T-shirts, but the possibility that I could run into one of my students while wearing them was unacceptable.

Beirutis were not shy when it came to staring at you. In horror, in shock, in mockery, a resident of the city would have no compunction about ogling. I must have been quite a sight, since every stranger I passed spent an inordinate amount of time looking and judging, but then again, it wasn't every day someone my age with my lighter coloring walked through the city with a huge broom and tiny dustpan. I had been taking walks forever and was used to being ogled.

❋   ❋   ❋

237

And sometimes, a walk allowed the memory of another to bubble up. On the same street, going in the opposite direction, toward home from school, almost eighteen, final year before graduation, delightful fall sunshine, quiet day, no shootings or explosions, snipers having a day off or something, I saw a red Datsun idling in the middle of the street, with three of my classmates, two boys and a girl, leaning on the car, talking to the driver. It was said during the war that driving a red car was the worst idea because snipers loved to shoot at them most. Apparently, the driver had no such concerns. The girl noticed me and giggled, a common reaction. Snickering and mockery walked hand in hand beside me in high school. I didn't mind. It was a relief that my inordinately stupid classmates shunned me. The boys looked up as well. All three chatted among themselves, shaking heads, gesturing, one boy more animated, the girl covering her mouth, in surprise or delight, I couldn't tell since I was yet to get close to them. I reached the car, passenger side, expecting one of them to hurl a hackneyed insult they'd been stockpiling for the last couple of years, softly though, barely loud enough for their friends to hear, maybe me as well, but not loud enough to be heard by strangers, for that would be classless.

But the boy, the one who'd been animated, said hello. First time ever. What was his name? Kamal, Kameel, Kamel, something like that. It was the first time he, or anyone in his clique, interacted with me, be it in or out of class. I nodded and kept on walking. He ran to catch up, the other two remained by the car.

"You're Raja, right?" KKK said, matching my stride. I decided that must have been a rhetorical question. It might have been answerable had we not been in the same class

238

for the last two years, or maybe if the number of students in our class hadn't shrunk because so many had left the country since the war started. We were in the same class because two were combined and still we were smaller. But then he said the strangest thing, which made me stop and acknowledge him. "Please," he said.

Need I remind you that Raja the Gullible was a sucker for a man asking for help?

He noticed I'd received the highest grade on our first philosophy paper. He mentioned that as if it were some revelation, as if I hadn't been the top student since that sordid summer. He, on the other hand, had received the lowest. It wasn't his fault, since he was good in every other subject. Something about philosophy was not making sense, probably because he couldn't figure out what it had to do with his life anyway. Our next paper was due in three days. Would I let him read mine before I submitted it? Basically, he wanted to cheat off me. I began to walk away.

Let me say here that I loathed KKK, hated every studied thing about him. The haircut, long of course, as was the fashion, shaped to look as if he jumped out of bed that morning and it simply fell that way; the three or four gold chains around his neck, minimum eighteen carats, and none more than a few millimeters thick or they'd cross into feminine; the stupid shirts with the tiny crocodile gnawing on the left nipple; the dockside shoes as if he'd spent all his time on a yacht. And I hated him because he probably had, even during a civil war. I hated him because he, like the rest of my class, considered me a leper, banishing me to a colony of my own, an island, never willing to row over until he thought he could use me to improve his grades.

239

But he followed me, trying to get me to slow down. "I'm asking for your help," he said. "If I fail the class, I won't graduate, and my father would kill me."

I still wouldn't stop. We could no longer see his other friends. That was when he apologized, and that surprised me enough for me to stop and look at him.

"I'm sorry," he said. "I know I haven't talked to you before and I should have. Maybe I should have said hello or good morning every now and then. But can you turn the other cheek?"

And I said my first words to him. "No, but I can turn my ass to you," and I walked away once again.

But he wouldn't take a hint, or maybe, as I would discover later, he was relentless as most men when he didn't receive what he thought he was owed. He made the mistake of grabbing my arm, and I snapped, "Don't you ever touch me."

"I'm sorry," he said. "I was trying to slow you down. I want to talk. I'm desperate. I'm asking for your help, and you keep walking away."

"You're not asking for my help. You're asking to cheat."

"Well, don't give me your paper if you think I'll cheat off it. I'll take whatever help you can offer."

"You would?"

"Yes, anything. I'm not good at this stuff. You are. We all heard what the professor said about you. Help me. I'll pay you."

"You will?"

"You can be my tutor."

"You're Kamel, right?"

"Kamal."

And that was how it began. I was hesitant that first time, since I had never tutored before. I wanted his money but I also wanted to make sure that he got his money's worth. We agreed I would tutor him for seven dollars an hour, and he would pay me if he received a grade of ten or above on a paper. He'd have to pay for every paper, since the lowest grade he would go on to receive was a twelve. I tutored him for the rest of the year.

My parents were shocked the first time I brought him home — my mother ecstatic, my father his usual asshole self. My academically challenged brother had already left for Baghdad. My father insisted we couldn't use the dining room or the living room to study because that would impinge on his space. He made sure to tell us that he felt leery about my taking Kamal into my room — the room I shared with my mother — if the door was shut. But we couldn't leave the door open because the monster of all monsters, Mr. Cat, might escape into *his* space. My father's solution was to use a doorstop to keep the door ajar, enough for him to be able to peek inside but not enough for Mr. Cat to wiggle through. A teeny crack that he could peep through. As if I were such a pervert that I would fuck a guy while my parents were in the apartment, as if I would fuck a guy in the room I shared with my mother. Yuck.

I began to change my opinion of Kamal because of two things: He said something like "And I thought my dad was a son of a bitch," and as soon as he sat on my bed, Mr. Cat jumped on his lap and settled. We did not become friends. And when more of my classmates asked to be tutored, I did not make friends with any of them either. At first, mostly because I didn't trust them, but after that because I was charging them. I wanted our relationships to remain professional.

I started having an income, not steady, since many tutoring sessions were interrupted when fighting would restart. It turned out I had a certain gift for teaching. Who knew? When I entered university the following year, my school referred nineteen students to me, twenty-two the year after. I was able to afford, if barely, moving out on my own after college. In 1985, when the school had a sudden opening because the philosophy professor had finally had enough, packing her bags and emigrating to Canada, I was the only person called. Job offered and job accepted.

I should say that I ended up using my room to tutor only a few times. By the time I was tutoring a bigger group of students, I ended up going to one of their homes. And yes, I admit to having had sex with Kamal that first year. It was a mistake, even though it happened toward the end of the year. What can I say, at that age, my libido vampired me. He fucked me in his car, though, obviously not in my room.

I had never been in a nuclear explosion. The destruction of the neighborhood next to the port, the one not protected from the blast by the concrete grain silos, might not have been as terrible as the flattening of Hiroshima, which I'd seen in photos, but then I hadn't stood in the midst of the Japanese city the day after the bomb was dropped. I had stupidly thought I would come down and help clean up whatever I could, but I could barely move a muscle. Like a sudden rainstorm appearing out of nowhere, veils of sorrow overwhelmed my heart. I had lived through a civil war, I had crossed the infamous green line of Beirut several times, but nothing—nothing had prepared me for what I saw. As if the war years, the numerous Israeli bombings, the Syrian destruction, the car bombs, were lease installments to the lords of grief, but now the balloon payment was due. My legs trembled, I felt dizzy. I ended up sitting on the hood of a crushed silver Mercedes of all things, as if it were a Hadean throne, my brush broom a scepter.

I was twenty years old in 1980 when the Panamanian boxer cried *no más* and the fans and media were so offended at his quitting the fight. I knew nothing about boxing, then or now, but I remembered thinking at the time that if someone was raining blows on me, I too would want the world to stop, to stop rotating and give me some time to catch my breath. Forty years later, on the hood of a Mercedes weighed down by a chunk of concrete on its roof, I was whispering no más, no más, no más.

The sullen buildings of the neighborhood, forcibly divested of glass and slabs and facades, felt as if they were taking their last breaths, as if they were trees after a forest fire had passed through. The blast had happened the day before, yet dust danced everywhere, refusing to settle. The structures continued to crumble. An aluminum frame fell from some floor up above, after which a half-burnt curtain floated down, landing not more than two meters away from my throne. Shards and scraps and blood covered everything. My gaze relinquished one atrocity for another, one horror for another. And people—people like me who came to see, standing in groups or not, together yet all alone. We, the shocked, the horrified, too stunned to do anything but gawk.

Ours is a tale of unremitting death, violence, and destruction, narrated with apathy.

I was in my city yet I wasn't. When I ascended from the garage apartment that summer in 1975, the city felt strange. What was familiar became alien, and now the alien had become oh so familiar.

I shut my eyes. No más. I took a slow, unfaltering breath, but how much grief could one inhale? My heart split like a melon. And I began to tear up, slowly and gently at first, and then I wept. I couldn't reopen my eyes. I no longer wanted to see what was around me, and I felt embarrassed, I didn't wish to know who was seeing me crying, and I couldn't stop. The humiliation of weeping in public was bad enough, but more, much more, I was overwhelmed with the ignominy of living Lebanese. I wanted to move, to get away, to stand up at least, to stand up and walk away from the flattened Mercedes, but I only cried harder. And then the worst thing: I felt a hand on my shoulder, a light but firm touch. I was forced to open my eyes. Of course it would be one of my students, Randa, the impressive Randa, whom I had not seen since she graduated more than thirty years ago, the attorney who became my mother's friend during the demonstrations, possibly the last person I would want to see me in this state. I tried—I desperately tried to control myself, but she was so beautiful and her new blue Adidas sneakers were covered in newer dust and everything was so wrong and if I had thought my predicament couldn't get worse I was wrong because she leaned over and hugged me and wouldn't let go and I was Alice-lost in grief. I was lost, and I lost the battle of maintaining any dignity. How could one preserve grace in this age of relentless humiliation? I strayed within my feelings for what seemed like an eternity. She shouldn't be so close to me, since neither of us had our masks on our faces. I was crumbling, like my city, nothing left. I hated that one of my brats was comforting me, even if she was an older, mature brat, but she wouldn't let go until I calmed. "Breathe," she kept whispering, "breathe," until I did. She pulled back and stared at my face. I must have looked quite the sight. I inhaled, exhaled, realized that I could now speak, and I began to apologize. "Don't," she interrupted. "Don't even think about it." Wait, I shouldn't do what? Not think about what? I tried to ask, but she shushed me.

Me? She shushed me? My brat shushed me.

"I wouldn't advise saying anything when she's in this mood." A tall, gray-haired man towered over the two of us. He was weeping and smiling at the same time. He looked familiar, but I couldn't place him. "Trust me, I know. Let her do what she needs to do and only talk when she gives you permission."

"That's my husband," Randa said. She poured water from her stainless steel bottle onto her handkerchief. I realized her husband was also a well-known human rights attorney, but I had no idea they were married. I couldn't tell him I recognized him, because Randa covered my face with the wet handkerchief, wiping and cleaning.

"It's a pleasure to finally meet you after all these years," her husband said. "She talks about you . . ."

"Now, you shut up," Randa said. She removed a brush from her handbag and began to comb my hair. "Oh, this is hopeless," she said, giving up. She smoothed a couple of strands away from my eyes. She held my chin with her thumb and forefinger, moved my face to the right, to the left, and nodded to herself. "Thank you for letting me do this," she said, as if she had given me a choice. "Shh, don't say it. Now listen, I called your mother this morning to check on her, and she invited us to dinner, something about finding the greatest cook ever. We can't do it now because of the situation, but sometime soon, when the pandemic is over and things settle down and if we still have a country, we're coming over for dinner, and you're going to be there. I will make sure to tell your mother to not listen to any of your excuses."

"Once again," her husband said. "I suggest you do what she asks."

"Don't tell my mother," I said. "I mean, you can tell her we met, but please don't tell her about the state I was in when you found me."

"Oh, Virgin, Mother of God," she said. "Zalfa is right. You must remove that stick out of your butt. She's your mother. She knows every state you've ever been in."

Early morning on the balcony, August 6, 2020. Nahed and her mother had invaded my home and I had not seen them since. I stayed away all day, and they stayed in the room all evening. My mother explained that Nahed was being extra cautious even though she and Aunt Yasmine had tested negative yesterday. I explained to my mother that extra cautious would be staying in a hotel, anywhere but here. As usual, she called me stupid, but she didn't yell because she didn't want to disturb our new guests. I'd had a rough night because I had so many thoughts and feelings tumbling in my head, but she didn't. She woke up this morning after I did, threw out the coffee I'd made for her, and brewed a new kettle. She knocked on the little room's door. I heard her earnestly whispering something before she appeared on the balcony, carrying our silver tray with two cups of Turkish coffee. I couldn't gauge her mood.

"Your aunt must be feeling better," my mother said. "She asked for a cup of coffee, which made Nahed happy."

"Let me buy a cake to celebrate."

"It's too early in the morning for your bad attitude," my mother said. "We have a lot to deal with right now. Let's have our peace agreement. Four hours?"

"Do I have to be nice?"

"Yes, of course," she said. "That's the whole point. We have to be nice and we can't fight. Sign it."

We raised our hands, pretended to hold a pen, and signed the air. She always insisted on the gesture. She believed oral agreements to be worthless and air-signed ones binding, or at least that was what she said.

"Why didn't you tell me you went near the blast site yesterday?" she asked.

"What? Did Randa already talk to you?"

"Randa? I didn't know she saw you. I'll call her. It was a friend of Madame Taweel's eldest daughter who saw you. She told Madame Taweel's daughter, who told her mother, who told me. I can understand why you're feeling bad. It seems you were noticeable because you were clutching a long broom but you weren't sweeping. I too would have felt awful had I been there. Why didn't you ask me to come with you?"

"What's the point of both of us being miserable?"

"You would feel better because you would have had to make me feel better."

We were still out on the balcony an hour or so later. I wasn't paying attention to much, since I was engrossed in a Nishida book. My mother's face was attached to her cell phone. She asked if I wanted breakfast. She stood up but sat right back down. I turned and saw a woman in a face mask and pajamas, hair shorter and whiter than mine, walking into my mother's room.

"She probably wants to take a shower," my mother said.

"And that would stop you from making us breakfast."

"Oh, shut up."

"We're still under contract," I said. "Be nice."

"You're right," she said. "I'm sorry. I'm going to wait and see if she wants anything to eat."

We didn't have to wait long—a quick shower, a pair of wine-red cotton pants, a sweatshirt, sandals, wet hair, and she appeared at the balcony door. My mother stood up, not very subtly making her chair available to Nahed.

"Breakfast?" my mother asked.

"I can make it," Nahed replied.

Her voice was higher than I expected, which made me consider my biases. She looked like she could still punch my fluorescent lights out. In my prejudiced mind, her voice should match, should be deeper.

"Don't be silly," my mother said. "Just sit and I'll take care of everything. You and your cousin can get reacquainted after all these years. You have so much in common, after

248

all." She moved to the kitchen but quickly turned back and pointed at me. "You," she added. "Contract."

"What does that mean?" Nahed asked when my mother was out of earshot.

"We have a contract to be nice," I said.

"You need a contract for that?"

"Oh, yes," I said. "And it's valid for another" — I looked at the time on my phone — "hour and twenty-two minutes."

"So, I should be wary." She showed an ever-so-faint and beguiling smile.

She took off her sweatshirt. Her T-shirt lifted, revealing a glimpse of her tight abs, followed soon after by her muscled arms. With arms like that, I too would wear sleeveless shirts. It seemed that she wasn't wearing a bra. Not that she needed one. She looked amazing, as if she'd jumped out of one of those *Healthy Living* magazine ads.

"Exactly," I said.

I could only look at her askance, since I was pretending to contemplate the building across from the balcony. She wouldn't look at me either, probably contemplating the same building. I felt, more than I saw, that she was smiling more fully.

"Well, I should take advantage of this time while you're still under contract," she said. "I must apologize, both for my mother and myself, for imposing on you."

"There's no need," I said. "We do what we must."

"No need to apologize? Are you sure? I was right outside the door when you were yelling that my mother and I should stay in hell and not in your apartment."

"We need a soundproof door." I suddenly noticed that her jaw was incredibly square.

"I'm trying to say I'm sorry," she said. "I promise I'll do my best to find somewhere else to stay, but in the meantime, I don't want to impose further by making you pretend you're okay with all this. I don't want you to have to lie."

"I'm not lying," I said. "Not in this case. You don't have to apologize for staying here. I would do the same if I were you. My mother is the one who needs to apologize. Your brothers need to apologize. You and your mother have a lot to answer for, but not for coming here. I passed by your building yesterday. I don't know how you survived."

"Pure luck," she said. "I was giving my mother a bath. We'd have died instantly had we been in any other room in the apartment."

"I'm not pretending I'm okay with this. I'm not happy you're here. But you don't need to apologize for that. For everything else, yes, but not for that."

Her right hand left her lap and gripped the chair arm. I noticed her short, well-manicured nails, chartreuse, and I was envious. I'd always loved that color, considered it both beautiful and ugly, yet I'd never tried it as nail polish during my geisha days.

"Still as rude as ever, I see," she said.

"Hey, that's not fair. You told me to stop pretending, and when I do, you accuse me of being rude. I can't win with you people."

I could see her cheeks turn redder—no, darker, not redder. She had her mother's—and my father's—coloring, bronze skin that tanned perfectly, but its blushing wasn't easily discerned, unlike my mother's and mine. She looked more like my father than I did.

"You people?" she said. "I am not my family."

"I didn't mean it that way."

"You certainly did. Don't lie."

"Still as rude as ever," I said.

This was the moment my mother chose to check up on us, pretending to update us on the state of our breakfast. Her head appeared through the balcony door. "We're going to have a light breakfast," she said, "because Mounira is delivering a big lunch. Now, are you two behaving yourselves? Would you like me to referee? Maybe you should draw up a contract between the two of you."

Neither of us replied. She withdrew and we heard her chuckling as she did so. I returned to studying the building across the street.

"I expected a different apartment," Nahed said. "When you first moved, I was so envious. I desperately wanted to live on my own but couldn't afford to. I got married to move out of the house. I imagined you living in a fabulously decorated apartment, with gilded mirrors, sequins everywhere, furniture upholstered in ermine."

"Sorry to disappoint."

"I'm crushed," she said. "You have a wonderful home, tasteful and comfortable. I expected campy trinkets but got divine Japanese vases. And the bonsai, stunning. Shame on you. Meissen plates? Come on. The apartment's saving grace is your crazy dining table. How do you expect me to get to the kitchen? I'm not sure I can squeeze my big dyke butt through that space."

"Well," I said, looking at her eyes for the first time, "I seem to have a similar problem. My stupid mother keeps saying we should butter the wall."

And she started laughing, a big, loud belly guffaw. I joined her. She wouldn't stop. We infected the neighbors across the street, the entire family on their balcony began to laugh. My smiling mother appeared to inform us that breakfast was ready, but we weren't. It took us another minute or so to gather our wits.

Aunt Yasmine didn't leave the small room for another twenty-four hours. I had suitable warning. Nahed came out first with the bedpan and returned after washing it in my mother's bathroom. On her second appearance, my mother asked if she wanted coffee. Nahed said she would love two cups. My spine straightened by instinct. Sitting on one of the rattan chairs, I tried to calm my suddenly taut nerves. Nahed rolled out the wheelchair that was stored in my mother's room, leaving it outside the door. My mother asked if she could help. Nahed carried her mother out of the room effortlessly. She was mighty and her mother practically weightless.

"To the balcony," my mother said loudly, like a queen's herald directing the rest of the court to the table. "Let's all have some fresh air with our coffee."

The air, still traumatized by the blast, was nowhere near fresh. It would nibble at nostrils.

Nahed pushed the wheelchair out, followed by my mother with our coffee tray. Surprisingly, my mother seemed nervous, a little jittery. I couldn't figure out why exactly.

Aunt Yasmine ended up farthest from me, but my mother and Nahed made sure all the chairs formed a semicircle, made sure we were all sitting together, and in case I didn't get the hint, my mother said, "Turn your chair around and be with your family. Enough with staring at the beyond."

Once she had us all where she wanted and we all had our first sip, my mother began. "Yasmine, do you remember Raja, my youngest? He's so happy to have you staying with us."

Aunt Yasmine couldn't possibly still be smoking, especially not during her latest bout of Covid, yet she smelled of smoke and vinegar. Her dark eyes kept blinking in and out of attention. My seated mother had her hand and arm directed toward me as if she were an advertising model pointing out the properties of a product — but in this case an old, worn product that might still have some use. I thought for a moment that Aunt Yasmine was in some fugue state, not knowing where she was, but then she snapped, "Stop asking if I remember. I remember everything." She squinted, made a visor with her liver-spotted hand to block out a sun that had yet to reach our balcony, and then snarled, "I can't see anything anymore."

She no longer had all her teeth. The face was a maze of wrinkles that Theseus would have never been able to navigate. Her voice might have been a little weaker but sounded just as mean as I remembered it, just as nasty. Nahed reached over, took an embroidered case out of the pocket of her mother's house smock. Aunt Yasmine tried to pull away from Nahed, and her bones seemed to creak when she shifted her weight. Nahed handed her mother a pair of cat-eye glasses. I had never seen her in any other eyeglass design. As soon as she put them on, Aunt Yasmine seemed to transform, almost a full human once more, no longer as vulnerable. She glared at me and yelled, "Did you steal my money?"

I wasn't sure exactly why, but helplessness slapped me. I had no desire to interact with her this morning. My mother's left hand clutched my arm before I had a chance to stand up.

"No, no," Nahed said. "The government and the banks stole our money and theirs. Raja is your nephew, your brother's son. Do you remember him?"

"Of course I remember him," Aunt Yasmine said huffily, with quite a bit of disdain. She had no equal when it came to snapping at others. A cat that bristled and scratched you when she didn't wish to be petted, a dog that bit you when he was annoyed—that was Aunt Yasmine. "He's the one who stole his mother's money."

"No, no," Nahed said. "It wasn't Raja. But I told you this morning that we don't talk about the other one."

"So, this is the nice one, the one we like?"

"Yes," Nahed said. "That's Raja."

"The faggot," Aunt Yasmine said.

"Mother! How many times have I told you that you can't use that word?"

"Why not? You are one," she said to me, "aren't you? You take it up the ass, so you're a faggot, right?"

I had not spoken to that evil woman for almost forty years, and the first words I ended up saying to her since 1981 were "You're quite right."

My mother didn't know what to do with her hands, so she reached out for one of mine and squeezed. Nahed didn't know what to do with her head, so she clasped it in her bent arms. Aunt Yasmine beamed. Her teeth, those that were left, seemed small in her mouth, nicotine-yellowed and sinister. She looked pleased with herself. Nahed looked as if she wouldn't be averse to having the ground open up and swallow her whole. I had to smile.

"So, when is breakfast?" Aunt Yasmine asked.

"You just ate," Nahed said.

"I did?"

She began to cough, the phlegm in her lungs rattling as she shook.

I was certainly surprised that we got used to living together in the same apartment rather quickly, mostly that I did. None of us were young anymore. We should have had more trouble adapting to each other's irritating habits, to having less space. My mother allowed Nahed to share her closet, her bathroom, and sometimes her bed, which was obviously more comfortable than the sleeping bag in the tiny room. For the first few days, Nahed worked judiciously on being unobtrusive, and Aunt Yasmine, who wouldn't know how to be so if her life was on the line, was not much trouble because she was happiest sitting by herself on the balcony, no matter how warm the weather was, staring at the mountain peaks, surveying the neighbors and neighborhood birds. Her moments of lucidity were rare.

Aunt Yasmine lived in a different era. I would say she lived in her memories, but that wouldn't be true. Her past was her present. She asked about her sons all the time. If I sat down at the table for lunch, or came out of the kitchen, or if we were watching television, she'd ask me, "Where's Toufic?" or "Do you know where Kareem is?" I had to bite my tongue not to say that Kareem was in prison in Egypt and her other sons rarely asked after her. She didn't ask about her husband, but she did want to know where Nahed's was. And me? She insisted I was her favorite nephew, how she admired me, how courageous she thought I was. I was flummoxed. It wasn't true, I knew it wasn't. Confabulation was what it was. I wondered whether her lush life had caused Korsakoff's syndrome. She certainly had filled her brain with enough alcohol, as had her mother before her. She was proud of me, she said. I broke the rules. What she liked best about me was that I was family to the marrow, profoundly attached to the bloodline, and yet hated everything about it, loathed the relatives and wanted nothing to do with them. I had to let her be. She lived in a fantasy.

On the other hand, I couldn't let Nahed be. She tried to leave me alone at first, and I tried to reciprocate, but my mother and the fates had other ideas. Nahed tiptoed around me in the beginning, and it was glaringly obvious that tiptoeing was not her strong suit. But then on the third or fourth day she apologized that she couldn't contribute to the financial expenses of the household, since she wasn't working and her brothers weren't willing to help. She didn't need them to, she said. She'd been taking care of the two of them for years, but she couldn't return to work until the pandemic was over. Even though some clients still called, she couldn't risk infecting her mother. She had to tell them she wasn't ready yet.

Her clients?

She was a masseuse. She was surprised I didn't know. She was quite good, didn't need to brag or anything. Just a fact. Before Covid, she would be booked months in advance, even after the financial collapse. Would I like a massage? No happy ending for me, though.

She was shocked, if not horrified, when she found out I had never had a massage, never thought I needed one.

All the wasted time, the wasted years. A life without massage is an unlived life.

Her table was destroyed in the blast, along with most of her belongings, so I had to lie naked on my bed so my body could become ductile, for my experience of bliss. It took less than a minute for me to start moaning ecstatically. It took less than a minute for her to realize she no longer needed to watch her step around me, that she could stomp on me, and I'd allow it. I began to understand why so many believed in heaven. And we began to talk—well, she talked a lot more than I because my face was usually buried in the pillow. We talked about everything, not just catching up, but explaining ourselves, trying to understand ourselves. With every knot she worked on, she would release pain and endorphins, feelings and stories.

She remembered our first day in school. I held her hand so she wouldn't feel all alone even though I did. Not true. I didn't remember it that way. I remembered my brother having ringworm when he was eight, the lurid red circle on his butt, one on his arm. Her father scratched his balls a lot. She didn't understand why he had to do that so often. Elastic book bands. They held our schoolbooks, and girls held them to their chests whereas boys carried them on the side. I had to train myself to do what boys did. She loved her mother's pink angora sweater. She didn't want one, just loved how it looked on her mother. She was ten. I loved chewing on flavored toothpicks, mint or cinnamon, and had to stop because my mother warned me the gap between my teeth would expand. Her mother told her a lady never chewed gum. My brother told me that if I swallowed chewing gum, it would block my butthole and nothing would be able to come out and I would explode in a million pieces of shit. Why did I give my brother the nickname "Starfish" when I was twelve? I had read in a book that a starfish had no brain and no spine, so it seemed appropriate.

I remembered having to wear my brother's hand-me-downs and hating it. She remembered wearing her brothers' hand-me-downs and loving it. I remembered taffeta and how it crinkled. She remembered beanbag ashtrays that would stay level on any surface. We remembered round playing cards and round tables with green felt.

She accused me of stealing her Barbie dolls. I didn't. She gave me one and I didn't get to play with it. I didn't think she liked playing with dolls. She most certainly did, though not in the traditional way. She liked rubbing Barbie on her vagina.

"Do you remember Salma? She was a couple of years older than us, but for some reason didn't mind playing with me. Our favorite game was removing all the heads off the Barbies. I would hide one or two heads in her underpants, wait a few seconds, then put my hand in and pretend to search for them. We played that every chance we had, until one day her mother walked in on us and had a conniption. Salma was no longer allowed to talk to me, let alone have me over to play."

❉   ❉   ❉

We had to get together for our first school meeting: the faculty, the administrator, the director. We exchanged emails: Should we meet in person, online? This went on forever, back and forth and back again, the usual. Something that would take an hour for a regular committee to agree to would take five or six if a cohort of high school teachers had to decide. The director finally declared that it would be a hybrid. I decided to log on to the meeting, but my mother insisted I attend in person. I was by myself all the time, she said, and we didn't know when the pandemic would relent, so I should take this opportunity to be with my colleagues. I'd feel better. I had to make sure the meeting room was ventilated, everyone masked and seated apart.

She turned out to be right. Even the walk to school was salutary, lifted my spirits. The meeting was as boring as every other one had been. I realized I missed my colleagues, or to be more precise, I missed being constantly irritated with them. We had to plan a follow-up meeting because we couldn't come to a decision on whether to bring the brats back to school.

I returned home to a hushed apartment. I assumed my mother was with Madame Taweel, but where was Nahed? I poured myself some fresh juice before checking in on Aunt Yasmine. I opened the door quietly, peeked in, and found my mother sitting asleep on the bed holding Aunt Yasmine's hand. My mother's head rested in an illuminated halo coming from the only light in the room, her old reading lamp. Unshoed and unsocked, my mother wore her favorite blue dress, her back to the wall, her legs at an angle, her feet on the floor. Aunt Yasmine wore her ancient nightgown and a miserable rictus of a frown. My mother and her sister-in-law

259

looked dramatically incongruous, the former exhausted, as if drained after offering so much blood.

Brick by brick my wall crumbled. I meekly shut the door and withdrew. I took deep breaths, in and out, in and out, until I calmed my overwhelm. I was surprised that I could still surprise myself at my age. I was disappointed that I could still disappoint myself at my age. I wanted my mother to hold my hand and that was the last thing I wanted.

The first thing I did when I returned to the apartment that summer was crawl onto my bed, over the covers, wearing the white shirt and gray pants that my mother had brought to the hospital for me to change out of the infamous dress. I faced the wall, cradling a frightened Mr. Cat in my arms. There was not much I could add to the argument outside my bedroom door. My father and brother ganging up on my mother and screaming that they did not want Mr. Cat in the house. How would they feed an animal while a war raged outside our door? I had laid down my ultimatum: If I stayed, Mr. Cat stayed, and if he left then I would as well. What I didn't know at the time was that my mother had laid down her own ultimatum. There was absolutely no way Mr. Cat was going anywhere. If they gave her any more trouble, she would pack me and my cat and move in with her sister and the two men would have to wash their own underwear. That was the first time I recalled her ever disagreeing with my father. To keep the peace, she promised her dependents that she would be the one to make sure Mr. Cat was kept clean, fed, and confined to the bedroom. Oh, and my brother did not have to stay in the room with the beast, as he called him. She would move in with me, and my stupid brother would sleep with his even more stupid father.

She moved into my room—she and her clothes, her jewelry and trinkets, her favorite pillow, the family photos, the reading lamp she loved. Of course, she had to move out my stupid brother's stuff as well. She did all that in one afternoon, under the watchful eyes of Mr. Cat, who, from behind my prone body, kept peeking each time she moved.

She stole his affections that first evening. She fed him before going to bed, and the betrayer moved to her bed as soon as he finished scarfing his meal.

She always said she didn't sleep that night but watched me the whole time. I couldn't confirm that, but the first thing I saw when I lifted my lids in the morning was both my mother and Mr. Cat studying me as if I were some new species they'd just discovered. She tried to engage, but I couldn't. I didn't even reply to her good morning.

"You should say something," she said, but I didn't.

"You were talking in your sleep all night," she said. "Why stop now?"

But then she always knew how to get me to talk. She stood by my bed and woke me during the second night.

"You're shivering," she said. "You don't stop shivering. You don't have a fever and it's too hot, so why are you shivering?"

I didn't think I was. I ignored her, kept my back to her. She climbed onto the uncovered bed with me. Before I could do anything, she had her arms around me, pulling me and my back to her bosom.

"Get off me," I said, my first words.

"No," she said.

I tried to push her away, tried to get up. I struggled, but I couldn't budge her. She was strong. I was weak. My incarceration had enfeebled me. She held on all night. I was no Jacob. My mother matched her breathing to mine until we established harmony and she kissed the crown of my head.

And when she decided that I'd moped enough, that it was time to kick me out of bed, out of the room and into the world, she forced me to tell her everything that happened. And I mean everything. Who killed whom, who kidnapped me, the layout of the garage apartment and its location, the dance lessons, the drugs I used, the sex I engaged in. She didn't relent until I told all. I was so mortified I couldn't wait to run out of the room.

"When I was ten," Nahed said, while kneading my hamstrings, "we were having a picnic on the mountain. I found a tiny bird on the ground, probably a sparrow or something, obviously injured. I picked it up, and the poor thing couldn't move. It was trembling, so frightened it was. I wasn't sure it would ever fly again, but I thought I would take care of it. I could feel its palpitating heart. I showed the bird to my mother, telling her I was going to call it Raja because it reminded me of you. She wound her arm back to slap me but stopped midway. She told me I was too old to be slapped anymore and that I shouldn't name an animal after you. But you were a broken bird, so terrified most of the time."

I certainly was terrified as a child, like many gay boys of my generation. Somewhere around the age of five or six,

I instinctively understood that adults no longer found my effeminacy endearing. What was once cute abruptly and without warning became despicable. And I didn't know why and had to adjust my sails. I spent most of my childhood worried I might slip, that I might do something that would expose my disgusting wickedness.

"I couldn't understand you. You sat at your desk in class, so quiet, never volunteering anything even though we all knew you were the smartest boy by far. Did you have any friends? I found you frustrating. I tried so often to involve you in things I did, but you wouldn't budge. But then you'd do the nicest thing, like helping me with our French homework. Always a broken bird, but then something happened. We were teenagers, and while many kids were cocooning, reconfiguring themselves, you jumped out of your shell. It was as if all of a sudden you no longer cared. You started dressing distinctly, walking confidently. I remember a cool evening, seeing you leave school to walk home. You took off the uniform, had on a white shirt with sleeves rolled up to your elbows. And weird moccasins with tassels. You looked so dramatic. I thought you'd grow up to become a movie star or something. That walk, light and sassy with a slight bounce. Theatrical. Did you know my father and yours were conspiring to have us marry? They thought we'd make a great match. Not that I would have agreed to it, but still my father mentioned it more than once. And when I saw you walking that day, I thought I could marry a boy who could walk like that. But then you disappeared that summer and returned as the biggest tight-ass in the universe. You looked so different when you showed up to collect the Japanese books, so proper, no flair at all."

What would you do if you found yourself back in a world you no longer trusted and no longer fit into, and where you no longer wished to speak to anyone? How would you deal with living in a city where your countrymen were trying to kill each other? What would you do if you were fifteen or sixteen with no outlet for seething hormones? I mean, my mother was sleeping in the same room. I couldn't possibly masturbate there. We had one bathroom. We had to ration water. Long showers were out of the question. The only place where I felt comfortable masturbating was in one of the little-used school bathrooms during lunch hour, which was one of the reasons why, war or no war, I refused to miss school when it was open.

What would you do in such a world? I read Dostoyevsky, of course. I read all his novels, one after another, and then reread them. He made me feel supersmart. That was his great talent, making teenage boys feel righteous. At that age, and only at that age, I considered his philosophical questions to be deep and poignant, and the fact that I understood them meant I was superior to everyone. Please remember that my brother's greatest intellectual achievement during those years was turning up his shirt collar in the back. My father congratulated him for thinking of such a brilliant thing. So of course I felt superior, and that feeling was almost superior to jerking off.

I went on a mission. I was going to become the greatest man I could be and everyone else could go to hell. Now, finding books in Beirut during the civil war was no easy thing, and finding Japanese books impossible. And I decided reading Dostoyevsky in Japanese was what I needed to do to become the greatest man I could be. Forget that my

Japanese at the time was barely at kindergarten level, I needed the Japanese Dostoyevsky books.

Mrs. Murata had returned to her country. I had no one. I tried the Japanese embassy, but the guard there thought I was insane and wouldn't let me in. I begged him to find Mrs. Murata's address in Japan. He asked someone who asked someone. I wrote to Mrs. Murata, pleaded with her to send me the books. I promised I would pay her back with interest when I turned eighteen. But I didn't send the letter because it occurred to me that we didn't have a functioning postal service and I wouldn't be able to receive the books. My depression returned, dramatically, of course. I didn't come out for dinner. I wouldn't speak to my mother. And of course she forced me to reveal what was troubling me. I shouldn't worry, she said. I could give Mrs. Murata the army address of her brother-in-law, Aunt Yasmine's husband. The books would be certain to arrive there. No postal worker, or anyone else for that matter, would dare steal from an officer.

It worked. I received a wonderfully encouraging letter from Mrs. Murata as well as all thirteen novels, the novellas, and the short stories in Japanese. She not only refused payment but would continue to send me books on a regular basis for the rest of her life. Obviously, my mother insisted I send her thank-you notes as well as little gifts whenever I could.

Remarkable generosity, and a timely present. The big problem was that my mother insisted I had to go with her to pick up the package.

"I wish you could have seen my mother's face when my father brought the Japanese package home," Nahed said. "We were expecting it, but still, having this thing from

all the way at the end of the world was terrifically excit-
ing. There was fighting outside, and we were all claustro-
phobically cooped up. My brothers were still at home. My
father brought this box, carrying it as if it were some fragile
treasure. The box was classy and colorful, you see. I'm not
sure you remember it as well as I do. You were probably
interested in the content, but the box was the mystery for
us. Even the label was beautiful, the script so precise. It was
addressed to you, of course, and because of that, my mother
had to temper her curiosity for a whole thirty minutes or so.
She then rushed to the kitchen, returning with a chef's knife,
and we all watched her surgically cut into the tape. I guess
we were expecting to find some splendid art or maybe something valuable, so we were disappointed to find out that the
only thing the box contained was books in a language none
of us would have any idea how to decipher. I don't think I
was as disappointed as my brothers or my mother, but I was
shattered seeing you when you arrived with your mother to
pick them up. I felt you had shut up shop. You were dressed
like every good boy in town, the blue button-down shirt, the
pants perfectly pleated. Wingtips, I think you wore. It was
almost as if the colorful box was meant for someone else. I
didn't think you'd become a movie star anymore. I thought
maybe a lawyer or an accountant. I was so sad."

They upended my quiet life. You would think that having
a ninetysomething-year-old woman in the house would not
add noise, but you'd be wrong, of course. Aunt Yasmine
might not have said much, spending almost all her time in
torpid contemplation, gazing into oblivion, her aged hands

constantly worrying her spindly fingers or tugging at the leather strap of the broken watch she refused to take off, but life buzzed around her. My mother spoke loudly to her all the time. As did Nahed. Truly, it was more like yelling because she was so hard of hearing, as was my mother, who at least wore her hearing aid every now and then. With Aunt Yasmine almost immobile, my mother left the apartment less often, which meant Madame Taweel spent almost all her time here and conducted most of her business in our living room. Running her business consisted of yelling at her thugs. Incessant noise day and night. I even lost full access to my own bathroom. With so many people in the house, if someone was in my mother's bathroom, another would use mine, without even asking me first.

At some point at the end of the boisterous day, almost every evening after dinner, Nahed would notice the encroaching panic in my eyes, would drag me into my room, shut the door, and force me to breathe before massaging me into rapture.

School, my salvation, would start in a few weeks, but how would I deal with the insanity until then? Weirdly, it turned out that Aunt Yasmine would save me. When she sat on the balcony, everyone would go back and forth checking on her. My mother, Madame Taweel, and my cousin preferred to stay in the air-conditioned living room. I took my book and joined my aunt. I became her official caretaker during those morning hours. Peace and quiet. My mother and Nahed checked on her less often. Not that I had a lot to do. We didn't interact much. Every so often Auntie Yasmine's fugue would glitch and she'd look at me, puzzled. Every now and then, maybe every hour or so, she would utter something baffling. I wasn't sure she knew who I was most of the time. She would mention how hot it was, then tell me how much cooler it was on her wedding day. She'd disappear after that. She almost always brought up that her savings had been stolen, asking if I knew how she could get her money back. And even though she got so used to my being around her, she remained mostly in her own universe.

And it turned quieter still when my mother and her entourage began to go out more often, leaving me with Aunt Yasmine. Not too often, but enough for the house and my nerves to calm.

I'd have glimpses of the Aunt Yasmine I used to know, the not-so-quiet Aunt Yasmine. One morning, the two of us were sitting outside, each nestled in our world, I in a book, she in a fantasy. A loud horn interrupted our dreamings, then again, and again. Someone had parked a car in the middle of our street, another car kept honking for the first to move. She didn't get up from her wheelchair, didn't even look down. She yelled at the world, "Stop all that noise." The honking caused a crack through which the woman with the intimidating sneer peeked. Toward me, she snapped, "What's the matter with you? Stand up and use your big-boy voice and order them to stop. Are you still afraid? Stand up, I said."

I believe Aunt Yasmine had spectral visitations from departed family and friends. I noticed her mouthing words a couple of weeks after we began keeping company. I wasn't sure whether that was something new or if she'd been doing it for a while. I hadn't been paying attention. One time I was trying to figure out if she wanted something when she blurted out that her mother kept asking her why her grandsons—Aunt Yasmine's sons—turned out to be ungrateful jerks. From that point on, I was able to decipher snippets of the conversations she was having with her dead relatives. I understood that she spent most of the time justifying her life. Her past flinging accusations, her present attempting to explain.

I slowly snuck into the small room feeling like an intruder, a burglar, a thief searching for souls to purloin. Aunt Yasmine slept deeply and vehemently, her eyebrows furrowed as if she was squabbling with Hypnos, or maybe Thanatos. Her slack arms clasped the pillow as if comforting an infant. She wasn't snoring exactly, yet she emitted a mild gurgling sound with each inhale, like an air pump inside an aquarium. When my mother slept, she looked as if she was soaking in a healing bath. None of that for Aunt Yasmine. Her sleep seemed like a sinking, like a brush with annihilation. I walked the narrow space toward her, sliding along the wall so as not to wake her accidentally. I had promised I would check in on her while both my mother and Nahed were out. I squatted down, my butt on my heels, my palm on her forehead. She had no fever. And she surprised me by sighing contentedly. I didn't remove my hand, left my touch for a few seconds more before standing up and leaving the constricting room.

VI
(2021)
Virginia

You thought I'd forgotten, didn't you? I had to tell you what happened before I received the email for you to understand what happened after that curse.

I read the email from the American Excellence Foundation three times in a row to make sure I didn't miss anything, to make sure I didn't have to produce any work for my three-month stay. They would put me up and feed me, allegedly farm-to-table and organic, and they would pay me nine thousand dollars. How could I possibly say no? Still, that was Friday evening. I could consider the pros and cons over the weekend before replying on Monday. Though really, what cons? In July 2021, my country was spiraling down a shithole sinkhole. My apartment was stuffed with people. Granted, after a year of living with Aunt Yasmine and Nahed, I had grown inured to all the inconveniences, but that was akin to getting used to a splinter under the skin of your finger. It still wasn't comfortable. A three-month break would be most welcome. Being paid a lot of money to be by myself was my idea of a godly blessing. I could take long, solitary hikes in nature. I could sleep whenever I wanted, wake up whenever I wanted. I would be fed fresh food. I would be away from my mother and her coterie.

My mother and Madame Taweel were all for my going, suggesting that getting away from the misery that was Beirut would be good for me. And if three months proved to be too much time, Madame Taweel said, if I became bored or I missed my mother terribly and realized I couldn't live without her, then Madame Taweel would arrange my return. It seemed her organization (whatever that meant) had branches (whatever that meant) everywhere, including the United States. She even had one man working for her who lived in Virginia, no less. I did not wish to know anything about her organization, so I tried to change the subject.

Nahed was more equivocal. She thought it was a great deal, maybe a too-good-to-be-true deal. "I mean, why you?" she asked. "Your book came out long ago, so it's not as if you're on everyone's mind. Why now? You haven't been invited anywhere in years, and then, all of a sudden, this organization decides you're the one to whom they should offer this residency?"

She wanted to make sure there wasn't anything fishy. So, she researched the organization, this American Excellence Foundation. This was what she discovered: The founders of the organization were a married couple, wealthy obviously, unreasonably so, and somewhat famous. The now-deceased husband, Peter Rutledge, was an oil magnate of some sort, and the wife, Victoria, or Vicky as she liked to be called, was from an even wealthier family. Both were quite active in the social scene of Washington, D.C. Nahed found nothing untoward except for a rumor, which had circulated way back when, that the mature Peter and Vicky had taken in a young cowboy to satisfy their sexual needs, a holy trinity with the bronco rider as the son.

Nahed decided that at least the foundation was on the level. I decided they were wonderful, and that I, Raja the Worthy, deserved this generous gift.

And Nahed and I finally discovered why I was invited. It seems Vicky's mother, a well-known philanthropist and fashionista, was not born to wealth but married into it. She was born Hiyam Ayoub, daughter of Zeina and Akram Ayoub, immigrants from the old country. Of course, Vicky, a daughter of Lebanon, would pick me.

Of course, I was a fool—a stupid, stupid fool.

It took forever to pack my bags, what with my mother hovering and pestering. She insisted I take two large bags, one for me and an empty one to be filled with goodies I was to bring back: cat food and toys for Monet and Manet, a nice tracksuit for her, a good but inexpensive house cardigan, hair dyes, and medicines—all kinds of medicines that didn't need prescriptions: ibuprofen, antacids, Tamiflu, anti-diarrheal pills, you name it. The pharmacies of Lebanon were all out of drugs. My mother gave me a long, extensive shopping list even though a month earlier, the first week of June, one of Madame Taweel's minions had returned from the U.S. with a suitcase full of pills and another filled with our cats' favorite cans of wet food.

And everyone wanted to offer unsolicited advice. I should insist to be paid in cash. I couldn't possibly accept checks. Where would I deposit them, in those sinkholes of institutions that stole all our money? I should spend some money, but only on essentials, i.e., what was on my mother's list, so I could return with some of the aforementioned cash. Advice on what to pack because I'd be arriving in early September and returning in December. It seemed fall in Virginia was hotter than Beirut in summer and colder in winter. Did they have washing machines at this farm? They treated me as if I were a teenager on his first trip abroad, in spite of the fact that I'd traveled more than all of them combined. Granted, I hadn't left the country in years, but it wasn't as if any of them could remember what jet lag felt like. They wouldn't leave me alone.

Every time they talked about my going in the presence of Aunt Yasmine, she would ask if I was coming back for a visit. I shouldn't be like her sons who never visited. I was a good boy.

After reading a few online interviews with the Rutledge woman, Nahed decided she didn't like her. Apparently, after visiting India sometime in the late seventies, Vicky had a Paul-on-the-road-to-Damascus moment — revelation, fireworks, and all that. She returned home to Washington, D.C., with a sari, a jar of spicy lime pickles, and her personal guru. In one of the interviews, she said that she'd "embarked on this never-ending journey of enlightenment and self-love."

Nahed couldn't stand those interviews yet kept reading them. She was offended by the fact that Vicky Rutledge used the word *process* extensively, in almost every sentence both as a noun and as a verb. Nahed wanted to make sure I didn't talk much to this Vicky. If I had to have dinner with her, I should speak little and avoid divulging anything about myself. Be wary at dinners was Nahed's advice. She needn't have worried. I would end up not having a single meal at that ranch or horse farm or whatever the fuck they called it.

My contact at the foundation, a woman named Wendy, promised a business class roundtrip ticket, but it turned out not to be so. I wasn't paying much attention. I arrived at the airport at three a.m. on a Saturday to find out that only the middle leg of my trip, London to New York, was business class. The first and last legs were economy. Gullible me didn't mind. I didn't freak out or anything. Economy offered enough space for my short legs. The longest flight, London to NYC, was business class with lie-flat seats so I'd be able to sleep. Who could ask for anything more? Well, I could have asked for what I was promised, but it was too late for that. Stupid me was still excited, looking forward to an adventure. I even congratulated myself for becoming so blithe in my old age, better able to weather annoyances and incompetence.

The flight from Heathrow was delayed. When I arrived at JFK, I barely had enough time to transfer to the second airport, LaGuardia, to make my flight to Charlottesville. Even though I had my passport, my visa, and everything in order, the Homeland (didn't the Nazis have a patent on that term?) guy threw questions at me, spoke without moving a muscle that wasn't strictly necessary, and kept me waiting for an hour while he searched his databases to find out whether I was a terrorist. Of course, by the time I reached LaGuardia, I had missed my plane. I was tired, grumpy, and sweaty—no longer blithe. The airline put me up in a nearby motel. If they paid more than twenty dollars for the room, they were robbed. I would have to take the same flight leaving the following evening. I had twenty-four hours to kill. I thought I'd go into the city in the morning, spend some time at the Met or MoMA before flying out. That was when I discovered that my credit card was not working. I had given the bank cash to make sure I'd be able to use my card, and still they screwed me. I would have to wait for Monday before I could call them and handle it. I'd only brought just over a hundred dollars in cash, which should be enough for a few days. No going into the city for me. I ended up spending the day reading in my room and in an uncomfortable plastic seat at LaGuardia. What drove me crazy at the end was that the airline forced me to pay for my two suitcases. Apparently, you paid for each suitcase unless you were traveling business class or internationally. I kept trying to explain that my flight was both, that I'd arrived from London on a business class ticket, but the agent would have none of it. What she was looking at was a newly issued ticket. I could write to American Airlines, and they might reimburse me, but she couldn't allow me on the plane without payment. I paid her in cash, begrudgingly, of course, and with no little resentment. Oh, and the flight was two and a half hours late.

I arrived in Virginia with a kilnish disposition.

I was sure no one else was up at three in the morning, whereas I woke up bright-eyed and starving, a near-euphoric alertness. I had slept deeply if not long. The Stetsoned man who picked me up at the airport explained that the dwelling I was going to be staying at was called the cottage and not a house or guest house, and the property was called a horse farm and not a ranch. I was too exhausted to ask how one farmed horses. He dropped me off at the cottage, suggesting I rest first, and I could get the lay of the land—the horse farm—after breakfast. He had a weird beard, long and white, filled and braided with colorful beads that looked like a rainbow of lichen. And speaking of lichen, as I entered the cottage, I was entranced by an ancient white pine covered by the stuff a few steps from the door. A good omen, I thought at the time.

It was dark outside, not so much inside. Every room in the cottage had at least two night-lights. I explored this cottage, my Ithaca for the next three months. It looked better than it did in the online photos, less tacky than I thought it would be. Haute rustic was how I'd describe the décor, a wealthy person's idea of a lumberjack's cabin. Cool and cozy, sparsely and elegantly furnished. Light-hued wood was the predominant theme. Above the fireplace mantle hung a framed macramé flag of Virginia, and on the wall across, its U.S. counterpart. The one thing I was most grateful for in the cottage was the air-conditioning system—silent, efficient, unvarying temperatures.

The kitchen had a fancy espresso machine but no kettle. I turned on the burner, heated water in a two-quart saucepan. I'd brought a bag of loose-leaf sencha and my drinking cup, but not my teapot. I should have. I decided to drink my tea on the veranda, or the porch, as yesterday's colorful cowboy called it. I hesitated as soon as I opened the door. It might have been a pre-dawn dark, the temperature not yet broiling, but the air was leaden, the humidity ponderous. My lungs already felt as if they needed a rest from breathing. And quiet it was not. The piercing cicada chirping was almost insufferable. Still, the Adirondack called my name. *Come keep me company*, it said.

Even without light, I could see how beautiful the area was. The trees: so many varieties of pines, the birches, the red maples, and dozens I didn't recognize. My butt melted into the chair; my mind tried to slow down. Another American flag, not macramé, this one high on a pole in the middle of the lawn. Another bigger one hung on a longer pole in front of the main house. I'd always wondered about Americans and their obsessions with the flag. Were they afraid someone might forget what country they were in? I might one day walk from the main house to the cottage, no more than a minute at most, and have a dissociative fugue. *Where am I*, I'd say, and then look up and see the American flag. The one nearest me drooped about itself, immobile for the lack of a breeze and barely a fold because of the wetness.

I didn't hear any but felt a mosquito bite. Nothing could get me running away quicker than the presence of a single mosquito. I sprinted inside. I was not going back to that Adirondack until mosquito season was dead and buried.

I walked around the cottage again, making sure I had what I'd need. The bedroom was ideal. A king-sized bed just for me. The linen was top-notch, the pillows goose down, and the towels chinchilla-soft. Wonderful. Should I unpack or should I make myself another cup of tea to watch the sunrise? If these were the kind of decisions I was going to be making for the next three months, I was going to be very happy.

I didn't risk going outside to watch the spectacular sunrise. Through the window was good enough. Headlights interrupted the idyllic scene. A truck slowed not too far from my window. Four men with gardening implements jumped off its bed while it was still rolling away with the rest of the workers. All four dispersed in various directions. One short man, with a hoe and a spade on his shoulder, walked toward me. I waved hello when he noticed me behind the window, which seemed to surprise him. He smiled and shyly waved back. He looked young, probably the same age as one of my brats, and Latin American.

I spent the next half hour or so lying on the couch and reading Cyrulnik but couldn't concentrate because of my hunger. I sat up, noticed two monographs on the maplewood coffee table, one on the horse farm, the other of the foundation, both replete with photographs. I imagined the books were vanity projects. I perused the farm one, many photos of beautiful steeds, pretend stable boys and farmers. I almost dropped the book when I came across photographs of a fox hunt—dozens of photos of riders in full regalia, the four-buttoned red coats, the five-buttoned beige ones, the black high-crown caps, even a top hat or two, photos of dogs, English foxhounds, beagles, terriers. It was as if those were pictures from Imperial England. I studied the people. Here was a younger Vicky Rutledge, another one when she was older. Peter Rutledge made many an appearance. I counted two American presidents and three celebrity actors. Then, without warning, my heart dropped almost to my ankles, my blood stopped flowing, and my mind hit the panic button. There, in a picture dated 1982, standing between the Rutledges, smiling in a hunter's coat, stood a young Boodie.

Okay. So, I freaked out. I shouldn't have but I couldn't help it.

I didn't know what to do first. Should I pack my bags before figuring out where I was going? Yesterday's drive from the airport took about forty minutes. How far was I from this Charlottesville town? I couldn't call a cab. I had no credit card and forty-three dollars in cash. I was a walker. I could walk all the way to the town or the airport, whichever came first. I needed to settle my nerves. I took long breaths. I tried to convince myself that it was a coincidence. The photo was from 1982, after all. Maybe he was just invited here once. I was going to consider this rationally and calmly. I sat on the couch again and opened the monograph. Yes, that was Boodie all right. I turned a few pages. There he was again in 1989, and again in 1990. While I was living through a civil war, he was frolicking on a horse farm. There was a list of names at the end of the book—the names of the board members of this American Excellence Foundation. At the top of the list was A. "Buddy" Baroudy, president since 2004. He must have been the bronco.

Calm and rational? I needed to break something. I lifted a fruit plate that lay on the partition between the kitchen and dining room and threw it on the floor. The damn thing bounced. I hated everything. I went into the bedroom. I hadn't unpacked much. I still hadn't brushed my teeth.

I called my mother.

All I had to say was I saw a picture of him in a book about the history of the horse farm I was staying at, didn't even have to mention his name, and she went berserk. For the first time in a long time, probably since I was still a teenager, I welcomed her insanity, soaked in it. Chaos reigned on her side of the line, yelling and imprecations. She was going to fly a plane herself and come kill that son of a bitch. She was going to roast his testicles. She went on and on with her detailed plans for murder while I panic-packed. But then Madame Taweel came on the line. Was I sure he was there at the horse farm? I told her it was a setup. I'd been an imbecile. Did I know where I was? I had a general address, but the place was huge. I couldn't stay here, I told her. I was going to walk away. She suggested I stay. I couldn't do that.

"Talk to your mother for a minute," she said. "Let me deal with this."

My mother returned to the call, a bit more rational, if not completely so. "Tell me everything," she said. "Are you sure he's there?"

"He's the president of the board of the foundation. Of course he's here."

"Tell me about the photos," she said.

"He's in many, always with the husband and wife. He's dressed for a fox hunt in one, in front of a horse, and he's holding a fox horn."

"Fuck his mother. I'm going to shove that horn up . . ."

And Madame Taweel took over once more. "You must hang up now," she said in a tone that brooked no argument. "You're going to be getting a call from someone who'll take care of everything. You can trust him completely. He'll make sure you're back here in no time."

I received the call as soon as I hung up. A Lebanese man with the deepest voice introduced himself as Firas. He asked me about the farm and why I was there. He was so slow, an interminable pause between each question. He was less than two hours away, maybe ninety minutes, maybe even less. Could I wait in the cottage? Did I have to leave, could I not lock the door and wait till he got there? He was already in the car with his kids when Madame Taweel called him. How did he know where he was going? Google, of course, but could I share my location on WhatsApp? He would be able to pick me up wherever I was, but I should stay in the cottage until he showed up. He then proceeded to tell me I was famous in his household. Did I know why? I didn't, but I didn't ask how in the hell I would know. His wife was one of my students some twenty-five years earlier. Did I remember her? Yes, I did. I didn't tell him she wasn't the brightest, of course, but she was a hard worker and a diligent student. He wanted to thank me, he said, because he woke up every morning not believing his luck that he was

283

married to this extraordinary woman. I had a lot to do with who she was as a person. I didn't understand why he was telling me all that. He then began to tell me the stories his wife had told him about me, one by one. He prattled on for a half hour or more. He even made his son tell me what he heard about me. He had his son tell me that he was accepted to the school of foreign service at Georgetown University and how much he was looking forward to that.

Okay, so I was dense. I didn't consider that this Firas guy was intentionally slowing me down. Yes, I was stupid. I thought he was just being Lebanese. It was only when he started telling me he hoped his son would do good in this world that I figured out the game. And I hate to admit it worked. I was calmer, almost serene. Until I looked out the window and saw the lights on in the main house. I told Firas I had to leave and hung up.

I ran around the cottage making sure I had everything. I wore the same outfit I had on the day before. I probably looked like a vagabond on methamphetamine, but I didn't care. I thought of stealing one of the bath towels because they were so soft and that would be exacting some measure of revenge, but I couldn't do it. Years of teaching ethics. I carried my two bags and walked out never to return. I didn't even lock the door behind me. The trouble was that I had to roll the bags on a mixture of gravel and dirt until I reached the road to the main house. I couldn't stop, though. It would have been more comfortable if I did, if I repacked my two bags into one. But I wasn't going to stop. It took me twenty minutes to reach the stupid gate with the galloping horse in rusted metal. One car rushed past on the main road. I crossed the road and began to feel better. I didn't stop, needed to get away from him.

The sun, though not high, was broiling already. I felt as if it was counting every drop of my sweat. I had still not walked far enough from the infernal property when I began to encounter other houses. I passed one, then another, and at the third, a beautiful, small house that had seen better days; two aging women wearing matching T-shirts and shorts sat in its front yard on red plastic chairs, passing a cigarette back and forth. Next to them, a man on a horse—a grizzly old man in a white baseball cap atop a tall chestnut with black mane and white socks, bareback. He looked like a mythical figure, one of the four horsemen on his day off. I didn't understand why he was on the horse, since with one or two gallops, he'd go from one side of the enclosure to the next. Between the rider and me, a wooden fence that was probably older than the house, a small ditch, and the asphalt edge that seemed to have been nibbled at by rodents. Even without so much as a feathery breeze, the smell of stale smoke reached me. They asked if I was okay, if I needed help. I thanked them but declined the offer.

I walked for a few more minutes before deciding it behooved me to repack my two bags into one. I unzipped both bags. I had to decide which one to keep. The big duffel bag was cheap, but its wheels handled the rough terrain better. I chose it for its rolling prowess even though everything would have to be ironed when I got back home. But then I saw a shiny black truck turning onto the road out of the horse farm's gate.

"Shit," I said, loudly, to myself.

The coruscating truck stopped not two feet away. Because of the ditch, it blocked almost half the road. The Stetson guy, wearing nylon shorts instead of blue jeans this morning, walked the four or five steps to me. I'd always hated the slap-slap sound of flip-flops, and his sloppy steps that morning made me wish for a worldwide ban. I did not stop moving clothes from one suitcase to the other. He hesitated for a moment.

"Are you okay?" he said.

"Fuck off," I said.

"Excuse me?" he said.

A silver sports car approached from the south, slowing down as it passed us. The look on the two young men's faces, the driver and his passenger, suggested confusion. One assumed they had not encountered someone repacking his bags on this road before.

"What are you doing?" drawled Stetson.

I ignored him. He walked briefly behind the truck, which unsurprisingly had a gun rack on its rear window, with a rifle, of course. He used his cell phone before returning. I considered telling him to put on some long pants because his hairless legs were disturbingly ugly. The purplish-blue veins covering his ankles looked like stitching that kept the feet connected to his body. "All you had to do was ask and we would have driven you wherever you wanted," Stetson said. "Mrs. Rutledge wants to know why you're behaving like this."

"Mrs. Rutledge can lick my butt," I said, while still repacking.

Stetson went back and forth, behind his truck then back to watch me pack, but he no longer said anything. I zipped up the duffel bag, prepared myself to move on, when another car, a fancy, latest-model Mercedes, stopped in front of me at an angle, its trunk and three of its wheels on the asphalt, trapping me between the vehicles. From the passenger side, a thin, overstyled woman exited. My mother would have thought of Victoria Rutledge as a stupid fake-phony, since nothing about her seemed natural. And from the driver's side, Boodie.

I refused to look at him, refused to acknowledge his existence. I was peeved because he looked younger than I, but I wouldn't glance his way. No looking. I would not respond to anything he said. I would not respond. I had to keep calm for less than half an hour now until the rescue arrived. I should concentrate on the monotonous sound of cicadas.

I grabbed the duffel's handle, needing to go around the Mercedes.

As she walked to me, Vicky said, "My name is —"

"Fuck off," I said.

"I told you I will handle it," Boodie said in a strange American drawl particular to the Lebanese, which sounds as if the speaker had unhinged their lower jaw, like a snake that wished to swallow something big. I hated emigrants to the United States more than any other kind of Lebanese.

He approached cautiously. I picked up the now-empty suitcase to use as a weapon. I could cause damage with a good swing. Maybe he would bleed if the rolling wheels struck his temple.

"Can we talk?" he said in Lebanese. "Just you and me."

"Why the fuck would I want to do that?"

"I want to make things right between us."

"Great," I said. "Now get out of my way."

"Will you please talk to me? I want to apologize."

"He wants to make amends," Vicky Rutledge said, joining her hands before her breasts as if she was praying to some Christian saint, or all of them, or the Buddha, or Vishnu, or every damn deity in all the pantheons for all I cared.

I had to recoil. Up close, she looked inhuman. She'd had more cosmetic work done than a Lebanese pop singer.

"She understands Lebanese," Boodie said, "but doesn't speak it well."

"Why would I give a damn?" I said.

I started to move around him, but he blocked my path.

"Wait, just wait a second," he said. "Why won't you talk to me?"

"Because I don't want to."

I did notice the gray hair up close. Not on top, just on the sides, and the brushed gray ribs across the width of his head, as if he had given himself a wreath of ash. The fucker had had his hair dyed and styled.

"You need closure," he said. "I hurt you and I want to apologize."

"You have no idea what the fuck I need," I said. "I haven't thought of you in years. What does closure even mean?"

"You're still upset about what happened."

"Whether I'm upset or not doesn't concern you," I said. "Fuck off and leave me alone."

"You're yelling. You might not think so, but what we did then still makes you angry."

"I'm angry because you lied and brought me all the way across the world without ever considering what I want. I put my life on hold to come here. You're such a narcissistic son of a bitch. For the first time in more than thirty-five years, someone else is going to take care of my brats. My brats. I let them down because you want to make amends. Fuck you."

"Your brats? I don't understand."

"You never did, so get the hell out of my way."

He looked so dejected that for a microsecond I almost felt sorry for him. But then he said, "Look, I'm sorry we lied to you. It wasn't my idea. It was hers, but I went along with it. You didn't give me any other choice. I've tried contacting you so many times. You wouldn't let me."

"And you wouldn't take a hint."

He sighed. "You haven't changed."

"You wouldn't know if I have or haven't. You don't know anything about me."

"Now you listen," Vicky Rutledge said, as she maneuvered herself between us. "Buddy here is the most decent man I've ever met. As long as I've known him, I've watched him suffer because of what happened between the two of you. No, wait. Let me finish. He's done a lot of work on himself, but he can't evolve into his full being until he resolves the issue of you."

"The issue of me? Are you serious?"

"Yes, of course," she said. "He needs to make amends for his own well-being, and you need to forgive him for yours. Once you forgive him, your life will open like a flower."

I stared at her, then at Boodie, and I realized they believed this shit. And for some reason, I found that amusing. "That might be the stupidest thing anyone has ever said to me, and I teach teenagers."

Stetson scowled, shuffled closer to the truck's door. I felt as if I had somehow landed in a soap opera about a clown alley. I desperately needed to move on. Another car passed by, had to slow down and maneuver around the Mercedes. I tried once more to drag my duffel around chubby Boodie and scrawny Vicky Rutledge.

"Please," Boodie said. "Please don't go."

"Get out of my way."

"But where are you going? You can't walk along this road."

"Watch me."

Before I had a chance to move, a black Range Rover with dark windows stopped on the other side of the road. No cars could now pass, the entire road blocked. The rear window came down, revealing a teenage girl in pigtails recording a video of us on her cell phone. We were a spectacle. But then out of the giant vehicle emerged a small man, probably shorter than me, in a black suit and tie. His eyes scoured the scene. Firas must have been in his late forties, yet he looked like a boy wearing his father's clothes. On the phone, he sounded larger. He approached, ignored everybody, and the first words out of his mouth were in Lebanese. "Are these your bags?"

"Just you wait a second," Vicky Rutledge said huffily. "Who are you and what are you doing here?"

He ignored her. He asked me again if those were the suitcases I was bringing with me. I told him they were, and that one was empty. He gave me an odd look. He grabbed the duffel's handle, picking up the second.

"You can't take him," Vicky Rutledge yelled. "Who do you think you are, coming here as if you owned this land? He's supposed to stay with us for three months."

Firas nodded his head toward the Range Rover. "Yalla," he said, "into the car."

I had barely gone a step before Boodie said, "Don't go. I love you."

I halted, turned around. "Did you really just say that?"

"I've always loved you," he said, "and always will."

"And that matters to me because?" I realized I was about to lose it just as I did. My veins swelled and distended.

"I stopped giving a damn about you on the day you left. You think I'm going to care now, forty-six years later? Get over yourself." I was screaming, gesticulating like a maenad, performing a bizarre play in the middle of a long road leading nowhere, in Virginia of all places. "What has you loving me got to do with me?"

And that was when the situation degenerated.

An apoplectic Vicky Rutledge began yelling that I was heartless, repeating it over and over. Firas demanded I get in the car. Boodie looked crestfallen, commenced chewing his lower lip. Stetson stood still next to his truck with his head tilted to one side, looking as stupid as ever. And the teenage girl recording everything. A young man ran out of the car; unlike his suited father, he was still in his pajamas, shiny silk no less, and flip-flops. He held out a phone, telling me my mother wanted to speak to me.

"You have no idea what love is," I shouted. "Well, no one does, but you specifically have no clue."

"Listen, you," Vicky Rutledge said, as she committed the egregious error of trying to grab me.

I had never seen anyone move so fast. Firas dropped the bags, grabbed her arm in one swoop, twisted it, and in a continuous, fluid motion, his left hand went behind his back, returning with a big-ass gun, which looked like five or six times the size of his hand. No one carried dainty guns anymore. Vicky Rutledge hit the ground on her knees, crying, unable to get her arm loose. Boodie remained motionless in shock, his face bewildered. Firas wasn't pointing the gun at either of them, but at Stetson across the way.

Everything stopped. Vicky Rutledge's wails softened into a whimper. All remained still for a moment, not even a cicada dared make a sound, so I was able to hear my mother's voice piping from the young man's phone. "Put me on the speaker thing! Put me on the speaker thing!"

The boy had to explain that she was already on speaker. "Boodie, fuck your mother," she began. "You horsefucker. I'm going to kill you. I'm going to take your stupid name and shove it up your ass. I'm going to roast you over a fire. I'm going—"

"Hang up now," Firas told his son, "and carry the bags to the back." Firas let go of sniffling Vicky Rutledge's arm and grabbed mine.

"Don't take both bags," I told the young man in silk pajamas. "I only want the duffel."

"Get in the car now, professor," Firas said.

I did try to follow him, but I couldn't help myself. When we reached the car and his hand relaxed, I shrugged it off, turned around, and with a hoarse voice, I shrieked, "You should have finished your baccalaureate in Lebanon instead of coming here and becoming a cowboy. Even stupid Sartre would have helped you." I was yanked backward by my shirt collar. "Even Nietzsche could have pointed you in the right direction, and that's saying something." Firas dragged me around to the passenger side. "You're a cliché," I screamed at Boodie. Firas shoved me in the back seat beside his daughter.

We drove into the next house's driveway to turn around and passed by the troupe again as we headed north. They were on my side, so I lowered the window, and yelled at a forlorn Boodie, "You should at least try to read Jankélévitch." The young woman moved almost into my lap, still trying to record everything. Her pigtail slapped the back of my head.

"Buckle your seat belts," Firas said sternly. My window rose shut, and I couldn't do anything about it. "Child lock," he said, measuring me in his rearview mirror.

"But I'm not done."

"Oh, yes, you are."

The son in the front seat decided it was time to stare at nothing but me. He had a killer smile. His father stuffed an earpiece into his right ear and pressed a button on his cell phone. The daughter said, "This is the best video ever. It would go viral for sure, but he won't let me post it."

Firas had booked me on a flight to Beirut through Paris at ten that evening, first class all the way. Following Madame Taweel's instructions, he had reserved a room at a much too fancy hotel so I could spend the afternoon in high comfort before boarding the flight. He had accomplished all that while driving with his kids down to the farm. However, I did not get to use the hotel room because he decided he could not leave me to my own devices. I was to stay at his home with him keeping an eye on me until I boarded my flight. He believed that left unsupervised I would find a way to get back to the farm and curse everyone once more. Patently untrue, of course, but I couldn't convince him. His home was lovely.

He drove me to the airport and witnessed my slow slog through security. I couldn't be sure that he didn't wait until the plane took off just in case I came back out or something. I had never flown first-class before and I must say, it was the best airline experience I'd ever had. I was administered a champagne gavage upon being seated. I was asleep before dinner was served and woke up in the Paris airport. I repeated the process on the Beirut leg. Sixteen hours that felt like mere minutes.

Madame Taweel's big thug drove me home from the airport. He didn't say anything but from his smirks and cheeky smiles, I figured that news of my escapade had reached him. I was curious to know whether he was friends with Firas, which was how he heard, or whether it was Madame Taweel who was regaling her minions with the tale. I didn't ask. Maybe it was my mother. I wouldn't put it past her. It didn't take me long to find out.

I heard their giggling before I opened the apartment's door. My mother, Madame Taweel, and Nahed didn't even hear me come in. They were cracking up with uncontrollable biblical mirth. All three of them were oblivious and obviously stoned, higher than helium balloons. It seemed Nahed decided that a little bit of weed might help her mother's appetite and sleeping, and my mother decided she needed to sleep better as well. As if that was not strange enough, I, Raja the Fulminant, was up there on our giant television screen, shouting out names of philosophers at a befuddled Boodie, and ignoring a kneeling Vicky Rutledge. Look, there I go again, returning to yell once more. Look, there I go again, trying to shout across the roof of the Range Rover. Look, there I, Raja the Neurotic Clown, go again, lowering my window to scream at a man, now called Buddy, in the middle of nowhere, clutching an empty suitcase, going nowhere.

You would think that spending a little more than a day in a different time zone would not cause jet lag, or at least not too much, but I slept around fifteen hours as soon as I went to bed. I woke up discombobulated around noon the next day to an empty apartment. Even Aunt Yasmine was gone. I made myself a cup of tea to settle my mind, sat down at the dining table to deal with the most urgent matter. I called the school to inform the administrator that I would no longer be needing anyone to take over my class. I carried my teacup out to the balcony. I surprised myself by wishing Nahed was around so I could talk to her. As soon as I thought of her, I received her text. Aunt Yasmine was in intensive care, not doing well at all. Nahed and my mother wanted me to know so I could figure out my own lunch.

I showered, got dressed, and walked out of the apartment. My favorite eatery was on the way. I bought half a dozen sandwiches with all the trimmings and went to the hospital. I didn't bother checking the waiting room. I went to Aunt Yasmine's room, where I knew Nahed and my mother would be. The big thug stood guard outside the door, which of course meant that Madame Taweel was inside as well. I was glad I brought extra sandwiches.

The official hospital policy was that visitors were not allowed in the ICU. You couldn't say that it was ignored because that would imply that the Lebanese had ever followed a policy.

Into the macabre scene I entered. Aunt Yasmine, at death's doorstep, wore a heavy-flow oxygen mask as if it were a niqab. Only her eyes with their febrile stare could be seen. Her face seemed to have shrunk. A nurse was changing her IV. She had to maneuver around Nahed, whose chair looked like an extension of the hospital bed. I was welcomed wordlessly. I distributed the sandwiches and was about to go find another chair when I saw the big thug carrying one for me.

We sat, ate our sandwiches, and we waited.

And waited. Nurses came in and out. They prodded and probed and changed tubes. Doctors came in and out. My mother seemed filled with consternation. "I'd forgotten how horrid hospitals are," she said. "I would not want this for me."

Once someone was delivered into medical hands, they were drained of both individuality and dignity. No nurse or doctor said anything directly, but they weren't doing much more than pain management, awaiting her final breath. My mother called Aunt Yasmine's sons, who promised to fly from Saudi. And we waited. At exactly 6:42 p.m., Aunt Yasmine exhaled a short, last breath, nothing dramatic and no gnomic utterances. Nahed, who had been holding her mother's hand since I'd arrived, broke down. My mother jumped up to comfort her, Madame Taweel to comfort my mother. The doctor came in. She declared Aunt Yasmine dead and offered her condolences. "May we all live as long as she did."

The swarm of orderlies arrived. Everything blurred. I didn't remember much of what happened except for noting that before Aunt Yasmine was transported to the morgue, one of the orderlies had stuffed her nostrils with cotton, which for some incomprehensible reason seemed to me like the utmost violation. When her corpse was wheeled out, Nahed reignited another weeping bout. My mother and Madame Taweel enveloped her and consolidated their tears. I felt awkward. I realized I hadn't said a word since I'd arrived. I was sad that Aunt Yasmine had died, but I couldn't cry for her. So, I remained seated. That was not acceptable to my mother. With her arm behind her back hidden from the other two women, she kept gesturing for me to join them. I had to.

I envied Nahed's placidity in how she handled all that happened afterward, as well as her ultracompetence. She dealt with her grieving brothers and sisters-in-law firmly and without rancor. She explained to them, as their mother was being laid in the ground, that there was no inheritance: no jewelry, no hidden cash, and no secret property holdings. No mementos either, everything was destroyed by the big blast. Would either of them want her eyeglasses? Her housedress? Her broken wristwatch, her wheelchair? Maybe Nahed should send the wheelchair to their incarcerated sibling in Egypt.

My mother stood beside Aunt Yasmine's orphaned offspring to accept condolences. I refused to stand next to her. I would have if my cousins weren't there, but I couldn't be around them. I wouldn't talk to my brother either when he made the obligatory sympathy call. My mother was able to for a bit before she passed him on to Nahed and the brothers. I was surprised how many people showed up at the obsequies. We weren't a big family, and I didn't think Aunt Yasmine knew that many people. There were one or two old army veterans, friends of her deceased husband, as well as a couple of my mother's friends, but most of the attendees were Nahed's friends and massage clients, and they filled the rented hall. My mother was happy. She believed, like many in her generation, that dying might be bad but not the worst thing to happen to someone. Dying and nobody showing up to your funeral was glaringly worse.

It would be almost a month after the funeral before Nahed would bring up what became known as the American Excellence incident. My mother and I discussed it briefly, but it seemed neither of us felt the need to talk about it in depth. Nahed did. I sat on the balcony one evening, admiring the incendiary, ochre-gold beauty of my city. Phoebus Apollo still needed some time to reach our horizon. She joined me, a cold beer in her hand.

"So, he told you he loves you," she said, sitting down, "and that didn't affect you."

"Of course not," I said. "Why should it?"

"I don't know. I always assumed he disappeared and that was it. Now I find out that he'd been trying to reach you all this time. Why didn't you let him talk to you, at least once?"

"Because I didn't want to." I grabbed the beer bottle out of her hand and took a sip. Begrudgingly, I had to admit I didn't find its taste as disagreeable as I used to. "Wait a second," I said. "Are you suggesting that because he said he loves me and always will that I should run to him so we can frolic in the meadows of that farm? Are you? Because there's way too much horseshit in that grass."

"Stop it," she said. "You're so frustrating at times, and annoying. The idea that forgiveness as a cure for everything is silly, but—"

"She said if I forgive him my life will open like a flower. A culture that serves and protects the perpetrators of crimes will always try to convince its victims that they will feel better if they forgive and move on."

"Are you going to lecture me on philosophy again?"

298

"Sorry, but you have to admit it's kind of appropriate."

"I'm not trying to tell you forgiving him is good for you." I loved the way she nodded her head whenever she wished to make a point. "Maybe I'm saying that if you're able to forgive him it will make him feel better. Is that so bad? I mean you forgave my mother. Why can't you forgive him?"

"I'm not sure I've forgiven your mother, but that's irrelevant. She didn't ask me to forgive her, nor did she care to. This guy lied to me, promising a residency and money, in the hope of possibly feeling less guilty. That was a horrible thing to do."

"It was."

"It was a violation. That shook me. I was devastated. Did I overreact? Of course I did. Should I have behaved more rationally? Of course I should have, though I'm sure I wouldn't have talked to him had I been calmer. I was furious, still am, but that doesn't mean talking to him would have made me any less angry. And I find the fact that he thinks his happiness is dependent on my telling him everything is okay to be very childish, and I hate childish. Fuck him."

"Maybe he knows no other way."

"And I don't care. I really don't."

"Maybe you should train him," she said, "like you do your students."

"Stop that."

There was something intense about her eyes, more so than usual, something questioning, something beseeching, daring me not to look away.

"Look, maybe you have made peace with what happened," she said, "but he hasn't. If your talking to him might alleviate his suffering, is it such a bad thing?"

"Yes, it is," I said. "It is for me. You think working things out with him could be helpful for me, but that assumes I can deal with going over the hell I went through. I can barely manage my life as it is, and you think opening Pandora's box is worth the risk because he will feel better? I should suffer over and over again to make him feel better and maybe after all my suffering, I might heal in time. You shouldn't be defending him."

"I'm not, I swear. I'm trying to understand what's going on with you. The way I see it, he kidnapped you thinking he was saving your life, which might be true, or maybe forgivable."

"But that's not it," I said. "I wasn't that upset about his locking me in the garage, not then and not now. Although I must say I couldn't risk feeling trapped again in that cottage. I had to get out. Seriously, the garage was not the problem. We were both kids, and as you said, we knew no other way. You, my mother, everyone assumes that the kidnapping traumatized me. It didn't, or at least not much. Some things during those two months were horrific, but quite a bit of that experience was exhilarating. I'm not going to bring up Sartre again, I promise, but let's say that in some way, I felt free in that situation. Maybe even happy. What was traumatic was returning to this reality. I ascended from the underworld into a world, into a culture, that would do everything in its power, everything in its considerable power, to crush me. Being with him in the garage allowed me to set the boulder aside for a moment. I had to pick it back up when I emerged, and it had doubled in size because, oh my god, I wore a dress. I don't blame him for that. It's not him, it's not me. It's this world we live in. Is that enough philosophizing, my dear?"

300

"Not even close," she said, "but you haven't answered my question. If you don't think he traumatized you, why can't you forgive him?"

I saw golden clouds reflected in the windows of the building across the street. Our balcony felt larger, enormous and airy and blue.

"I didn't say I can't. I choose not to. I wasn't hurt because he kept me hostage. I was hurt because I realized I couldn't participate in a system that seeks to destroy people like us. I had to resist, to live life my own way. He chose to take part in that murderous system, decided to wallow in that pig trough, and continues to do so to this day. From the beginning, he chose war. He chose to kill people who were not like him to fit in. I'm sorry he's not happy now, but I'm not asking for him to apologize, nor do I want to forgive him. You know, that photo of the fox hunt was from 1982. From 1982! While I was hiding in this corridor and Israel was trying to obliterate us and then Reagan decided that his battleships should join in the bombing merriment, Boodie was on a fucking fox hunt, probably cavorting with Reagan himself. I should forgive that? Fuck no."

"Fuck him."

"Are we done talking about him now?"

"Absolutely. We're done with him."

"I wash my hands of him," I said. "Out, out, brief Boodie."

"Out, out brief *bougie*," she said.

"You didn't just say that."

"I certainly did."

"That's a horrible pun."

"That's a great pun."

She handed me her beer. I took a big swig.

VII
(2023)

My mother died on August 13, 2023. She simply didn't wake up. She was a healthy eighty-five, and her cardiologist had given her a clean bill of health a week earlier. Yet her heart stopped during the night. She'd received her wish of dying in her own bed and not a hospital.

I woke up that Sunday morning in a tranquil apartment. I was beginning to get used to the fact that Nahed had moved out. The world outside flushed with a promise of pinkness. I assumed my mother was with Madame Taweel, but that assumption didn't last long. As I brewed my tea, the hum of the fridge the only noise, a frantic Madame Taweel called. She hadn't been able to reach my mother, who wasn't answering her phone. It was then that I noticed she hadn't fed the cats. I darted to check on her as Madame Taweel kept repeating, "Tell me she's okay, tell me she's okay."

My mother looked like she always did when sleeping, on her back, serene and angelic, but the world seemed wrong—cold and dark and unfamiliar. She had shrugged off the weight of life. Manet and Monet were beside her, but they weren't napping. They were observing her. Monet emitted a heart-wrenching, plaintive meow. My knees went weak. I sat down on the bed next to her. Madame Taweel was yelling and crying on the phone. I couldn't talk. The relentless sun played havoc with the bedsheet. I wiped my clammy hand on the side of my pajama pants. I had trouble moving. Madame Taweel on the phone was telling me that she was driving over. Next to the bed, on the nightstand, the two pill dishes: the lotus leaf porcelain for the "when you wake up" pills, and the square wooden one for the "after you eat something" ones. The unsipped glass of water to their left. She hated drinking out of plastic bottles and she allowed Monet and Manet to share her glass.

The gray roots had begun to make their monthly appearance. It would have been time to help dye her hair.

I wished for a different day, for a day of snow and frost, for a thunderstorm to end all storms, for the sky to unzip itself and release, but it was August.

I lay by her side. I tried for a last hug, but it was impossible. It felt all wrong. A sourness. I couldn't touch her. I couldn't.

The world should have raged, raged.

I, the bereaved, was treated as a child, and a not-too-bright one at that. I wasn't allowed to make any adult decisions. Nahed and Madame Taweel took care of everything. Even the big thug had more input on the funeral procedures than I did. Shunted to the periphery I was. Force-fed when I wasn't hungry. Talked to, talked at when I would have preferred solitude. They were efficient and capable. Madame Taweel's boys performed their assigned tasks like soldiers preparing for a barracks inspection. They brought up chairs, a dozen silver trays filled with sweets, another dozen for the coffee. She even had a young woman log on to all my mother's social media accounts and close them. Flowers began to arrive within an hour of my mother's passing. Another young woman was assigned the task of recording all the names on the cards so that when the senders arrived to offer condolences their bouquet would be in a prime spot.

I made one decision. I insisted that we hold the formal obsequies in our apartment, not in a rented hall. This was where she lived, this was her home. This was where she was happy. No, of course not, we were not going to move the dining room table. We would not need the space. We could place chairs out on the balcony if needed. Not everyone had to squeeze into the kitchen. We'd be able to slide trays of coffee back and forth. We would manage. Not all mourners would come at the same time. They would stagger in over three days. Yes, my mother had quite a few friends, and many were going to come to pay respects to Madame Taweel and Nahed. We should be able to work with that.

I was right. My mother would have wanted everything to be in our apartment.

And as usual, I was also wrong.

I should have figured something was off when we returned from the burial later that afternoon. The apartment was a beehive, which was not right because only close friends and relatives were supposed to show up the day of the death. Nahed's lesbian friends took over coffee duty, treating our kitchen and dining table as their own. They had known and loved my mother for years. One was insulted I didn't recognize her. My mother was her surrogate mother, had loved her for over thirty years. She had been to our apartment a dozen times. Had I not been paying attention? Then there were the minions. It seemed Madame Taweel's men adored my mother, even though she mocked and cursed them on a regular basis. They would be taking care of logistics for the next three days. I shouldn't worry about anything. But for that evening, they brought their families to say goodbye.

The big thug sat with his wife in one of the corners next to a fiery bouquet of tiger lilies. And he was weeping. I walked over to check on him. He was all right. His wife with the sand-colored, straight hair assured me he was. He just loved my mother. I had to force myself to remember his name, their names. Hassan and Najwa.

He told me not to worry. He might be relaxed that evening, but he would be at his "organizational best" the following day and he would make sure everyone else was as well.

Madame Taweel, in all black and black Balenciaga mesh sneakers, sat next to me and told me not to worry. Everyone kept telling me not to worry. She tried to explain that it was decided that the mourners were now organized into Whats-App groups and a schedule was set up. I had no idea what she was talking about. What WhatsApp group? "We don't want you to worry," she said. "Everything is taken care of."

Then it was Nahed's turn to inform me I shouldn't worry. She was going to spend the night in the apartment. She didn't care that I didn't need her to, that I enjoyed being alone. "Well, the cats need me even if you don't," she said. "And I don't particularly like my place, so I might stay here for a while."

The next morning, I woke to a buzzing apartment, Monet and Manet refusing to leave my bed. Too many people hurricaning outside my room. Madame Taweel's men in dark suits and women in all black lined up folding chairs in a circle with two rows. Nahed wore the same black dress she did for her mother's funeral. She never wore dresses otherwise. She was directing a hanging of two sizeable, recently printed and framed portraits of my mother. A black and white, as a young woman posing for a professional photographer, probably around the time she was married, left shoulder at an angle, almost facing the camera, her head turned in an attempt to be seen as seductive; the second one—the second pierced like a bullet. I had taken the photo a month ago on a trip to a lavender farm in the mountains. She looked exuberant because she was surrounded by her favorite scents, the lavender bushes at her feet, a jasmine trellis behind her, and gardenias around her neck. A galvanic smile that could power a Beirut blackout. Someone who didn't know her would be surprised at the contrast between the two photos. As an older woman, she looked happier, more alive, and so much more beautiful.

"Get dressed," Nahed said.

By a quarter to nine, I was seated next to her on the main sofa. We needed the most comfortable seats because we were going to be spending the day standing up and sitting back down every time someone arrived and every time someone left, up, down, up, down, all day for three days. Still, I, Raja the Dimwit, consoled myself by remembering that there would not be too many people. I suggested that Madame Taweel sit next to us, being my mother's closest friend, a member of the family. The smart woman didn't accept. Too much work for her old legs, she said. But she'd sit in the chair right behind me in case I needed help remembering who I was going to be talking to.

Randa was the first to arrive. It wasn't as if I could forget she was my student, but she had become my mother's friend. My mother loved her deeply. Randa hugged me, cried on my shoulder, then composed herself. She ended up sitting farther from Nahed and me, flinging her black linen jacket on her chair. She spent the next fifteen minutes, until other people arrived, texting on her cell.

There was a steady stream of people for the next hour or so, nothing too busy, but no lull. I didn't know half of them. Either Madame Taweel or Nahed would whisper their names in my ears. But then Nahed and I stood up to greet two men who looked vaguely familiar. She was no help, as she didn't recognize them. We exchanged the obligatory phrases. Unfortunately, I have an unsubtle face.

"You wouldn't recognize us," one of the men said. "It has been so long."

"Kamal," I said, recognizing him after he spoke. The countenance might have changed but the voice hadn't. "And Tarek. It took me a moment, but I would never forget. You were my first students."

"And classmates," Kamal said, "although I probably shouldn't remind you."

I was certainly surprised they showed up. More surprised when an older couple did that neither Nahed, Madame Taweel, nor I recognized. It turned out they were parents of one of my brats, Miriam, class of 2004, who introduced them to my mother. They'd had lunch with her a few times. I hoped my face remained stoic, but I wanted to kill my mother.

And then the woman said the oddest thing. I should have known. Madame Taweel told me, Nahed told me, Hassan told me. I wasn't paying attention.

"We wanted to bring Miriam, but she's coming with her class at three," she said. "We thought we'd get here before the rush. We tried to organize all the parents who are coming, but we're not as good at WhatsApp as the kids are."

I sat down, knowing I was about to weep. My mother did this, and I wanted to kill her again and again.

"How many are coming?" I asked Nahed.

"A lot," she said. "I told you yesterday. It's August. So many are back in the country for the summer holiday."

"Don't worry," Madame Taweel said. "The boys are handling everything downstairs. There are seats and coffee in the building's lobby. We even have cooling fans. We have it covered."

"Well, I don't have it covered," I said. "I don't think I can deal with this. It's much too much. Had you told me I would have stopped it."

"Oh, shut the hell up," Nahed said.

"What are you talking about?" Madame Taweel said. "I told you yesterday, three times. They're organizing themselves by class. Today is the difficult day. One class every half hour. It gets easier tomorrow and the day after. Only one class an hour. You'll be done at six thirty every day, seven at the latest. You can handle that."

"No, I can't," I said, in a not-so-mild panic. "I'll break down. No one can see me like that, and especially not my students. There are boundaries. There are rules. It's all her fault, flaunting my rules whenever she wanted. I can't do this."

"I told you," Madame Taweel said to Nahed. "We should have stuffed him with Xanax. I took two this morning."

"I don't need Xanax," I said. "I don't—"

"Be quiet," Nahed said. She gestured for Randa to come sit next to us. "How much time do we have?"

"The first class is almost all here," Randa said. "They're supposed to come up on the hour, so seven minutes. But we can delay them if we need to, of course."

"Don't tell him that." Nahed stared at me. "Go to the bathroom. Compose yourself. Do whatever you need to do and come back out in seven minutes. No more. You will deal with this."

I did as I was told, except I was only able to compose myself after eleven minutes.

I had barely sat down before I had to rise again. The class of 1996, both sections. Thirty-four out of the sixty. They walked into the living room in groups of six, the elevator's maximum occupancy. So charming, so polite, so beautiful. They were surprised I remembered them, as if I could ever forget. They may have grown older, in their mid- to late forties, but I remembered them all. I could probably remember the grade I gave each one of them, and how much they improved from first class to last. Of course I would remember.

Four of them made sure to tell me they had met my mother and loved her.

They filed into the two rows of seats reserved for them. They sat quietly, almost all of them grinning for some reason. I knew that manners suggested I saunter over there and engage them in chitchat for a few minutes, but I couldn't. I didn't trust myself to walk those few steps. Randa did. She went over, chatted for barely a few seconds before two girls — two women — came and sat by me, Amal and Sylvie. They were inseparable back then and apparently still were. They even carried the same handbag. Small talk was not my strong suit, but it certainly was theirs. They told me about themselves, about the group. Amal would point at someone across the room, someone beaming. Fadi was in Kuwait, working in advertising. Majida was a hotel manager in Istanbul. Sawsan, now Susan, was an executive at Apple in California. Did I need a computer, or maybe a new cell phone? Thirty percent off. They hadn't all stayed in touch, but everyone knew what everyone else was doing. Didn't I know about the Lebanese gossip tree?

Sylvie pointed at another ex-student, gray-haired Omar, who waved at me from across the room, looking as if he was a teenager once more. "That one's greatest accomplishment is having married my sister, class of 2000," she said. "Except he took her with him to Australia, and they only come to visit every couple of summers."

"I wanted her to come with me," Omar with the historical nose said from across the room, "but she wanted to come with her class."

I held it together, but barely. Luckily, Randa glanced at her phone and nodded her head. The entire class stood up in unison. One of Madame Taweel's men, Ziad, held an empty tray for their coffee cups. And the class lined up to shake my hand. As soon as they descended to the lobby, another group of six came in, class of 2008. And then more, and then more. Thirty-eight of them. They sat in the same area. I held it together. I did. I was even able to exchange a word or two with them. I also held it together for the third group, class of 2016, barely. They were younger, and it seemed shaking hands was not enough for them. They had no compunction about cheek-kissing or worse, hugging me. Those who crossed the Atlantic, living in America or Canada, liked to hug, whereas kissing was for those in Europe or the Middle East. They were a more loquacious group. At least half of them knew my mother quite well, having marched with her in the same demonstrations.

I broke down with the fourth group, 1986, my first official class. I was doing fine, I really was. I had better control of my feelings. Randa even joked that there were only seven of them downstairs, so they were all squeezing into the elevator. I thought she was standing up to greet them, but then a lightbulb moment—she was one of them. I couldn't explain why her walking over to line up and pay respects with her class tore my heart. They looked so elegant, so gorgeous, all eight of them. I couldn't bear it. I announced to the room that I needed to go to the bathroom, and tried to rush out before any of them could shake my hand or worse. But it was not to be. Randa grabbed my arm as I went by her, dragging me into her embrace. She hugged me worst of all. No space for me. I bawled. In front of everyone in the room. And if I thought things couldn't get worse, they most certainly did. The rest of her class—Janane, Joumana, Amer, Hani, Sofia, Mohammad, and Basma—decided that it was appropriate to have a group hug. Insufferable.

Wait. It got worse still.

I began to hiccup. Keening and hiccupping. Inexcusable.

Even though the huggers were all taller than me, I looked up, and through bleared eyes, I saw my mother, surrounded by fragrant flowers, having a laugh at me—a laugh so delightful, so impetuous, so luminous. I could imagine her running victorious laps around us.

I stopped struggling. It was too late. Probably every one of my former students would have heard about my breakdown within five minutes of its happening. I didn't bawl again, but every time I looked up at my mother's portrait, I would weep a little, and with every class that came up during the three days, I would weep a little more. I wept when I saw Ghassan Q. with his class, and again when I saw Mirna, Yusef, Mohammad, Manal, and the rest of their class. Umaya, Firas's wife, showed up with her group and then returned with her husband and their two kids. It was too much, way too much.

Couldn't my mother have hung on until fall, when all the emigrants returned to their new countries?

And somewhere along the line, all my ex-students decided it was quite okay to hug or kiss me, and there was no way I could stop these heinous acts without causing a scene. My cheeks had been tenderized with all the damn kissing.

I did cause a scene on the third day. I was sitting between Randa and Nahed. Madame Taweel and Randa's husband were behind me. And as the class of 1998 began to exit, Randa announced that the next group was the class of 2024. I couldn't believe they, whoever was organizing this wake, would do this to me. I stood up, rigid and in rage.

"I can't welcome them," I said, seething. I didn't yell because I didn't want the ex-students who were leaving to hear. "I will not have them meet me for the first time in my own house."

"Settle down," Nahed said. "They wanted to come. We're not going to tell them they're not welcome."

"Oh, yes, we are. How will I be able to grade them?"

"What?"

"I won't have it. I can't grade them if I have a personal connection with them. That screws up everything. I can't interact with them before class."

"He's being serious, isn't he?" asked Madame Taweel, her face contorting into a questioning, slightly dumbfounded look.

"Of course I am," I said. "I should have been consulted. I have rules. These kids will never listen to me if they see me now."

"Every day," Randa said, "and every minute, I think how right your mother was about everything. Are you dumb enough to think there will ever be anyone in any of your classes who won't do exactly what you tell them? After all this? Now, settle down because here they come."

"I swear to God," Madame Taweel said, "had I not made a promise to your mother, I would have one of the boys take you to your room and spank you so hard that you'd turn malleable."

They began to trickle in, a line of terrified kids. Not one of them in mourning garb, no black dresses, no dark suits, in all kinds of outrageous colors. The only thing I could muster to say to each one was "Thank you for coming." I shook one boy's hand before noticing he was chewing gum. I wouldn't let go of my grip. Thankfully, he was smart enough to take the gum out with his left hand and put it in his pocket. "I'm so, so sorry," he said. I released his hand.

There were so many of them. Probably all sixty of both sections. They sat in their assigned seats, not budging, not a hint of movement. They were so young, so gorgeous, so nervous. My babies.

I tried my best not to glower but wasn't sure how successful I was. Every time I looked their way, I could feel them recoil. They would have to get used to that sooner or later.

One by one, they lined up to say goodbye.

"I will see you in class," I said to each, just a tad gruffly. "Never be late."

The official obsequies ended, but people kept calling and sending emails of condolence. I wasn't allowed to be alone. I refused to answer any of my brother's calls. Nahed moved into my mother's room, forcing me to deal with all my mother's belongings. That wasn't easy, even though I didn't have to do much. Madame Taweel ended up clearing the room, or her minions did. She sat in a chair, shedding tears and pointing at things to be done.

Ten days after my mother passed, I received an email from an account I didn't recognize. "I'm sorry about your mother," it said. "I'm thinking of you." It was signed Boodie. I typed, "Thank you." I sent the email and then blocked the account as if I were the Grandmaster of Tech.

Things began to settle down about two weeks after my mother's death. Even though I objected, Nahed had moved back in with me. She insisted that someone had to take care of me. I explained that I had lived alone most of my life, but that didn't change her mind. We spent an entire afternoon discussing ground rules, which she wouldn't promise to keep. What was the point of rules if you weren't going to follow them? Unfortunately, I was grieving and didn't have the strength to argue or stand my ground.

I wasn't a weepy guy, but once people stopped calling to offer condolences, it felt as if I spent all my time weeping.

I couldn't understand why I was being overwhelmed with such hefty sadness, such a murky grief. I had always been able to store feelings away, but her absence buried me under an avalanche of sorrow. I had studied the machinations of grief for years, of course. I thought I understood the logic of it and the emotions behind it. I discovered that I understood nothing, and nothing seemed to help. I couldn't even bring myself to read any of the various philosophers who wrote about the subject. I just wept.

I blamed her.

One evening, just before sunset, Nahed and I lounged on the balcony. I was high, she wasn't. I was weeping, she was wondering what we should do for dinner. Madame Taweel called her saying she was coming over with a cauliflower-and-lamb stew. As usual, she didn't even ask if we would welcome that or if I had other plans.

I objected. "She can't come here," I said. "She can't see me like this."

"Like how?"

"I'm stoned."

"What the hell? She got high with you not two nights ago. In any case, she called from downstairs. She's already here."

"But I didn't invite her," I said, just as Madame Taweel opened the door with her key.

She was followed by Hassan, the big thug, carrying a giant covered pot. "Let's eat while it's hot," she yelled going into the kitchen. She sidled in with ease, but Nahed and I had to wait for a minute or two before Hassan could squeeze through. Madame Taweel, wearing a sundress with a sunflower print and designer combat boots in mock-croc, looked as if she was prepared for anything and everything. She noticed me looking at her boots, and a solitary tear ran down her cheek.

"Your mother loved these boots," she said. "I couldn't find her a pair. They're men's shoes and her feet were so small."

She set the table for four, obviously knowing the topography of our kitchen. Hassan took charge of the silverware. They were efficient. Our plates were full within seconds. I realized I was starving. Madame Taweel and Nahed sat at the head of the table, Hassan and I around the edge.

I'd taken the first bite when Hassan said, "I asked if I could join for dinner because I wanted to thank you."

"Thank me?" I said.

"My wife and I wanted to do it earlier, but it wasn't the right time with everything that happened. We are both grateful. If there's ever anything you want, all you have to do is ask. Even if you think it's impossible, I will do it. There's no favor too big."

"You're thanking me for what?"

"Your mother and the boss told me how hard you worked to get my son into your school. After all our history. I never thought you ever forgave me. Your mother kept telling me you had, but I wasn't sure I believed her. And then you do this."

"But I didn't do anything."

"Your mother said you would say that," he said, laughing uproariously. "She knew everything."

"But I don't even —"

"Don't listen to him," Madame Taweel said. "He always denies everything, and he's so stoned right now, he probably doesn't even remember."

I wished to object; I didn't remember because it never happened. I was about to say something else when Hassan smacked me on the back, almost knocking my head into my cauliflower stew.

"You don't have to say anything, my friend," he said. "Your mother said everything already. I miss her so much."

"We all do," Madame Taweel said.

"There was this one time when it was me and her in the car," Hassan said. "We were stuck in stalled traffic, and this guy in a fancy car was trying to sneak in ahead of us, inching slowly while pretending he wasn't doing anything. Your mother rolled down her window and yelled at the poor guy. 'Listen, you incontinent creep. You move forward one more centimeter and I'll come down and smack you with my umbrella, and I wouldn't even have to involve my bodyguard. Don't make me get out of the car.' I don't think the guy was scared of her, but he certainly was perplexed. He didn't move until we passed him. Your mother was insane."

"You don't have to tell me," I said.

"Tell us about how she broke her leg," Madame Taweel said.

"She told you that story?" I said. "She shouldn't have."

"I don't know it," said Nahed. "Tell us."

"No way," I said. "It happened so long ago. And I wouldn't anyway. I can't believe she told you that. She's not supposed to talk about my sex life."

"Oh, now I need to hear this story," Nahed said.

"Why wouldn't she talk about your sex life?" Madame Taweel said. "We all know you're gay."

"Everyone does," I said, "but there's no need to discuss my sex life. I know you're straight, but I don't want to know the details."

"Your mother certainly did," Madame Taweel said.

"She asked about mine as well," Nahed said. "I wouldn't oblige at first, but she persisted."

"Did you explain lesbian sex to her?" Madame Taweel said.

"Well, yes. That was so long ago. Maybe a few months after she returned from Dubai. She wanted to know everything. But really, all we ended up talking about was masturbation."

"So, you're the one who explained things to her," Madame Taweel said. "I was wondering about that."

"I can't believe we're talking about masturbation and my mother. You people are out of your minds."

"I would like to hear more." It was Hassan who said that, and he would be the last person in the universe to whom I would tell that story. No way.

"Tell us that story," Madame Taweel said.

I told them. "It was almost thirty years ago when I picked up a man on the corniche and brought him home. All he wanted was a blowjob, didn't even bother to pull his pants down. As soon as I was done, he zipped up and rushed out the door, slamming it on his way out. Not unusual behavior, but I was surprised when he rang my doorbell the next day. He informed me that he'd investigated who I was, knew my name, figured out the school I worked at. If I wanted my secret to be kept, I was to give him four hundred dollars a month, insisting on the American denomination. If I resisted, he said, he would tell my parents, since he now had their names. I was flabbergasted, not so much at the attempted blackmail, but at the fact that he thought I could afford four hundred dollars on a teacher's salary. I stood before him speechless for a while, couldn't wrap my thinking around what he was asking and that smug look on his face. I finally told him that everyone knew I was a faggot. He didn't believe me at first, but then my mother, on one of her daily impromptu visits, happened to get out of the elevator. I told the guy if he didn't believe me, he should tell my mother. He was mortified. I explained to my mother that this guy and I had sex and he thought she'd be surprised to find out her son was a homosexual. It became obvious that the guy wanted nothing more in life than to run away. My mother was many things, but stupid she most certainly was not."

I took a long breath and had to smile to myself, recalling what her face looked like as soon as she figured out the situation. It is said that a synaptic transmission occurs in less than one-thousandth of a second, but my mother was a hell of a lot quicker than that.

"She had one shoe in her hand," I went on, "and smacked him on the forehead before he had any idea what was happening. And he was a tall guy and she tiny. He ran away down the stairs, and my mother, like a cricketer, threw an overhead heel that whacked him in the back of the head as he turned the corner. But then this wasn't enough for her. She followed him down the stairs, mind you, while trying to take off her other shoe to send it flying his way. She stumbled and broke her leg. It wasn't a major break, a hairline fracture or some such thing, but at her age, she had to wear a cast for six weeks. Of course, she thought it was completely worth it."

Madame Taweel had laughed from the beginning of the story till the end, her loud getaway-car laugh. I didn't think the story was that funny, maybe slightly amusing. The lights flickered off as if afraid of the sound of her laughter. We waited six seconds for the building generator to kick in. Manet jumped on Nahed's lap. She lifted a piece of minced lamb with her forefinger and thumb. The cat waited silently, knowing what was coming his way. She spoiled him more than my mother did.

"I'm just glad your mother never hit me with her heel," Hassan said. He smacked my back in glee once again. Everyone was being way too familiar these days. I didn't like it.

Fuck my mother.

Acknowledgments

I am indebted

to those who read drafts of the manuscript: Lina Moun-zer, Raja Haddad, Samhita Sunya, Desi Isaacson, and Satya Bhaba—

to Joy Johannessen for her help with early edits—

to Sherrie Brown, librarian extraordinaire at the University of Virginia, for her research help—

to Rima Rantissi for telling a story that inspired the listless seal—

to Elisabeth Schmitz, Morgan Entrekin, Deb Seager, John Mark Boling, and everybody at Grove—

to Kelsey Day and everyone at Aragi—

to Nicole Aragi for everything—

to the Lannan Foundation and the Pen/Faulkner Foundation for offering me their fiction prizes, which allowed me to devote more time to work on this novel—

to the fabulous folks of the Lannan Center at Georgetown University: Aminatta Forna, Carolyn Forché, and
Patricia Guzman, who must suffer working alongside me —

to the poetry unicorns for having me in their midst —

to my mother, who keeps inspiring —

to my sister Raya, whose life and philosophy informed
this novel —

and to my sister Rania, who would break my legs if I
didn't mention her.

Thank you.